# CARTER'S
# UNFOCUSED,
# ONE-TRACK MIND

# CARTER'S UNFOCUSED, ONE-TRACK MIND

A NOVEL BY BRENT CRAWFORD

HYPERION · NEW YORK

Printed in the United States of America

First Edition
10 9 8 7 6 5 4 3 2
G475-5664-5-12260

Library of Congress Cataloging-in-Publication Data
Crawford, Brent.
Carter's unfocused, one-track mind: a novel/by Brent Crawford.—1st ed.
p. cm.
Summary: Fifteen-year-old Will Carter's sophomore year at Merrian High
presents new problems, from the return of Scary Terry to friends-with-benefits
negotiations with Abby, but when Abby considers transferring to a New York
arts school Carter's world is turned upside down.
ISBN 978-1-4231-4445-8 (hardback)
[1. Self-perception—Fiction. 2. Dating (Social customs)—Fiction. 3. High schools—Fiction.
4. Schools—Fiction. 5. Interpersonal relations—Fiction.] I. Title.
PZ7.C85415Cbu    2012
[Fic]—dc23    2012001231

Reinforced binding

Visit www.un-requiredreading.com

TO ALL THE GIRLS I'VE LOVED BEFORE . . .

WELL, NOT ALL OF THEM.

YOU KNOW WHO YOU ARE.

# FALL

# 1. FINALLY HITTIN' IT

My fist slams into Andre's ugly face, and he staggers back in shock.

"Dude, you're gonna pay for tha—!" he starts to say, but I kick him in the stomach to shut the noise down. He charges me with his head lowered. Everyone knows he's trying to take the fight to the ground.

My boys yell, "Get outta there, Carter!"

I'm already on it. I jump as high as I can and pull my knees up into my chest like I'm about to bust a gainer, and I sail over him. His big arms *whiff* beneath my Nikes, and he stumbles to the parking lot. I land on the asphalt and spin around, planning my next move. Everyone is shocked that I'm winning this fight. Andre is embarrassed and angry, but I couldn't care less. I've wanted to beat his ass for years, and it's finally (sort of) happening!

He was the one kid on summer swim team who I could never beat. I always felt self-conscious in that little swimming suit . . . but never as much as when I had to stand next to Andre. The SOB had pecs when we were ten years old! And it looked like he was smuggling a Snickers out of the snack bar in his Speedo while I was just working with a Tootsie Roll down there. I never even noticed that I had little boobies and a muffin top until this mutant came along.

His overdevelopment and athletic ability aren't the reasons I dislike him so much, however. Last year, he sold me down the river in an attempt to steal my girlfriend. He's a d-bag!

I admit that I initiated my own EPIC FAIL when I told Abby that I loved her and then asked Amber Lee to go to the homecoming dance in the same passing period. A few hours later I made another mistake when I bragged to my boys in the locker room that I'd gone up Abby's skirt. . . . That's on me! But Andre told a band geek about it, knowing full well that the band pipeline would pass the news to the drill team with Google-like speed. Then he broke the locker room code (for a second time) by twisting my words and telling Abby that I'd bragged about having *sex* with her in a movie theater. I may have *implied* it, but that's perfectly acceptable in a locker room, and everyone knows it.

*I* broke Abby's heart that day, but a case could surely be made that Andre made the situation a lot worse and way harder to recover from. Especially after he swooped in and asked Abby to homecoming. Yeah, Amber Lee is super hot, and I did ask her to go to the dance with me, but she tricked me into it just so she could meet up with her scuzzy, parent-not-approved boyfriend, Rusty. Her dad wouldn't let her go anywhere with ol' Rusty (I'm not being clever; he's actually old). I was an easy mark because I'd been in love with Amber for years, and her dad was right to try to keep that dirt-bag away from his angel, because Amber's now four months preggo with Rusty's seedy seed.

Logically, I understand that Andre had nothing to do with Amber Lee getting knocked up, but I'm not feeling logical tonight, so in honor of Amber's unwanted baby, I give him the sweetest roundhouse kick right in the jaw!

My boys cheer, "Ohhh, Carter! Where did that even come from?"

I wish I knew, but I'm just going on instinct here. I'm not thinking; I'm just doing! I'm really focused tonight for some reason (two liters of Mountain Dew), and when I'm focused I'm pretty tough to beat at anything.

I tag Andre in the ribs as he's trying to recover from the roundhouse, and then I drive my fist straight into his big nose. Blood sprays all over the place, and everyone laughs, except Andre.

"Sprrriiinkler, dude!" Bag roars.

EJ adds, "Don't get any blood in Carter's hair, he'll really freak out!"

Andre stumbles backward and examines his bloody hands. He starts hopping up and down like he's getting fired up for a comeback, and grunts, "That's it, fool! I'm 'bout to mess you up!"

I accidentally sweep his legs out from under him, but it looks like I totally meant to do it. I flip the hair out of my eyes and mutter, "Bring it, sucka!" as I approach a metal trash can off to the side of the alley.

Everyone gasps and Andre mutters, "Always knew you was dirty, Carter!" as I raise the can over my head. Everyone cheers as it bounces off his skull with a *CLANG*. The bleeding from his nose gets worse, but the real problem is the green stuff that's now draining from his ears (I'm no doctor, but I believe that might be brain fluid).

EJ yells, "NEXT!" as he pounces onto my back (in real life). I drop the game controller to the carpet and try not to fall down. I was going to toss my hands up in triumph, but I've got to use them to keep EJ from choking my neck as he rides me around Bag's basement and shouts, "Will Friggin' Carter, the Cinderella story! The Cinderella boy!"

We're playing the new version of Mortal Kombat, where the game takes a picture of you and creates a character in your image. My guy is wearing my same jeans, Nikes, and gray Merrian Football T-shirt. He's got my hair, but he seems skinnier and way goofier than I actually am. Everyone else looks about right, though. Andre's big nose and trademark buzz cut is perfect. So are his damn muscles.

I usually suck at video games. My fingers are kind of slow, but it's my attention span that really gets in the way of greatness. If I practiced more, I'd be better, but my parents have always discouraged this type of achievement. I know some guys who aren't embarrassed to brag that they played the same game for ten hours and then complain about how sore they are. I enjoy feeling like a champion as much as the next guy, but it seems the better you are at video games, the worse you are at life.

It's almost nine on a Saturday night and my whole crew is here: EJ, Bag, Nutt, Doc, Levi, J-Low, Hormone, Andre, Timberlake, The Ding-Dong, Coot, Lt. Dangle, Sloth, Hangin' Chad, The Devil, and TrimSpa. We are a mash-up of old and new friends, and I really like most of them. I actually came to this party with my sort-of-back-on-again girlfriend, Abby, and I need to remember to check in with her pretty soon. My sister, Lynn, always stresses the fine line between paying attention to a girl and stalking her. You want to blow her off a little, but you don't need to be an a-hole.

It's about time for me to bounce anyway, because this is the time of the night (six beers) when EJ starts to get obnoxious.

"WHO NEXT?!" he screams, and smacks my butt as I carry him around the room. "Who? Who? Who let an owl into the basement?" He starts cracking up. "BAG! Why do you have an owl? Are you a wizard? Do you go to the Ballwarts School of Wizardry?"

His sticky hands start pulling my hair, so I ram him into the wall and he lets go.

"Owwweeee," he cries as he crumples to the floor.

Whoops, I may have accidentally hurt him. All of the fake violence really does get to me.

EJ just lies on the ground for a while. I know he's all right when he puts on his gay-robot voice and says, "Your love is too rough, Will Carter!"

I jump on top of him and make him slap himself a few times. I like to beat on him when he can't defend himself (around six beers).

There's an actual party going on upstairs. We can hear the music thumping overhead, and I might even smell some food. My boys and I are sophomores now, and people seem to enjoy our company, but we're still more comfortable down here playing games and pretending to kick ass than actually getting in the mix. It's not like we're frightened. This is just easier.

Technically, this is Bag's older sister's party, so it's kind of a college gathering. It's the local junior college, so I don't think that counts. They all say they're saving money and that our local JuCo is really good, but I think most of them are scared to leave Merrian. They know they're cool right here, and there are no guarantees that their coolness will transfer.

Andre slaps my hand as if he's a good sport, then wrecks it by saying, "Can't believe you hit me with a friggin' trash can. I might have to go steal yo' girlfriend again! I'm just playin', dog."

"You know it's not really a joke when you've actually done the thing you're threatening to do, right?"

"I saw you walk in with Abby, all sly," he says.

"I gave her a ride. Nothing sly about—"

"Ahhhh, you finally hittin' it?" he asks.

"No, Dre. We're not doing this. She just rode my axle pegs."

He yells, "Yo, Abby rode Carter's axle!"

I cover his mouth and say, "No, no! Shut it down."

He wriggles free and asks, "Do you have any idea how many chicks I've banged since Abby?"

"Uhhh, you accidentally made it sound like you and Abby 'banged' when everyone knows you didn't."

Andre scoffs, "Well, maybe we did, maybe we didn't."

"You didn't."

He continues, "My point is, I'm not still hung up on her."

"Obviously . . . You just stalk her 'a little bit' and notice when she shows up and who she's with."

Andre pushes me and says, "So guess how many!"

"I don't recall anyone asking for your stats."

He shakes his head like I've missed his point. "All I'm saying is, if I'd put in the time that you have . . . I'd be up on Bag's mom's water bed right now surfin'!"

I try to figure out the surfing reference while I retort, "I haven't put in any 'time,' dog, she and I are *friends* . . . and she might be going away to some school in New York City next semester . . . so . . ."

Everyone settles down and EJ says, "Seriously?"

"Yeah, she told me on the way over. I guess she applied to this farty art school last year and she got in."

"Why didn't she start the school year there?" Bag asks.

"It's really expensive and she didn't get the scholarship she wanted, but the girl they gave it to had a nervous breakdown, so it's available again."

"When would she leave?" Doc inquires.

"I don't know. I kind of spaced off while she was talking."

They understand that I only get about half of what's going on most of the time, but they also know how much I care about Abby and how close I am to having sex with her, so they're kind of bummed out too.

Nutt exclaims, "Why don't you go with her?!"

"To New York City?! I don't know. Because I didn't apply to the school, I'm not an art fart, and I'm only fifteen and—"

"You're a pussy!" Andre adds.

Bag says, "You acted in a movie this summer, dude. They'll let you in. And you don't need a scholarship because you got paid all that money."

"Yeah, but that money is for college."

Nutt is from a family of schemers, so he observes, "No, that's for *school*. If you went to some *Fame* high school, maybe you could skip college and just go pro."

That *sounds* nice, but unfortunately, working with Hilary Idaho on a movie allowed me to see how much "going pro" as an actor can screw you up.

Bag suggests, "Maybe you and Abby could get an apartment together!"

"Her mom would love that," Doc scoffs.

I start to imagine our little love den. It's in an old

building, but it's nice. Some people call it a loft, but Abby and I call it home. It's got lots of huge windows and a king-size bed that squeaks when we—

*WHACK!!!* EJ slaps the back of my neck and says, "You aren't going to New York City, dumbass! You'd get run over by a taxi on your first day."

He may have a point, but I playfully shove him to the ground. "I'll run over you like a taxi, bitch."

"That's what I said to your mom last night!" he replies.

I pounce on him. "My mother is a lady, damn it!"

EJ and I slap each other until Nutt says, "You know, Abby might break you off some good-bye booty if she leaves."

"You think?" I hadn't even considered that this could be a good thing.

Andre breaks back into the conversation when he yells, "Eleven! I've doinked eleven chicks since I got with Abby."

I finally let go of EJ and stand up so I can clearly explain to Andre, "Dude, you never 'got with' Abby!"

He says, "Only 'cuz I cheated on her."

"But mostly 'cuz you're a doofus, right?"

Andre's cheeks start to turn red, so I punch him in the chest to let him know that I'm kidding (not really). He punches me back a little too hard and gives me a cold stare. It occurs to me that he might really like Abby too, and he'd be upset if she left. All I know is: I don't want to get into a real-life fight with Andre, because I would lose. Badly.

Just then, a gang of flip-flops come slapping down the basement steps. I toss the hair out of my eyes to get a better look at thirty painted toes and six tanned feet, shapely calves, and strong thighs descending creaky stairs. Nicky is wearing a miniskirt that you can totally see up. Abby is behind her (in khaki short-shorts) and Amber Lee is bringing up the rear (in frayed Daisy Dukes). Amber's legs always look great, but everyone is gawking at her swollen belly tonight. I know that we all went silent because of Nicky's skirt, but it probably seems like we shut up because a pregnant girl just walked in and we're grossed out.

Abby breaks the uncomfortable silence. "Hey, what are you geeks doing?"

Andre replies, "I was just beatin' Carter's ass in Mortal Kombat."

I'm about to give the actual details of the fight, but stop myself before the dork instincts kick in. I just point to the screen, where the video game image of Andre is still lying on the ground, leaking brain fluid.

No one says anything else until Amber giggles. "Look what the game did to Carter's hairdo!"

Everyone laughs, so I say, "It's not a hairdo, Amber! You're the one that got tiger-striped highlights in eighth grade! Remember that?"

My boys start making fun of me. "You should totally get highlights, Carter! You could be a country singer!"

So, one of the only things I have to remind me that I was an actor in a movie this last summer is a new "look." The set stylist felt bad for me because I worked so hard on a film that's never going to be seen, so she gave me a free haircut. It's a big deal because she's like, a grand champion. Her cuts run about five hundred bucks (for people she doesn't feel sorry for). She didn't trim that much off, even though I hadn't had a proper haircut in nine months. (I'd shaved my head for a swim meet in February and then let it grow out so I could slick it back for the spring musical, then the character

I played in the movie was supposed to be a homeless kid, so I just let it keep growing. It wouldn't have looked right if I'd just gone to the barber.) She snipped and clipped for more than an hour and transformed my shaggy-dog mop-top into what my boys call a "flop-do" or a "Skate-Bieber." I think it looks awesome, but everybody loves to hate.

They gather around the screen and hopefully recognize that I won the fight. Bag observes, "Your avatar looks like Bon Jovi, dude."

Nicky says, "Yeah, but like old Bon Jovi."

"Or an anorexic Conan the Barbarian," Nutt adds.

Levi yells, "Conan the Gaybarian!"

"Okay, we get it."

My boys don't like anything out of the ordinary . . . like private schools or fancy jeans. They view self-expression kind of like a cancer. If they can make fun of it enough, maybe it won't spread. God forbid this hairdo takes off and people start copying me! They've been wearing me down for about a month now. They can tell that I'm getting close to cutting it, because they share DNA with sharks and bees.

EJ says, "Scary Terry is about to get out of jail, and if he's been thinking about killing you AND ME for the last six months, I'd prefer it if you didn't look like a Gossip Girl when we see him for the first time."

I push him down again and everyone laughs.

EJ and I were forced to fight a guy called Scary Terry in the halls of Merrian High last year. Terry is a loon who'd stolen my bike the weekend before. My sister briefly dated the nut ball, and she took it upon herself to bitch him out in front of a bunch of people, so he was already pissed at me when I accidentally ran right into him in the hall. He wanted to fight, but I was obviously not into it. The problem was that all of these kids had gathered around to watch us brawl, and he didn't want to let them down. He took off his shirt and started to do all these karate moves, and then EJ came up behind me, like, *I got your back, no matter what!* and I started to think, Why not? But then a teacher showed up and Terry started crying and backing out of the hall brawl. But he was still threatening to kill me at my house later, so I decided to get the fight over with. *Allegedly*, I called him a pussy for crying. I don't remember doing it, but I do recall EJ making a kissing noise and Terry dropping him like a Popsicle onto the linoleum. While he was following through with his punch, I knocked Terry out with my five-pound Intro to Science textbook. Terry had been in a few fights before that one, so he had to go to a juvenile detention center for a while.

Abby tousles my flop-do and says, "You guys, stop! Carter's hair is so cute!"

"You're not helping," I explain to her.

EJ jumps up, grabs my hair, and says, "It's sooo cute, I want to take it out to the shed and get it pregnant!"

Even Andre knows that EJ just shoved his foot into his mouth. It wouldn't have been so bad if everyone hadn't looked at Amber for a reaction and Nicky hadn't yelled, "EJ! Don't talk about getting things pregnant in front of Amber Lee! God!"

EJ and Nicky have an on-again, off-again relationship, kind of like Abby and I do, but unlike us, they have sex . . . and they kind of hate each other.

EJ wouldn't have said something like that if he was sober. But he's a pretty different dude when he's had a few drinks. "What'd I tell you about bitchin' at me in public, Nicky?!"

She snaps, "And what did I tell you about being a retard, retard?!"

Amber quietly says, "Okay, I'm leaving. I just wanted to say hello. . . . I'll see you boys later."

Abby replies, "You don't have to go," and shoots me a dirty look as she stops Amber at the foot of the stairs. They're having a hushed conversation while EJ and Nicky continue to flirt/fight and Doc and Nutt reboot the Mortal Kombat. I'm not sure where to look! I'm worried about Amber's feelings, but I'm very confused about how all of this just became *my* fault. Nutt's avatar looks like an anteater jumping around the TV. But it sounded like EJ just compared Nicky to his mother! I'm dying to see where he's going with this.

I've always wondered how the flirt/fight works. How can you tear a girl's heart to pieces and still get booty? I understand this phenomenon as well as I understand tornadoes. Mr. Bestos says tornadoes occur when a cold-weather front runs into a warm-weather front and all the energy gets confused and starts to swirl. But that doesn't explain the carnage or why they go after trailer parks. EJ and Nicky will keep hurting each other's feelings until the emotion reaches a fever pitch and someone shuts the other one up with their mouth. It just seems like there's more magic to these events than actual science.

Amber and Abby head up the stairs, and I decide to follow them because I'd follow Abby's butt almost anywhere, and they say the safest place to be during a tornado is right in the center. I may be thinking of a hurricane, but I need to deal with whatever this is before it gets out of control.

A DJ is jamming some old 70's funk, and the house is packed with people sort of dancing. A bunch of the seniors from last year decided that they want to be DJs; they're not even going to JuCo. They're way too committed to "the music" . . . and living in their parents' basements. I'm not really friends with a lot of these people, but I'm down with a few cool ones. Bag's older sister Kammie (known as Pam when she's in a swimsuit) dances up to me as I watch Abby and Amber salmoning their way toward the front door. I *should* tell Kammie, "I'm too busy to drool over you right now!" but I'm unable to speak because she's showing a fair amount of cleavage tonight.

"What's goin' on, heartbreaker?" she asks.

Kammie is the exception to the rule that only dorks go to JuCo. She's majoring in public relations and plans to become a reality TV star or marry a professional athlete; I don't think you need Harvard for that.

"I'm cool . . . you know . . . just maxin' and re—"

She cuts me off. "I saw Amber Lee crying. Did you guys call her fat or something?"

"Uhhh, no. We just kind of ignored her."

She makes a face like, *That's way worse!*

As I turn away from the cleavage, I run into a wall of muscle. My sister's boyfriend, Nick Brock, is one of the graduated seniors who has left for college. He's on a full scholarship to play football for Nebraska. He's home for the weekend because he didn't make the travel team. Which is insane! He lifts me off the ground as if I'm a rag doll and almost slams me into the ceiling. "What's up, you hippie?!"

I try not to sound whiny when I say, "S'uuup, Niiiick?"

Lynn appears from Nick's shadow. "Put him down! Carter, did one of you little cretins say something mean to Amber Lee?"

"No, none of us said anything to her!"

She rolls her eyes around so aggressively that I worry they're going to fall out of her head.

I point to the front door as it slams behind a pair of khaki short-shorts. "I was just trying to catch up to her and Abby right now!"

Lynn takes a dramatic breath, contemplating her next statement. She usually gives great advice, so it's probably worth the wait. She's a *selective feminist*, which means she cares deeply about women's rights but has no patience for girls who wear sport sandals. I know it's difficult for her to look out for me the way she does, but she has always felt a responsibility to do so. She's never allowed my mom to buy me Under Armour gear or cowboy boots (even though I know I would look awesome in them). She tries to keep people from seeing what a geek I really am, and she's tried extra hard to help me win Abby back.

"You need to slow down, turbo!" she orders. "What have we talked about when you feel yourself rushing into situations?"

I'm silent for a moment, so she continues. "Exactly. We take a breath and try to see the problem from the other person's perspective."

"Well, I can see that she's mad at me, but I don't know why, and she might be going away to some private school in New York, and she's pissed because she thinks we were mean to Amber . . . and they're getting away. . . ."

She shoots Nick a look of shame before she says, "Just

stop! Give 'em a few minutes. First of all, you're not going to try to stop her from going away to school, are you?"

"No."

"My brother will not be the guy who stops a woman from pursuing her dreams!" she barks.

"I am not—"

"Amber lives a few blocks from here, so they're probably headed over there," she explains. "And Abby's mad at guys in general, not you. You're all obsessed with sex, but as soon as there are consequences to your actions you all freak out. Abby is obviously frustrated with her friend's situation. I heard that Amber and Rusty are living with her dad."

Both Nick and I say, "Yikes!" at the same time. I assume Nick is picturing himself eating the last bowl of Mr. Lee's favorite cereal and getting his balls cut off for it, because that's what I'm doing.

My sister continues, "So just let them talk about what a bunch of jerks you guys are, and then show up at Amber's house in fifteen minutes with some Diet Cokes like you're the exception to the rule."

Nick gives me a fist bump (ouch) and says, "Like me."

Lynn's eyeballs get another workout as she says, "Yeah, just like this one . . . who doesn't call for three straight days!"

"My phone was broken!" Nick protests.

I'm really going to miss her when she leaves for college next year. And she *will* be leaving, though I don't think Nebraska is very high on her list. She loves Nick, but a good football program is not one of her priorities. She seems to be looking for things to get pissed at him about lately.

I give Nick a good-luck nod and head for the kitchen to

steal some Diet Cokes from Bag's fridge.

Lynn knows that I'm in love with Abby, but she's warned me to keep that crap to myself. According to my sister, Abby is not a very good starter girlfriend. She's too smart, tough, and beautiful to put up with my playa training wheels. Lynn has always advised a tightrope approach. I'm allowed to *show* my love for Abby, but not say it out loud or cry in front of her or anything. Apparently, weakness pushes strong girls away. This is problematic if you're a boy who finds himself crying all the time. And I feel like a gymnast, just swinging around on this damn tightrope.

I remember a time when Lynn was a freshman and she was totally into this guy Rhett. She'd get all giddy whenever he called, and she tried on fifteen different outfits just to meet up with him at the mall. Then ol' Rhett had the nerve to buy her flowers or a teddy bear or something and she completely shut him down. She tried to explain it to me like, "It's not the gifts, Will, it's the timing!" but I was only in seventh grade so I didn't get it. But I'm starting to see why Nick doesn't return her calls right away and why he doesn't do everything she asks him to do. Sure, she gets mad at him, but she stays interested as well. I guess I don't have to understand the power of the tightrope; I just have to try to stay on the damn thing.

As I head for the door, Lynn reminds me, "Ask Amber questions about her health . . . and don't forget to listen!"

I'm feeling good as I step outside. I know that swooping in with these Diet Cokes is going to get me closer to having sex with Abby than if I rolled up in a Ferrari. All I've got is a bicycle and a dream. How the hell am I going to ride with these stupid cans in my hand? I'm standing on the porch, looking down at my bike and trying to work out the geometry equation . . . when Scary Terry Moss comes walking up the driveway! He's alone and seems like any other teenager with a buzz cut and thugged-out clothes. He's got three lines shaved into his left eyebrow. His look suggests he's ready to dance but might also have a gun in his pocket. Nobody was trying to be ironic when they saddled him with the nickname "Scary Terry."

You might also think he's one of those annoying aspiring rapper dudes, the way he's talking to himself, but I don't think he's working out a rhyme. He's having a serious discussion . . . with himself. If it happens to rhyme, it's just a coincidence. It appears that juvie didn't help with the crazies.

He doesn't see me, but a girl standing in the doorway says what I'm thinking: "Oh, nooo!"

## 2. FIGHT OR FLIGHT

I drop the sodas, and of course one of them blasts open and sprays suds all over the place. I don't know if Terry saw, because all of a sudden I'm pulled back into the house like a stunt man in a Jackie Chan movie. Nick's big arms are wrapped around me as if I'm a football and he's rushing for a touchdown. We hustle through the crowded living room and down a hallway before dashing into the little bathroom. I kick the door closed as he's setting me down. Nick tries to latch the worthless lock, and I tell him, "Dude, you gotta push in and then twist!"

He seems panicked when he replies, "No, it's this button!"

I don't want to criticize a guy while he's rescuing me, but I have to explain, "That button hasn't worked since this ratty house was new."

"I used to date Kammie, I know this lock!" he replies.

"And I've taken at least a hundred dumps here, Nick!"

I stop my own ridiculous argument to ask, "What the hell are we gonna do?" and "When did he get out of jail?" and "Do you think he's still mad at me?"

"I don't know. Just hang out in here for a second and I'll try to find out," Nick says.

"Y-y-you're leaving me?! I mean, I should warn EJ . . . don't you think?"

A girl's voice comes from nowhere and says, "Excuuuse me!"

We both jump and turn to find a chick hunched over on the toilet with her pants pulled down. We apologize, but we don't leave. I say to Nick, "Yo, we've got to fix that lock."

"Focus, Carter!" he barks. "Get in the shower. Lynn'll warn your boys; I'm gonna figure out what's up with Terry."

I climb into the shower. My heart is pounding out of my chest. Nick is probably just earning points with his girlfriend here, but I'm stoked that he's involved. He rushes out the door, but the drunk girl stays put, and I'm feeling a little awkward.

Eventually she clears her throat and asks, "Did, did he locked the door?"

"Uh . . . I don't think it matters."

"Are you guys playin' hide-and-seek?" she asks.

*Drunks are retarded.* "No, Scary Terry Moss just walked in."

"Ohhhh," she slurs. "He's in juvie, right?"

"He's obviously *not* anymore."

She lets that sink in before asking, "You're hiding from him?"

I don't say anything to that one.

She adds, "He's cute."

"So are pit bulls."

"That's what I mean," she says. "He's got abs!"

"Yeah, crazy people are almost always ripped."

She continues, "I saw him fight in the hall, at school. I

think it's why he got sent to juvie. It was right next to my locker."

"Yeah, I was there too."

"You were?!" she asks. "I'm Cher . . . Chery-llal . . . HA! OMG, I drank so much, I can't even say my name! Cheryl . . . Cheryl. Yes! He was, he was punching himself in the face, right?! And his shirt was off, and he's got abbbsss!"

"Yeah, we covered that."

She keeps going. "Then these little freshman pricks started making fun of him and shi—"

"What? No, we . . . no, *they* didn't."

"Yu-huh! I thought you were there, man? They called him a 'scared bitch'!" And the bigger one, like, taunted him with a kissing noise and got punched the fu— Wait a minute! Peek your head back out here!"

Other reasons I don't like drunks: They're shameless. And they're easy to underestimate. I open the curtain, and she gasps. "I knew it was . . . *You* sucker punched him with a textbook!"

"You really think *we* were picking on *him*?"

She closes her eyes for a second and leans back on the toilet tank before she jerks forward and barks, "Yes! Hell, yeah! He was crying and then he had to go to jail over it. You guys were the a-holes!"

I don't even know what to say. I can't just discount this as the ramblings of a drunk on the toilet, because this is her memory of something that took place six months ago.

We just hang out in silence for a moment, and I wonder if Terry has a right to be mad at me. Maybe I was an a-hole. Kids who didn't know me really started to respect me after that, and I was kind of proud of the outcome of the fight.

Maybe I should just go out there and apologize to Terry. I wonder if that would make it all better.

"A-a-are you about to wrap it up out there, Cheryl?" I ask.

She laughs. "I can't remember if I went. I fell asleep."

I lean out of the shower and turn on the sink faucet. As the water starts to run, her body remembers what to do and she starts to tinkle. She says, "Thanks . . . you're sweetie." Then she rips a monster fart that echoes off of the bowl. "Whoops!" She giggles.

"Yeah! Go ahead and drop a deuce. I'm not trapped in here or anything."

She tells me to shut up as she flushes. I gawk out of my polyurethane prison to watch her struggling to stand and untwist her panties. She finally gets them under control, but the jeans are giving her trouble, too. She's got the coordination of a baby horse, but her panties are kind of cute—black, boy-cut (Victoria's Secret, summer catalog, pages 7–9). Her booty is not as nice as Abby's, but it's right there, and that is awesome! "These pants are sooo tight!" she complains.

With so much going on, I really shouldn't be turned on right now, but I've yet to find an OFF switch on this thing. I finally decide to take pity on her and offer some assistance. I step out of the tub and say, "You're standing on your pant leg."

I grab the back of her waistband—just as my sister and Nick come barging back into the bathroom. "What the hell are you doing?!" Lynn barks. I panic and fall into Cheryl . . . whose jeans are still stuck at mid-thigh. Nick raises his eyebrows in shock (or playa admiration).

23

Then six more dudes barge into the small room and ram Nick into Lynn, who pushes me into Cheryl again. All of their eyes immediately lock on to the exposed black panties.

Bag cheers, "Carter, you old dog!" as he shuts the door.

Lynn considers slapping him, but instead lifts me off of Cheryl and tries to assist her with her pants. Nick tries to get us back on track by saying, "Yo, we have a problem."

Other than the obvious: ten people in a two-person bathroom. Lynn explains, "Terry is still mad at you and crazy as a loon!" She buttons Cheryl up as if she's dealing with a toddler.

EJ asks, "Mad at who? Me or Carter?"

"I didn't ask about you, idiot!" Lynn yells. "But it's not much of a stretch to think that you're somewhere on his list. Surely, you guys can see this isn't about you. It's about him still being in love with me!"

Even Cheryl rolls her eyes at that. Nick looks back at me and says, "Just stay out of his sight, man, and it shouldn't be a problem."

EJ asks, "Nick, don't you think Carter should just fight him again and get it over with?"

"And where are you in this plan, wingman?!" I ask EJ.

"Right behind you, like always!" EJ says.

"Back that thang up, boy!!!" Nutt laughs.

Bag smacks EJ's ass and says, "You love gettin' behind dudes, don't you, E?"

EJ grasps for Bag's nipple and replies, "I've had just about enough of your lip, young man—"

Lynn starts hitting us like a mom at the supermarket. "You idiots better straighten up! You do not want to mess with Terry Moss!"

"Nick, you said if I stood up to him last year that he'd like, r-r-respect me and we'd become sorta friends?" I ask.

"Well, yeah," he explains, "but you knocked him out in front of the whole school, and then he had to go to juvie for six months. I also fought him three times before we became friends."

I clarify. "He went to jail because he knocked out EJ, not because I hit him!"

"I wasn't knocked out!" EJ barks.

"Duuude, we were all there," J-Low says.

"You were twitching and gurgling like a baby!" Doc adds.

Even Cheryl goes, "True that."

"He looked like a dog running in his sleep," Levi says.

Nutt says, "Remember how swollen his lips were? Like Angelina Jolie on 'roids!"

We all laugh at EJ until Nick asks Bag, "Does this window open?"

"Yeah, it really stinks in here!" EJ says.

"Carter, did you crap your pants?" Bag asks.

"No, that chick was takin' a dump. And Nick is thinking of how to get out of here, not—"

Cheryl gasps. "I was NOT taking a dump, you little—"

"Sorry, I forgot you were still here. She did not poop, she just farted really loud."

My sister whacks me on the back of the head, and my boys crack up as Cheryl pushes her way out of the crowded room, muttering, "You're a jerk!"

My boys mock her in high voices: "Carter, you *are* a jerk!"

Bag pries the window open and climbs through it, landing in the backyard.

Nutt snaps his fingers and yells, "You should pay him off! Even psychos like cash."

EJ agrees, "Yeah, Richie Rich, give him some of that movie money!"

"That's ridiculous, and I don't have any—"

Doc says, "I thought you got paid a buttload to be in that movie."

"I did, but it was like, too much. My parents put it all in a savings account, and I can only access a little bit at a time."

"Don't make out like you're poor, though," Lynn says. "You have that debit card, and they give you two hundred bucks a month."

"Shut up," I scold.

My boys gasp. "You do?!"

Great, I'll be buying everyone's snacks and movie tickets until graduation.

"Well, I spent all of my money for this month and next, so I really don't have any, and I don't think Terry—"

Bag sticks his head back through the window and asks, "What did you spend it on, Carter?"

"On stuff I needed!" I grumble.

EJ pipes up. "He accidentally joined a whole group of porn sites."

"What?" Lynn barks.

My boys laugh . . . the kind of laughter that you only get if you've been in the exact situation.

"You hit the 'watch full video' button, didn't you?" Bag asks. "You greedy bastard!"

"You're sick!" Lynn says. "Don't ever touch my laptop again."

"Always delete your history," J-Low adds, like he's making a public service announcement. "Just make a habit of it."

Doc starts to do an impression of my mom looking at the Road Runner bill, but I cut him off by yelling, "Yo, we gotta get outta here!"

Doc worms out next and falls into the yard. It feels pretty crappy to have your tail between your legs, but it's always nice to have your boys with you. Of course they make fun of the way I climb out the window. "Stop dry-humping my house, Carter," Bag says.

"Don't ever become a burglar," EJ adds.

"You guys are dicks," I say, tumbling into the backyard.

A few people are smoking and laughing at us as the rest of my crew jumps into the grass. The smokers probably don't know that Scary Terry is here and think we're up to some run-of-the-mill tomfoolery, not running for our lives. We creep around the house, and I look in all the windows as we go. My sister and Nick are talking to Kammie in the kitchen, and we're pretty sure somebody is having sex in Bag's bed. He's so mad, but we won't allow him to yell at them. There is no sign of Terry Moss. My heart is pounding with fear, but shame and guilt are also in the mix, so my stomach hurts. I probably shouldn't have eaten that whole bag of Doritos and sleeve of Chips Ahoy or drunk that two liters of Mountain Dew. I start wondering again if it was wrong to hit Terry with a textbook . . . even if he is crazy . . . especially if he's crazy? Was I defending myself or beating up a handicapped guy?

As we peek around the side of the house, I whisper to EJ, "Hey, you know that girl in the bathroom?"

"The hammered one with the black boy-cut panties?" he asks.

"Yeah, she was there, at our fight with Terry, and she actually thought that we were picking on him."

"WHAT?!"

"Shhh!" I say. "That's what she said! What if we just go up to him and apologize?"

EJ retorts, "Yeah, but he's crazy . . . like the Joker in the Batman movies. He just wants chaos."

"Maybe they changed him in juvie?"

He whispers, "I don't think that's what they do. They just try to teach them how to be plumbers and not kill each other. I bet he's gotten worse."

"You're not helping."

"I'm just keepin' it real," he says. "But if you want to walk up to him, I've got your back."

We're all attempting to hide behind a tree that wouldn't even cover one guy, so we start laughing. Bag and Nutt are doing ninja somersaults and Doc starts climbing the little tree. No one is taking this retreat seriously except me. I pick up my bike and glance around nervously. EJ swats at my bangs and whispers, "If you don't get your hair cut soon, I'm gonna have to start calling you Floppio. I'm not kidding."

Before I can throw a leg over my seat post, the screen door on Bag's house crashes open and Nick Brock tumbles out. His huge arms are wrapped completely around a squirming Terry Moss as he yells, "Calm down, bro! It's not gonna happen! Carter, get outta here!"

Terry starts dragging the two-hundred-and-fifty-pound linebacker. He scans the yard with wild eyes and finds my boys and me frozen like deer in headlights.

He screeches, "CARTER?!"

Against my better judgment, I drop my bike into the grass and try to take a deep breath. My dad always says, *An apology never hurts anyone and usually helps everyone.*

But Nick seems to have the better insight for this situation. He yells, "RUN!"

I'm walking in reverse when I say, "Terry, I believe I owe you an—"

"Come here, boy!!!" Terry yells.

I feel my fight-or-flight instincts kick in. I'm so proud that my hands instinctively draw up to protect my head. I'm a fighter, after all. But I've really got the urge to flap my elbows like a chicken and attempt a takeoff!

Kids are pouring out of the house to watch the ruckus. Terry doesn't disappoint. He wriggles free of Nick's grasp and spins around to punch him in the mouth. It's a hollow, smacking noise and sounds nothing like the Mortal Kombat game.

I've almost backed myself into the street, so I've got a great view. From the ground, Nick grabs Terry's shirt. Terry jumps like a scared cat before he viciously punts his friend in the ribs. The thud of the contact and the groan Nick makes are awful. A girl screams, and it's like a starter pistol in my head.

I take off running, leaving my boys for dead. Terry starts to chase me. I glance over my shoulder just as my sister flies out of nowhere and jumps onto Terry's back like an angry monkey. She fishhooks the side of his mouth and takes the screaming boy all the way down to the grass. How am I such a pussy if *that* is my sister? How can I leave my friends like this? I don't know, but I'm sure doing it, and fast!

I'm usually kind of slow, but with my life on the line I'm pretty speedy! I'm imagining how bad I'll feel if Terry hurts my sister or one of my friends, but I keep running like a coward. The thought of Terry mowing me down with his old Cutlass keeps my feet churning, but I don't hear anything except the sound of my heart pounding out of my chest. I've probably run about a mile when I finally allow myself to slow down. I try to catch my breath, but it won't be caught. I've run sprints a million times, but I've never actually run for my life before—this is some cardio, dude!

A wave of frustrated emotion washes over me, and I double over to start sobbing when Abby's voice floats out of the darkness. "Carter?"

"Nuuuaaahhh!!!" I gasp, and leap into the air. "Hi there! S'up? S'up?!"

Dang it! I appear to be standing right in front of Amber Lee's house. They must've just arrived, because Abby, Nicky, and Amber are standing on the steps of the front porch. It seems as if I've chased them down to say something important, but I can only gasp, "Running! Running is hard!"

Abby replies, "Are you okay? What's going on?"

"H-h-hell yeah. I uh . . . uh . . ." I don't really want to get into how I just ran away from a fight, so I stutter, "I uh, I w-w-was coming over here to bring you some diet . . . to apologize . . . to Amber, for the way we acted, or uh, *re-reacted* in the basement. We're just not cool enough to deal with the . . . baby situation, I think. We're just like, really focused on sex, you know? Like all the time . . . That's, that's what we're doing when you came down the stairs. We weren't having sex, that sounded weird. But all of your legs were out and it was more about Nicky's skirt than . . . and yoouu . . . and your, uh, bump are, you know, they're really throwing a wrench into our sex machines."

Abby has a hopeful look on her face, as if she's sure I'm about to get to something good, but Nicky and Amber seem skeptical as I clear my throat and continue. "You see, uh, pregnancy is like a consequence of the action we want to be doing all the time, and we're not ready to handle that yet. I mean we're ready physically, like our sperm can probably do it, but our brains are like, *AHHHHHHH!!!* You know?"

The girls are looking at me with disgust. Amber Lee asks, "You think *I'm* ready to handle this?"

"No, I really don't."

She laughs. "Well, thanks for the vote of confidence, Carter."

"Sorry, I've been running. But I'm sure you'll figure it out, and I, uh, wasn't trying to compare my boys and I's issues with what you and Rusty are dealing with. I-I-I was just attempting to make an excuse for being rude and I wanted to apologize for it. The rudeness."

The girls are backlit and staring down at me like hot assassins. All the sudden I see Abby's teeth, as if she's smiling. Maybe I said something good.

Amber tosses her hair and says, "Well, thank you. I appreciate that. I've never known what it felt like to be an outcast."

"Well, I'm an expert, so . . ."

Abby defends me. "No you're not."

I wipe some sweat off my face, and Nicky asks, "You ran all the way over here just to say that?"

"Yep . . . Nope . . . I was gonna walk over and bring you some Diet Cokes and say something like that, but then

Scary Terry showed up at the party and I fumbled the Cokes and there was a brawl, and Nick Brock told me to run, and what am I gonna do, disobey him?"

I tell them about the fight until a police siren starts wailing in the distance. We all know where they're headed, so Amber says, "Let's get you inside."

I've never been inside Amber's or any other pregnant girl's house. I bet there's some weird baby stuff already set up, and a funny smell. I know her dad has guns and probably hates boys more than ever, but I accept the invitation just to get off the street.

I step in and gasp. "Wow, your house is really nice."

It smells like flowers and has high ceilings and dark wood floors and cool lights.

"Why do you sound so surprised?" Amber asks. "My dad made a lot of this stuff." She guides us into the kitchen and we sit down on old red lunch counter stools.

Abby says, "Haven't you been here before?"

"I've never made it past the porch. Amber's dad doesn't just make cool furniture, he also intimidates people."

Amber and Abby smile. Nicky is not in the mood. She snottily says, "So where are the other dwarfs?"

"I thought they were right behind me, but . . ."

She continues, "So you just ditched them? You left them to deal with a psycho who was looking for you?"

I don't know what to say. Thankfully, Abby says, "Nicky, you don't need to be a bitch all the time. Nick Brock told him to run."

"Nicky's right, though, I shouldn't have just taken off," I say.

Abby argues, "Carter, you did the smart thing. You

were the catalyst of the situation. The fight probably stopped when you left."

She really shouldn't call me *smart*, because I can't remember what *catalyst* means, but I don't say anything.

Nicky scoffs. "If the fight stopped, what do you think those sirens are about, Abby?"

"Carter doesn't have anything to prove to anyone!" Abby snaps.

I nod in agreement, but I feel like even more of a wuss being defended like this. I also know that if I hadn't bumped into these girls, I'd be crying in the street right now.

It's quiet for a second when Amber asks, "Do you want a Diet Coke?"

"I'd better not. I already had a two-liter of Mountain Dew."

"Why were you gonna bring us Diet Cokes, then?" Amber asks.

"I don't know . . . Oh, hey, how are you feeling, Amber? My sister wanted me to ask . . . because I want to know . . . how you're holding up . . . physically and all that."

She laughs and then tells me a bunch of gross stuff that I don't want to know. She describes an "abnormality" in her "fallopian tubes," and I try really hard not to puke or make a face. Then she shows me a sonogram picture of the baby. It looks like she's pregnant with a sea horse, but I don't say that. It's kind of sci-fi cool, actually. The four of us eventually start gabbing like old friends. We talk about how "swollen and sore" Amber's boobs are, and I am only slightly aroused!

The conversation intensifies when we start to discuss baby names. Amber is all excited when she explains, "Well,

Rusty and I are thinking Thor or Cadillac if it's a boy! And Dandy-Lion or Lilo if it's a girl!"

I think those are all fantastic choices and absolutely hilarious, but Abby can't handle it. "What?! You can't do that!"

"When you have a baby, you can name it something boring!" Amber yells. "But we want our child to reflect our values and aspirations!"

"Values?" Abby gasps. "How does Dandy-Lion—"

"It's nontraditional and artistic!" Amber replies.

Abby is forced to drop the subject because the baby-daddy enters the house looking like a defeated mud wrestler. Rusty's covered in grease from working at Lee Auto Body. He dropped out of high school so that he could work full-time and save up enough money to move Amber out of this very nice house and into some crappy apartment off Merrian Lane. I thought the Merrian Gardens required each tenant to have at least two illegitimate children and one nonworking car, but maybe they'll make an exception because Amber and Rusty are so young.

Rusty stomps up the stairs when Amber's dad waddles in the front door. I'd love to ask him, "What's up, Doc?" because he looks exactly like Yosemite Sam, but I just stand and say, "Hello, Mr. Lee."

He puffs his thick red mustache at me and scowls . . . Nope, that's a smile! He's chuckling. "Hey there, movie star! How the hell are ya?"

I don't get the chance to answer because Amber asks, "Daddy, did you make Rusty clean the grease traps again?"

"That good-for-nothin' says he wants to learn my business, and them traps don't clean themselves, darlin'," he replies. "Auto-body ain't glamorous work, and the only thing ol' Rusty's qualified to do is change oil and clean."

She grumbles, "I can't believe you made him clean those nasty bathrooms yesterday."

I believe he's about to call his daughter a varmint, but he stops himself and turns to ask me, "Why aren't you at that party? Rusty was pitchin' a bitch all day, how he can't go to this thing, and y'all already home?"

Amber and her dad are a lot closer than I thought, because she starts telling him all about the party. What music was playing, who was wearing what, and how my boys stopped talking when she came down the basement stairs. He puffs his mustache at me again, but this time it's more aggressive. Amber also tells him that I ran away from Scary Terry.

He can tell I'm embarrassed about it, because he says, "Ain't no shame in walkin' away from a dumb fight, son."

"Thank you!" Abby says.

But he continues, "If I'd pussed out a little more—"

"'Compromised' might be a better word," she adds.

"Yeah, that is better." He laughs. "If I'd 'compromised' more in my life, things might be a whole lot different."

He's not looking at his daughter, but I imagine the biggest regret he's dealing with lately is a harsh stance with boys that led Amber to have sneaky unprotected sex in the back of an old Ford and resulted in his becoming a grandparent without a gray hair.

Then he adds, "But sometimes you gotta fight . . . even if you lose, you gotta go down swingin' for something you believe in."

Abby argues, "But this isn't one of those times. Terry's

just an a-hole who's jealous and wants to hurt him."

"He's probably jealous of that Flock of Seagulls hairdo!" Mr. Lee cackles.

I laugh at the joke that I don't really get, and reply, "Sorry I'm not cool enough to grow a smooth mustache yet."

He snaps his thick fingers at me like I've crossed a line. I'm about to explain that I wasn't kidding, but Rusty comes stomping back down the stairs before I get the chance.

Amber asks him, "Where are you going?"

"Out," he replies. "I was supposed to meet you at the party. I can't just *be* in this friggin' house all—"

Amber's dad gets in Rusty's face and displays his aforementioned inability to compromise. "You too good for this house?! This 'friggin' house' where you don't pay rent and eat all the food and play video games all night long?"

It seems like I'm about to watch my second brawl of the evening, but Rusty just walks out.

The LTD's engine fires up and the cat tears off into the night. Amber displays her obviously inherited inability to compromise by stomping her foot and yelling, "Daddy! You can't treat him like an employee when you're not at the shop. All of this is very hard for him, and you are not—"

"This *should* be hard for him!" Mr. Lee shouts. "If he wanted it easy he should have thought about that before—"

"Daddy!" Amber yells, and shoves him.

Nicky mutters, "Here we go again" as Abby grabs my hand to leave. The three of us quietly say good night, but Amber and her dad are yelling over each other, so they don't hear it. They don't seem to care that they're embarrassing themselves. This is their family and their life, and I guess they're fighting for it.

As we walk down the street, I start wondering if Scary Terry is still on the loose and possibly hunting me, or if he's back in juvie. I'm also trying to figure out how to get rid of Nicky so Abby and I can make out for a while, but all the sudden, Nicky starts sobbing. "Abby, how can you even think of moving to New York and leaving me to deal with all of this by myself?!"

I hadn't even considered that Abby's leaving would affect other people besides me, but it obviously does. Nicky continues, "You're going to be partying at the Boom-Boom Room while I'm on diaper duty in that miserable house!"

Then Abby starts crying as she replies, "I'm so sorry, Nicky. I feel bad, but honestly, this is one of the things I'm dying to leave behind. It's just too depressing."

Well, I guess I won't be making out with anyone tonight, so I steer our course for QuikTrip while they yammer on about their feelings and blah, blah, blah.

My boys are already hanging out front when we walk up. It almost makes me cry because somehow they've brought my bike, but then Nutt yells, "Hey Floppio! The fastest hairdo alive!" and I remember what a bag of dicks I hang out with.

They tell me that Nick Brock started beating the crap out of Scary Terry once my sister got involved, and then the Merrian P.D. swooped in just as Terry was leaving. Which means I'm still being hunted.

A cop car pulls into the parking lot and chirps its siren at us. When we don't immediately take off running, a deep voice comes over the loudspeaker and says, "This a no-loitering zone. . . . Move along."

Whatever "loitering" means, my boys and I are accused of doing it all the time.

My dad calls the Merrian P.D. "lazy" all the time, and I'm starting to see what he means. Some drill teamers are parked at the gas pumps, so Abby and Nicky just climb in with them, and my boys and I ride toward EJ's house. EJ thinks his dad has some old boxing gloves, so we're going to start a fight club. We'll practice beating one another up so we'll be ready the next time a psycho comes after us. Terry won't be the only trained fighter around here!

We take a shortcut behind the school and discover a huge party going off in the faculty parking lot (no teachers are present). A group of seniors has decided the best place to get drunk is on school property, and a hundred other kids have joined them. It sucks because my boys would rather do this than teach me how to fight, and I'm going to have to wait for at least an hour for the cops to show up. Rusty is also here, and he's staring at me kind of aggressively, but Abby and the drill teamers eventually show up. I somehow manage a few moments of alone time with Abby, so I try to make the most of it. "We should really kiss good night now. Because the cops are going to be here any minute, and this is highly illegal, and we probably won't get the chance to make out with everyone running and screaming and stuff . . . although that would be pretty badass."

She smiles, and I take it as a green light.

# 3. A PIECE OF MY FART

I just sat on the flowers! I was yapping with my drama friends, and I didn't want them to make a big deal that I'd bought Abby flowers, so I casually set them on my chair. But then I forgot about them and plopped my ass down on the custom mix of lilies and baby's breath!

Lynn told me I *had* to get them for Abby because Abby and I have been a little bit *off* since Bag's party. I didn't even notice until Thursday, but then we ran into each other at a field party on Saturday, and I asked her a few questions and everything seemed cool. One of my questions was, "Will you go to homecoming with me?" And she said yes and we made out again . . . but then back to silence this whole week at school. I don't know if it's her possibly leaving me that's making me weird, or if *she's* being weird about it. It could be that I ran away from a fight and she's lost respect for me. . . . Whatever it is, we've found it easier to not talk about it and pretend everything is fine. Lynn thinks I can get the ship back on course by giving her these (now mangled) flowers and just asking her what is up.

I got the flowers because it's opening night of the fall play and Abby is one of the lead actresses in the show . . . and when my sister tells you to do something, it's just easier to do it than deal with the repercussions of not doing it. I rode my bike all the way to Hy-Vee after football practice (because apparently you can't buy flowers at QuikTrip) and paid twelve bucks for them. Of course I had to make my own arrangement because all the premade ones were like twenty bucks and were better suited for a funeral than a school play.

The old lady at Hy-Vee was kind of flirty with me, like, "You have exquisite taste!" and "Are these for your *girlfriend?*"

I almost launched into a monologue about how Abby and I are still in this weird place because of some dumb stuff I did last year, and how she's leaving me, and how I was hoping these flowers would assist in getting her naked . . . but the lady started to get creepy on me, like, "I wish I'd had a nice boyfriend like you when I was young." It was like the opening scene to every sketchy cougar porno (that Nutt has made me watch).

I hustled back to school to make the seven o'clock curtain. I only thought I was wrecking the arrangement on the bike ride. If I'd known I was going to ram my butt cheeks into the flowers, I would've just jammed them in my backpack. I wasn't even that late. I was riding fast because I was nervous . . . Obviously I still am. For the first time, I'm not even worried about my own problems. I'm actually worried *for* other people.

The fall mainstage is called *A Piece of My Heart*. The energy in the auditorium is nuts. The red curtains are drawn tight and everything looks normal out here, but I know that there's a tornado of activity going on backstage. Every once in a while you'll see a techie dart out of the orchestra pit and sprint toward the light booth or the drama classroom.

(Techies are drama geeks who didn't get cast in the show, so they help with lights and props and stuff. They wear all black, like ninjas, but most of them wouldn't do very well in a fight.) Drama geeks running are always funny because they don't do it unless it's an emergency. They usually have some high-maintenance hairdo (kinda like mine . . . ha-ha, not funny) that they have to hang on to while their legs attempt to move their awkward bodies through space. I don't mean to sound like a dick; I really dig the drama kids. They're all cool (in their own way), smart, and funny. They're also LOUD, so you never have to ask them to repeat themselves. But they don't play sports for a reason.

I'm not even in the play, and I had diarrhea this afternoon like an adventurous eater exploring a Third World country. I know almost every word of the show because I helped the actors run lines. If any of the actors fall into the orchestra pit (it's happened . . . to me), I am ready to jump onto the stage. It would be a little weird because this show is about six girls . . . but I could do it! There's only one role for a guy in *A Piece of My Heart*, and my boy Jeremy got it. He actually plays fifteen different parts in the show, but it's written for just one actor. If I tried to handle that many characters and costume changes, my ADD would have a meltdown. But Jeremy is an awesome actor. His only issue has been that there is just one of him, and six girls vying for his attention. This would be a dream come true for most guys, but Jeremy is gay and has been "constantly annoyed with these bitches!" So I rolled up my sleeves and pitched in. I ran lines with them on the weekends and after football practice. I also helped build and paint this set.

Even though I'm wearing a Merrian High football T-shirt and my body is bruised and swollen from playing football, I'm totally a drama geek at heart. Do I regret signing up to play football again? You bet your bruised ass I do! There are a few weird moments when there is no place I'd rather be than on a football field. I see the way other kids gawk at us when we're in the pads or when we come into the weight room. I know people call us "dumb jocks," but I also know jealousy when I see it. Nobody should be envious of football, because most of it suuucks, but I have to admit that some of the little stuff, like running out onto the field before games and blasting away your angst, is pretty rad.

The houselights finally dim and the auditorium quiets as the six girls step onto the stage and into their spotlights. They don't talk right away, to build the drama. Ms. McDougle is awesome with the drama. They just wrote an article about her in *American Theater* magazine (online).

Abby is playing an idealistic USO performer. She's rockin' this yellow dress that's super short and showing off her legs, like way up. Her makeup is on thick and her hair is all pulled back and up. Abby calls it a beehive, and says that a can of hairspray is required to make it work. She's wearing these knee-high white go-go boots, and a guitar strap is splitting her boobs down the center, making them even more pronounced. It doesn't hurt that she's wearing an old-school push-up bra like they wore in the '60s. She says it's uncomfortable, but from my perspective, it's worth it.

She has this little bit of extra muscle meat just above her knees from being a serious dancer. It's usually one of my favorite parts of her anatomy, but it's making me feel bad at the moment because I can see that meat trembling. I feel my mother's nurturing instincts bubbling inside of me, and I fight the urge to scream, "Relax, sweetie! Just let it flow! You're gonna be great!"

After the opening monologues, Abby smoothly rotates the guitar around from behind her back and starts to strum it. She learned how to play the guitar just for this show! She only goes back and forth between two chords, but I couldn't friggin' do it. She's been practicing so much—there is no way she's going to screw this up, but I'm so nervous for her! Then she opens her glossy lips, and the stage microphones pick up the most gorgeous noise my ears have ever heard.

She quietly sings, "'Come on. Come on . . .'" and then she gets a bit louder when she asks, "'Didn't I make you feeeel like yooouuu were the only maaan?'"

I want to say, "Yes you did!"

By the time she gets to the main part and tells us to, "'Take another little piece of my heart now, baaabay!'" I'm totally crying. I'm such a bitch, but I can't help it. It's just leaky eyeballs. I'm not blowing snot bubbles or convulsing or anything. Thank God none of my friends agreed to come with me tonight and that crying is so acceptable in the drama department.

Maybe I'm crying because she sounds so amazing and I'm proud of her, but it's probably more like a kid who's favorite toy has been taken away. She's leaving, and I'm never going to have sex with her. She's still saying she "might" go. She's waiting to find out about that scholarship, but come on! These people are going to bend over backward to get her. I know I have.

The song ends and everyone claps. This show is great and moving and all of that. We learn that war sucks for everyone, but people can come away from it stronger and more connected than if they'd never gone through hell together. I think that was the point of the play; I spaced off a few times, so I'm not positive. The acting was solid, but I couldn't help but judge the performances in terms of what I would have done differently (even the girl parts).

After the show, I help pick up programs like the drama geek I am. When Jeremy comes out into the auditorium, a few people clap for him again. He takes another bow and says, "Oh, stop. No, don't!"

He works his way though the crowd and says hello to a guy I've never seen before. I may not recognize him because he's wearing a bandana on his head, like he's an extra on an '80s TV show. Jeremy seems into him, though. I may not be gay, but I know flirting when I see it. Eventually, Jeremy comes over to me, and he's blushing like crazy.

"Breathe," I instruct.

He sees Abby's flowers and shouts, "Carter, you shouldn't have!"

"That's why I didn't."

"Let me hold them for a few minutes and then I'll give them back," he whispers.

"Okay," I say, and hand them over. "You did an awesome job, by the way."

He throws his arms around me and smashes the damn things even more. I don't hug any of my other guy friends, but it's cool in the drama department. In football you're basically hugging all the time, but you just finish the embrace by slamming the dude to the ground and saying something like, "Not in my house!"

I ask Jeremy, "So, what's up with Brett Michaels?"

"Who?"

"The bandana boy who's gawking at us."

"He does look like a rock star, doesn't he?" Jeremy giggles.

I was trying to make fun of the guy, but Jeremy is obviously in that phase of the relationship where he's so into the person that he can't even hear the sarcasm. He whispers, "He goes to Rockford Boys Academy. I met him at a show choir tournament!"

"I don't understand private schools. Are the classes that much better? They don't have girls at Rockford. I mean, I guess I would get more studying done, but would I even get out of bed in the morning?"

Jeremy laughs as if I've said something way funnier than I actually did. "You are too funny!"

"Ohhh . . . you're not even listening to me. You're just using me to make him jealous . . . trying to seem aloof."

He yells, "Totally!" Then mutters, "Just keep talking, please."

I do, because he's my boy. I've never tried to make another guy jealous before, but a good wingman is a good wingman, so I say, "Jeremy, your performance was dead-on. I'm really proud of you, man."

That may have been the wrong kind of "talking," because it makes him start crying. "I ap-appreciate that more than—"

I give him a playful shove and say, "Pull yourself together, dude." But then I keep saying, "I thought each character was totally unique and each guy had his own life and problems and—"

He shoots me a mean look and asks, "What are you

tryin' to do? My nose is starting to run!"

"Sorry."

Abby finally comes out of the dressing room and gives us a wave and a smile, but she doesn't come right over. And I don't run over to her because I'm a friggin' sophomore and I am now able to control my dork instincts. I try to seem engrossed in Jeremy's story about a costume change that almost went bad, but he's kind of rambling because he's keeping tabs on Bandana Boy, who seems to be leaving. I take a few deep breaths to try to focus. I've got to play it cool. I'm allowed to tell Abby how good her performance was, but there's no need to gush!

She's talking to someone's parents for a really long time, and she seems really stoked to talk to them . . . and that's fine. Jeremy hands me back my flowers and chases after Bandana Boy, so I'm in need of my own wingman all of a sudden. I see Ms. McDougle looking at Abby, so I walk over and ask, "What's up?"

McDougle replies, "Those are recruiters from the New York Drama School."

"Ohhh. Is that what it's called?"

She nods. "They're either breaking her heart or taking her away from us."

"The scholarship? When would she leave?"

"Next semester, I think." She sighs. "Shouldn't you know this? Aren't you her boyfriend?"

"We are not into labels. We're keeping it loose. It's a bit confusing, actually."

She smiles.

I ask, "Could I get into that school?"

"I think you're talented enough, but you have to have really good grades as well."

"Oh. Never mind."

Some people come up and congratulate Ms. McDougle on another awesome show, and she starts giving some techies "notes" while I stand around like a boob. Finally Abby comes over to us and I hand her the mangled flowers. She thanks me, but my thunder was totally stolen by those recruiters.

"What did they say?" McDougle asks.

"I got it!" she squeals, and jumps up and down.

Her boobs are like pistons . . . that I'm trying not to look at. I say, "That is great!" But it doesn't sound like I mean it.

She's beyond excited. "They want my mom and me to fly out there in a few weeks for a visit."

She's stopped jumping and I can't think of anything to say. McDougle is clearly bummed to lose one of her best actors, but she tries to act happy. "That'll be fun! It's a huge opportunity."

*Opportunity to remove my friggin' heart!* If I was truly Abby's friend I'd be stoked for her, but I'm obviously not much of a comrade. I am in love with her and I'll be destroyed if she goes.

The disappointment must be written on my face, because she gives me a tight hug and says, "I'll visit the school and . . . maybe I won't like it."

Now I'm disappointed in myself. She's not getting to enjoy this awesome moment because of my issues. I don't want to be this guy, so I say, "Shut up. It's a drama school; you'll love it. You're awesome and you deserve this."

She gives me another hug. "Thanks. I was so nervous that I barely listened to them."

*Welcome to my world!*

She notices Jeremy and Bandana Boy, and asks, "Is that the Rockford Academy guy?"

I nod that it is, and I try to gossip with her and McDougle for a few seconds, but my stomach is cramping like I need to poop, and my heart has been ripped out and I kind of need to cry, so I say, "Hey, I uh, gotta go . . . study, so . . ."

No idea why I said that. It's an excuse most people can break out, but Abby knows that I don't study unless somebody's got a gun to my head.

She asks, "Are you okay?"

"Yeah, I'm great. I just have a test I need to prepare for, you know? So . . ."

That's not a lie. I should be studying for a geometry exam, but we both know that's not what I'm going to do.

I don't run out of the theater or anything. I manage to say good-bye to a few people on my way out, but everyone can see that I'm acting weird.

The fall weather is starting to kick in, and it's a little crisp outside. I unlock my bike and take a few deep, foggy breaths before kicking my bike. OUCH!!! What the hell is the matter with me? Why am I so angry? Maybe I'm jealous. Surely I'm not mad at Abby for getting an opportunity, but I'm pissed off. I guess I'm annoyed with myself for wasting so much time. That's the one thing I do that pisses me off more than anything. (Instead of just riding home, I've started adjusting my front brake for no reason, and I'm picking at some loose rubber on my handgrips.) I should have focused all of my energy on Abby and told her how much she means to me, and I really should've made out with her more!

Everyone always says, "Carter, you have no concept of time!" and they're right. I honestly don't understand it. How can the clock move so slowly when things suck? (Geometry class is like a vortex!) And how can time just fly by when things are fun? An afternoon at the pool or hanging out with my boys or building a set with the drama kids causes everything to jump to warp speed. Maybe that's why adults take jobs that they hate or get married to people they can't stand . . . just so life doesn't rip right past them.

The sound of laughter pulls me out of my daydream. I assume someone is making fun of me for staring at a brick wall for God knows how long, but it's Jeremy, talking to Bandana Boy and leaning on a Mitsubishi Eclipse. He seems nervous, which is rare for Jeremy, but the other guy keeps insecurely adjusting his hair-to-bandana ratio, so things are looking good. They are obviously making the stupid talk everyone makes before they kiss for the first time. You'd think all of this would be easier with two dudes, but it seems like having balls still doesn't guarantee a game. Wooing is hard.

I'd like to channel my inner football coach and yell, "Green lights all around, LADIES!!! Less thinking; more doing!" But drama/choir guys might not respond to football pep talks.

I'm not even sure how long I've been standing there when Abby's voice rolls in from behind me. "Hey. What's funny?"

"Was I laughing?" I point at the Eclipse and say, "Jeremy and this time-traveler are trying to find the courage to hook up."

Abby sees them across the parking lot and laughs. "Aww!"

"So, New York is a go, huh?"

She says, "I'm sorry."

"Please don't apologize to *me*. You should be stoked, not worried about me. I'm a prick! I'm jealous of you for being awesome."

She gives me another hug and whispers, "I know. I'm not ready to leave you either."

Hey now! Boobs press into my chest like two firm (yet supple) green lights.

We slowly pull apart, and I touch her cheek with the back of my fingers (pimp!). She leans in just as I do . . . but her mom's voice cock-blocks me from behind. "There you are, darling!"

Dang it.

They hug. I point to her mom and mouth the words *Does she know?*

Abby shakes her head, and for the first time I feel some compassion for the old hag. She's not ready for Abby to be a teenager yet, let alone move to New York City.

Her mom ruins it by asking, "Did someone run over these flowers? What floral designer in their right mind would pair lilies with baby's breath?"

"Mother!" Abby says. "Carter got them for me, and they're beautiful."

"Well, I can see that they *were* pretty. That was

very thoughtful of you," she says, as if she's talking to a kindergartener.

I pick up my bike and say, "Okay, well, you guys need to talk, so, good night."

I ride past Jeremy and Bandana Boy and yell, "Somebody grow a pair!"

I'm trying to be funny, but I'm kind of serious. You never know how much time you have with someone.

# 4. OKLAHOMA ROAD

I only *thought* I was having a tough year before Scary Terry got out of jail and recruiters came from New York to steal my girlfriend. I decided to play football again, and I was kind of trying harder in school. What a pain in the ass . . . literally. At practice yesterday, Andre bruised my left glute with his helmet. And I've been spending a lot of my free time in either the math or writing lab. Sitting on a plastic chair for hours on end hurts your butt almost as much as a helmet.

I swear I'm always wearing these stinky pads and running into someone. Even though I bitched about football all last year, I still signed up to play again. I actually missed hanging out with these idiots. I barely saw them all summer because I was shooting that movie. But after a few weeks of football practice, I was over it. The part that sucks the most is just seeing the other kids hanging out after school. They just go do whatever the hell they want to, while I get yelled at. The only redeeming thing I've found is the ability to release your frustrations! When you've found out that the girl you love is moving, or that there is some psycho trying to kill you, you can smash into people as hard as you want! Eventually the part of your brain that worries about stuff just shuts off.

Coach is lecturing us right now while we warm up and

stretch. I seem to have missed the point of his rant. I think he's talking about staying focused, but I'm not sure. Coach is very passionate but a bit of rambler. Even the guys on Ritalin say he's tough to follow sometimes.

One fun thing is that the best guys from our class have all moved up to JV, which means I actually get to play in the sophomore games (sometimes)! I'm a linebacker on defense and tight end on offense. I thanked Coach for finally noticing my "tight end," but he didn't get the joke. Theoretically, I could now catch a pass, and if all hell were to break loose, I could score a touchdown. I've also hit a bunch of extra points and one field goal as the sophomore kicker.

We start rolling around on the ground to loosen up our backs and necks. At least I think that's why we do it. My whole body is yelling at me because it's so sore from this morning's workout.

As if Mondays didn't suck enough, our coach has figured out a way to make them worse: we have mandatory weight training sessions before school. They make us do CrossFit because it's quick and intense, and at 6:15 a.m., we're usually too tired to register how much pain we're in. We're never allowed to do anything like bench press or push-ups. They've learned that if we lie down, we just fall asleep. It sucks to get up early and feel like you're having a heart attack before dawn, but it's fun to hang with your boys and complain about it. I'd never do CrossFit voluntarily, but I usually have a pretty good day after those morning workouts. I'm very focused until lunchtime . . . and then it's nap time! And then it's detention time because teachers hate it when my nap time conflicts with their class time.

Next we stretch our legs, which also hurts like hell. I

didn't work out much this summer because of the movie. But I'm in awesome shape now, because whenever you screw up in practice, your punishment always involves more exercise. Let's say, hypothetically, you're tardy or you forget what you're doing for a second or you make a smart-ass comment to a coach . . . you get to run sprints or do burpees or somersaults until you can't see straight.

I may have picked up some bad habits working on the movie. The director was always telling me to "Stop thinking!" but football coaches are always asking, "What the hell were you thinking?!"

And coaches hate it when you bust out an acting term, like, "I was in the moment!" But remarks like that are the real secret to getting buff. I'm such a screwup that you can see my abs!

The team gathers around to jump up and down and yell for a while. My actor training comes in handy for this. I can scream really loud now, and it doesn't hurt my throat because I use my diaphragm muscle.

I must have spaced off for a second or two (thousand) because Coach has just smashed his whistle into my helmet and is yelling into my face mask. I'm not sure what I missed. He is bellowing, "You dad-burn-guckin foose, ejit!" (Without using his diaphragm.)

Nobody knows exactly what a "guckin foose" is, but he only says it when he's really pissed, and it's usually followed by this stupid hitting/punishment drill called Oklahoma Road.

My boys start lining up for it before he's even finished screaming at me. Oklahoma Road is basically a two-hundred-yard sprint where you have to blast your way through a group of guys every ten yards. It's exhausting. You just smash and smash until you get to the end of the road . . . or you die. The drill has no purpose other than to make us tougher. There is no practical application of this drill in a game situation. Guys never take you on in neat groups, and once you've dealt with a blocker or tackler, the play is usually over. But coaches seem to love this exercise.

Since it appears that I am the reason we have to do it (still have no idea why), Coach yells, "Carly, you're up first, you cooter box!"

I can only guess what a cooter box is, but I know I'm "Carly," because awesome hair is appreciated on the football field about as much as contemplation. Today was not the first day I've been snapped out of a daydream by a red-faced coach holding half of a whistle in his hand. I find this kind of anger silly, but I know better than to laugh (now).

Coach asks, "You want to line up, or do you just want to coach this one, dipstick?"

I also know that "coaching one" is not really an option, so I jog to the top of the road and get down into my three-point stance. Before blowing the whistle, Coach makes me wait until it feels like my fingers are going to break, but he knows what he's doing. I'm so pissed off by the time I collide with the first set of guys that I don't even feel the pain. After the twentieth *WHAAACK* the hurt actually feels good.

Before I know it, we're all limping back to the locker room and laughing about something. I'm either brain damaged or I had fun. I think I caught three passes while I was on the scrub team offense, and I got to kick field goals with the varsity kicker.

It's almost impossible to turn the shower knobs because

I jammed all of my digits during Oklahoma Road. And I loudly sigh, "Thank you!" when I finally get the buttons of my jeans fastened.

I flip the wet hair out of my eyes to see what my boys are laughing at.

Now that the season is in full swing, injuries aren't that much fun, but my boys never get tired of crowing on my hair.

"Does anyone have a blow-dryer Carter can use?" EJ asks.

"And some product!" Bag yells. "His flop-do won't cooperate without it!"

Doc adds, "I need ten cc's of gel and a can of mousse over here, STAT!"

My instinct is to tell them that I actually use a very expensive *pomade*, but I'm not that brain damaged. I still foolishly try to defend myself from their attacks. "I don't even own a blow-dryer."

This is true, but I've been using the crap out of my sister's lately. They don't care, though. I'm going to get made fun of for a while, and we all know it.

"How do you style your pubes, then?" J-Low asks.

"When are *American Idol* tryouts, Carter?" TrimSpa asks.

Andre sneers. "You look gay."

I just shake my head. "Good one, Mongo! Gold star for helmet!"

Everybody laughs at my joke, which diverts attention away from my hairdo just long enough to get them off track. Somebody tries to start it back up by saying I look like Ellen DeGeneres, but somebody else says that Bag's mom really looks like her, and that gets us discussing moms, and we debate who's got the hottest mother (mine would be pleased to know that she's in fourth place, but I'll be damned if I'd ever tell her). The subject of mothers somehow shifts into theories that college girls are easier than high school chicks, and then we dive straight into the age-old debate: boobs or butts? The gallery is divided, as usual, with powerful arguments on both sides of the issue. The only thing we can agree on is that it's definitely easier to be a butt man than a boob guy. Every one of us has been busted in a boob-gawk, but you have to accidentally make a noise to get busted checking out a booty.

Bag explains, "You just have to make sure the girl's parents or boyfriend are not watching you watch their girl's ass."

Nutt believes (because his brother Bart told him) that the whole idea of men opening doors for ladies is closer to a dog sniffing another dog's butt than it is to chivalry. He asks, "You think chicks can't open a friggin' door? You let 'em go ahead of you in the elevator, why? So you can check the bumper for dents!"

"Then they thank you for it!" Doc adds.

"You are welcome, lady!" EJ cheers.

The locker room falls silent again. I stopped paying attention for a second, so I'm not sure what shut them up. Somebody must be doing something stupid. I look beyond my reflection in the wall mirror to see a gaggle of eyeballs staring back at me. Dang it. They've caught me playing with my bangs again.

Bag breaks the silence. "Do you need some help, Carter? Should we call your stylist?"

I just shake my head, but hair falls into my eyes and I instinctively flip it away with a head toss. I must be doing the hair-flip thing too much, because twenty guys all do it right back, to mock me. As a sophomore, I understand that teasing isn't personal. When I was a freshman, I thought I could control this crap, but I've learned that a mob *has* to pick on something, somebody . . . anything. It's not real; it's sport. Everybody enjoys making fun of other people. Some do it behind the victim's back, but my boys like to keep things out in the open, and enjoy the entire show. I know the worst thing I can do is actually get upset (they love tears) or attempt any witty comebacks.

Bag says, "You know Scary Terry might not be so anxious to fight you if you didn't look like a girl."

"Nobody has seen Terry in weeks, dude," I reply. "And I doubt a friggin' haircut would help that situation."

"You'd look a hell of a lot tougher if you shaved your head again," Nutt says.

The whole team says, "Yeah!" like it's the greatest idea in the world.

I do look pretty badass with a buzz. But just as I'm starting to picture the David Beckham version of Will Carter (in this vision, I've got a tattoo on my neck and I'm wearing a white suit), Andre says, "You'll have to shave your head for the state championships in a few months anyway."

Hold up, now! That almost sounded like encouragement. Andre has never given anyone moral support, especially not me.

"That's not until February," I say. "And only if I make it to the state championships."

"You're totally going to!" Bag cheers.

I squint my eyes at him in response. EJ senses that I'm on to them, and quickly adds, "Look, my dad has those old clippers in the basement and we could finally break out the boxing gloves and practice for your fight with Scary Terry!"

"Why am I always alone in this imaginary fight? He went to jail for hitting you, you know!"

"Quit saying that. You know we've got your back, and we will help you with your boxing skills . . . after we give you a haircut."

I start to tell him to shut up, but EJ cuts me off. "AND!!! You guys gotta check out the new ride!"

"You got the car?!" I ask.

He nods and says, "Yep, the old man brought it home last night."

*New* is probably the wrong way of describing a 1969 Dodge Dart, but it is new to us.

"You gotta see the backseat!" EJ adds. "It's like a motel on wheels!"

Everyone sees the possibilities at the same time, and I say, "Awesome!"

He knows he's got me. He continues, "By the time we finish cutting your hair and kicking your ass, my dad'll be home, and we can take the old girl out for a spin!"

"Come on, Carter!" everyone pleads.

It's tough to resist people when they seem like they're looking out for you, and especially when things sound like fun . . . but I'm a sophomore now! I'm not falling for this old bait-and-switch routine. They do *not* have my best interests at heart; all they see is a cliff that it would be fun to push someone off, and I seem to be standing on the edge. My ears are way too big to rock a shaved head properly, and everybody knows it!

I grab my backpack and say, "No way! I've watched

your dad cut dingleberries off of your dog's butt-hole with those clippers."

They're still trying to sell me on the cleaning power of bleach and the benefits of a free haircut as we walk out of the locker room. Everyone sees Abby sitting on the bleachers reading a book, and they all know that she's waiting for me. It's a dream come true for *me* to be *the guy* that a beautiful girl is looking for! Everyone is jealous. Not only is Abby hot . . . she knows how to read!

My heart is pounding, but I fight the urge to run up to her yelling, "HIYA, ABBY!!!" I simply walk over and lightly kick her foot before asking, "S'up, nerd?"

She smiles and says, "Just finished drill team. Wanted to see what the cool boys were up to."

EJ explains, "We're going to my house to check out my new ride and shave Carter's balls."

"Really?" she asks.

"No. That is not what we are doing. They want me to cut the hair on my skull, though."

"But Carter is worried he'll get kicked out of the boy band he's starting," Nutt adds.

Everyone laughs, and I extend the appropriate finger. Abby gets serious when she asks me, "Can I talk to you for a second?"

My boys peel off for the parking lot. EJ has to come back and collect Andre, because he's staring at Abby like a lost puppy (pit bull).

She asks, "So, EJ got a new car?"

I know she has something bad to tell me, and the fact that she's not getting right to it is troubling.

"No," I explain. "The car is really old. It was his

great-aunt's, but she died. It's got a really powerful engine and a huge backseat." I raise my eyebrows suggestively.

She laughs as if I'm joking, and says, "That'll come in handy if he needs to transport a lot of cargo."

"Yep, that's just what we were saying."

"I'm sure it was." She touches my hair and asks, "Are you really thinking of shaving your head again?"

"I don't know, maybe."

"You'll look cute either way," she says.

I lean in and kiss her on the lips. I better get what I can get while I can still get it. She pulls back before we can start any tongue action. She's not looking at me, so I finally say, "You wanna tell me what's going on?"

"Sorry." She laughs nervously. "I think you're going to be mad at me."

"Only one way to find out."

"I can't go to homecoming with you," she says.

"What?! Who're you going with?"

"I have to go to New York that weekend," she explains.

Her mom is written all over this! She must have found out that Bag is getting a hotel room after the dance, and I was thinking about booking one too. I try not to show my disappointment when I say, "Oh."

"I have to check out the school and the dorms and stuff," she says. "And the city too. I've never been, so I don't know if I'll even like New York."

"You might hate it," I say hopefully.

She nods. "Or the school might change their minds and be like, 'You are uninvited, dork.'"

"I don't see that happening. And if it does, who needs 'em?"

She kisses me and says, "Thanks."

I love kissing Abby more than anything, but I'm so distracted that I'm kind of phoning this one in. The shadow of doom seems to be floating around us. I've always known that Abby was too cool for me . . . because people are always saying things like, "She's too cool for you." But I've allowed myself to believe that they're wrong and that we're meant to be together. She pulls back and says, "What do you think about coming to New York?"

"Instead of homecoming? With your mom? I don't know, dude."

She whacks my shoulder. "No, I think you should apply to the New York Drama School."

"Really?"

"Yeah. I've been thinking about it, and I know they would take you. You've got the tuition covered with your movie money. It seems like your creativity could really thrive in a place like that, and we could have so much fun together!"

I instantly picture us having sex in a dimly lit, small apartment with brick walls, and then on an old metal fire escape.

She asks, "What are you thinking?"

"Uhhh, just that it's a big step."

"Yeah," she agrees.

"I-I-I don't even have a driver's license."

She says, "Neither do I, but you don't need one in New York. You just take the subway or ride your bike."

"That's cool, but no . . . you're smart and like, organized. I don't even know how to make mac and cheese."

"What does that have to do with anything?" she asks.

"Well, my mom still takes care of a lot of my life for me."

Abby continues, "They have advisers to help you and a dining hall that feeds you."

"I-I-I just don't think I'm ready to leave home yet, Abby."

"You wouldn't even start until next year," she adds. "And you'll never be *ready* to leave your mom. She's too awesome. I just thought that you don't really like football or swimming—or school, for that matter. The only class you enjoy is drama . . . so—"

"And gym! They probably wouldn't even have gym at performing arts school."

"They have dance classes," she points out.

Oooh, that would be cool. I do love to dance. I picture myself sashaying across a large open studio with tall windows, and no one makes fun of me for doing it. Abby interrupts my daydream to say, "I just wanted to plant the seed. I think you'd rock in New York, and it would be so nice to have you there with me. And since I can't go to homecoming—"

I visualize us doing it in the back of a taxicab. . . . It's a minivan so there's plenty of space to—

Abby snaps her fingers in my face to regain my attention. "Huh?" I ask.

She says, "I said, what do you think about taking Amber Lee to the dance?"

"What?!"

She shakes her head and repeats, "I was just saying to you that since I can't go, why not take her?"

"Uhhh, well, first off, she's pregnant. And if you recall, I actually took her to that dance last year, and she ditched me."

"Rusty won't take her," she whines. "He's being a dick. He thinks everyone is going to stare at him like he's a loser who got a girl pregnant, dropped out of school, and now works at a body shop."

"I could see how that might happen."

"But who cares? Amber is *really* upset about it," she sighs.

"Going to a dance is her biggest concern right now?"

"She thinks everything is going to be different when she has the baby," she says. "Like she'll never go to prom and all of that, and she's pretty depressed. I just know that getting dressed up and dancing and hanging out with you would make her feel so much better."

"I am pretty awesome."

She kisses me again and says, "Just think about it. No pressure. If you ever wanted to recue a damsel in distress, this is your chance."

"Okay . . . I'll think about it."

"Thank you!" she cheers. "You'd better catch up with your friends. But be good, and don't do anything you don't want to do." As if she didn't just ask me to do a bunch of junk I clearly don't want to do.

# 5. SHAVING YOUR WIENER

Abby goes back into the halls. She's editing some video for the school newspaper. This place is going to fall apart without her. I peer out of the field house windows and survey the parking lot. These days, I like to make sure no psychos are waiting to take me out before I exit a building. My boys are waiting for me by the bike racks. It's nice to know that people have your back (even if they want to shave your head).

I don't tell them about Abby's ideas, but I do make the mistake of flipping the hair out of my eyes, twice, as I'm unlocking.

Bag asks, "Can we get you a scrunchie, Floppio?"

"Enough! Do you ever just stop?!"

Dang it. My boys can smell the weakness in me. They have shark DNA. EJ puts his hand on my shoulder and says, "Don't you think it's time we got rid of this thing?"

Bag adds, "You'll feel better if you just clean the slate."

"Fine," I sigh.

They roar with excitement. I don't blame them. We enjoy watching one another go through painful situations, and love to participate whenever possible. As we take off, I tell EJ about Abby asking me to apply to the New York Drama School.

"What are you gonna do?" he asks.

"I don't know."

He nods with empathy. "What do you *want* to do?"

I shrug my shoulders with indecision, so he pushes me into the drainage ditch at the edge of the parking lot. I avoid a wipeout, because this happens to me a lot. I have to really hustle to catch up with the pack, and I realize that they're riding faster than usual. They're also bunny hopping every crack in the road and they're giggling like girls. It's easy to see that my boys want this haircut way more than I do, so I decide to have some fun.

As we turn onto Merrian Lane, I exclaim, "Naahhh, I can't do it, guys; I've changed my mind!"

They wail like babies who've had a toy ripped out of their hands. I slyly add, "Well, maybe if I had some company . . ."

They look at me as if they don't get it, so I go ahead and spell it out for them: "I will only shave my head if everyone of you does too!"

How many terrible things have been unleashed on the world after hearing or saying something like that? Most rational humans would say no, because it's absurd to shave your head just because someone dares you, but no one has ever used the word "rational" to describe fifteen-year-old males. We are the guys who get the "If your friends are jumping off a cliff" speech from an adult on a regular basis. But we're sans grown-ups at the moment, and we don't talk each other off of cliffs . . . we push!

Andre yells, "Done!" because he's already got short hair, but the other guys drop their heads in defeat as we roll into EJ's neighborhood. They don't want buzz cuts just as it's starting to get cold, but they're powerless to say or do anything that will stop it from happening.

We ride in silence until Nutt asks, "Did you know that those sensors on auto-flush toilets are measuring your penis?"

"What the hell's the matter with you?" EJ asks.

Nutt replies, "Bart's writing a research paper about testosterone, and he stumbled onto these government reports that are documenting the shrinking of the American wiener. Think about it. No one is going to volunteer to get his dong measured."

"Especially if they're going to tell you it's too small," I add.

"Exactly!" Nutt says. "The government doesn't care if a urinal is flushed; that's just a bonus. The little red light starts flashing when you unzip your jeans. That's a camera, dude."

Levi says, "No way. That would cost billions."

"Why do you think our country is in so much debt?" Nutt asks.

No one says anything, so he continues. "Bart says they've been working on it for years. During World War II, the military conducted the same study on GI's because they'd noticed such a decline in size since the First World War."

Doc suspiciously interjects, "Wouldn't they have better things to do in a war?"

"I haven't noticed this chapter in my American history book," I add.

Nutt retorts, "It was top secret! They don't want other countries to find out how small we're getting! They think it's happening all over the world, but no one will talk about it. But it's like: why did dudes start wearing skinny jeans all the sudden? Old-time guys only wore baggy pants and they pulled them up real high so their meat couldn't fall out. Ancient men rocked kilts and robes because they couldn't handle pants at all."

I don't think trousers were even invented back then, but Hormone adds, "The Spartans sure would've blown out the crotch of some Emo-pants!"

We've all seen the movie *300* about three hundred times and it's obvious that those guys were tougher than us (even though they wore miniskirts). It stands to reason that they'd have bigger wangs too.

"Pee shooters started shrinking during the industrial revolution because of pollution and because we stopped hunting and fishing for our food," Nutt explains. "Dudes start working at desks and pushing paper, so their testosterone levels drop. Women are taking control because brute strength is basically useless in the modern world. So our king-size Snickers are shifting into minibites!"

We roll up to EJ's house and finally see *IT* parked under the basketball goal. FREEDOM!!! A poop-brown 1969 Dodge Dart, Swinger edition! EJ's great-aunt Jenny died last month, and his dad bought this car from her estate for a dollar! EJ's mom thinks they got ripped off, but the boys and I think *we* got the deal of the century. His mom wanted to get EJ a convertible Beetle, but that dream died when Aunt Jenny kicked the bucket, and EJ was able to retain his dignity for a while longer.

According to EJ, the Dodge Dart came with a 426-cubic-inch Hemi-powered engine. I don't know exactly what that means, but I try to seem impressed along with the rest of my boys. I gather that this car is very fast and we're going to become some of *those* people who bitch about gas prices (and speeding tickets) soon.

I love that it's got a chrome emblem on the side that says "Swinger"! It's just a special edition of this type of car, but it's also what my grandpa would say when he wanted to call someone a player.

Doc explains, "This car was made for free love, in the height of the Swinging Sixties! The backseat is just a twin-size mattress with safety belts!"

"Take it easy," EJ warns. "Nobody is getting any 'free love' in this thing except me."

Everyone laughs at him because we all know that EJ would never enforce a rule that caused the rest of us to not get laid. He's aware that this isn't just his car. The Johnsons may have some paper that says they own it, technically, and EJ will probably be the one that wrecks it, but this thing is public property. We're all going to take part in its destruction. It still smells like an old lady's perfume, but it'll soon stink like a locker room (a combination of Axe body spray and a homeless dude's armpit) and have a lot of questionable stains on the vinyl seats.

We're giddy with the thought of never having to cram into Hormone's CRX again. Bag pets the plush seat like it's a cat and gasps, "I'm gonna have so much sex in your grandma's ride!"

EJ clarifies. "She was my great-aunt! And at least let me be the first to use her."

We all seem to agree that this is a fair arrangement. J-Low shakes EJ's shoulders and yells, "Make Aunt Jenny proud, E!"

Just like that, a car that could be nicknamed so many things will be forever known as "Aunt Jenny." Good nicknames work like that.

We don't have her keys, so we can only give her a virtual test drive. We work out the geometry of the car (in our own way)—she can handle eleven dudes at once, and that's not including her massive trunk (the lewd jokes are endless).

Nutt is sitting in the driver's seat when EJ's dad pulls into the driveway. Nutt is wearing Aunt Jenny's old sun goggles, and he honks the horn and asks, "Hey, sonny boy, you wanna go fo' a ride?!"

EJ's dad seems happy that we like the car, but also a little nervous. It doesn't help that his son and four of his friends are climbing out of the trunk, and Doc asks him, "Do you know why they called it the Swinging Sixties, Mr. Johnson?"

He just walks past in silence. EJ asks, "Dad, where are the hair clippers and the old boxing gloves?"

Fathers are like natural-born detectives. He smells trouble, and stops to ask suspiciously, "Why?"

EJ assures him that it's nothing out of the ordinary. "We're just gonna shave our heads and start a fight club."

His dad peers into Aunt Jenny's rear window as if we're a pack of aliens that has landed in his driveway. You'd think he'd shut this whole operation down, and you would've been right last year. But EJ's family has been going to counseling for the past few months. I guess the therapist laid into his mom pretty good for "overparenting" and not allowing her kids to fail. This doctor lady warned EJ's parents that their kids might never leave the nest, because they give out the gold stars too easily. So both his mom and dad have been giving EJ a lot of freedom lately. (Notice the race car in the driveway. The one that says "Swinger" on the side.) Mr. Johnson just walks into the house without telling us where the clippers or gloves are.

EJ says, "I gotcha, Dad, we'll find 'em!"

I also think Mr. Johnson needs an excuse if anybody's parents (mine) want to bitch him out when they learn at whose house their son shaved his head and got a black eye.

We rip the basement apart for ten minutes before EJ remembers that the clippers are in the emergency kit (a plastic tub that holds a flashlight, duct tape, pudding, beef jerky, Band-Aids, and hair clippers). I guess the Johnsons worry about snacking and grooming during a crisis.

The shears are almost as badass as Aunt Jenny. They're big, old, and loud. We clean them with some bleach and an old toothbrush, and get to work.

EJ cackles as he shaves a tic-tac-toe board into the side of my skull and then "HI" into the other side. On some level, I'm being tortured, but on another, I'm having a blast. This is the junk I missed over the summer, and what I'd miss out on if I went to some private boarding school in New York City. Abby would be there, but there would be nothing like this going on, I'm sure.

I hate seeing the locks fall before my eyes, but I feel light as a feather when I'm back to stubble all the way around. We take turns with the barber duties, and J-Low gives EJ a rat tail that looks awesome. We almost convince him to keep it, but he eventually shaves it off himself.

I'm just finishing Bag's haircut, stripping the last bits

of fuzz off his oddly shaped skull and wondering if he was dropped as a baby. I'm also wondering how much barbers get paid when Bag suddenly whips around and says, "Yo, Carter—"

That's all he gets out before the old shears gobble up most of his right eyebrow. It sounds like a garbage disposal grinding up a baby bunny. Even the clippers seem to know they've done something they shouldn't have.

I scream, "Ohhhh, noooo!" before pointing at him and laughing my ass off.

"WOOOWWW!!!" EJ gasps.

Bag sprints into a tiny half-bathroom under the stairs. He looks in the mirror and cries, "DUUUDE!!!" before he starts moaning like a wounded dog. The rest of us are hysterically laughing on the floor. He's obviously not seeing the humor yet (probably won't until after Christmas). There are only about four hairs left toward the middle of his brow.

"You look like a mad scientist about to come up with a plan!" Doc says.

"You look cross-eyed!" J-Low adds.

EJ says, "Yo, you gotta shave that little patch off."

I remind Bag of the challenge he issued to me about an hour ago. "Clean the slate, bro!"

Bag is trembling with frustration. He wants to blame me, but everyone saw him turn right into the clipper's path.

"Okay, I'll shave off the rest of my eyebrow if you guys shave one of yours!" he yells out, like it's the best idea ever.

That trick seems to work only once a day and doesn't apply to essential face hair. So Bag raises the shears to his forehead and strips off what's left of his right brow. It doesn't help the crazy factor. Now he just looks very suspicious of everything.

We giggle like a pack of skinhead schoolgirls. We all look strange, but Bag looks *ri-dic-ulous*!

"I'm not gonna get laid for months!" he whines.

*Join the club, and replace "months" with "ever."*

EJ observes, "It's like your left eye is wearing a fake mustache as a hat."

"What the hell am I gonna do?!" Bag asks.

I yell over the laughter, "Get me a Sharpie! We'll draw it back on."

Andre finally says what we're all thinking: "You gotta get rid of the other one, dude."

"Clean the slate!" I cheer.

Bag reluctantly shaves off his other eyebrow . . . and normal appearance. Who knew eyebrows were so important? He's on the verge of tears, so we try not to laugh for a second. But then he looks up at us like a puppy that's returned from his first trip to the groomer and asks hopefully, "Is it that bad?"

We fall all over ourselves. Bag has no sense of humor about this because he just broke up with this girl, Kathy, and he was a total dick about it, so he won't be able to get her back. And now that he looks like a giant newborn baby, he's as dead meat with the girls who don't know him as he is with the ones who do.

EJ's dad is in the kitchen reading the newspaper when we come up from the basement. Bag is the first guy he sees. He drops the paper in shock and gasps, "Oh, lord!" I don't think their therapist has covered the possible negative side of "freedom," because Mr. Johnson just gets up and heads for the door. "I wasn't here. You didn't see me."

"Hey, we can't find those old boxing gloves, Dad," EJ says.

His dad stops to considers his next move. EJ continues, "We really need them. I told you that guy Scary Terry got out of juvie, so we're going to practice fighting. Maybe you could show us some moves from your old boxing days?"

His dad rubs his face in frustration. "I don't know how to box, Emilio! Those are antique boxing gloves. Your mom got them for decoration when you were a baby . . . and they've been hanging on the wall of *your bedroom* ever since, genius!"

The old leather boxing gloves are indeed hanging above EJ's dresser. They're mixed in with a whole collage of other old sports crap, but we still tease him mercilessly for not knowing where they were. The gloves are rad. They're deep brown and soft as hell. The only problem is there's only one pair, so on the way to the backyard we snag a pair of his dad's ski mittens. The plan is that one guy gets the left boxing glove and the other guy gets the right, and we switch between rounds to keep it fair.

We mark off our ring with a garden hose and we time the rounds with my watch. Real boxing matches have three-minute rounds, but ours are only two because no one can keep his hands up for that long. Sometimes our rounds last four or five minutes, though, when I space off and start enjoying the show instead of doing my job and banging the pots together.

EJ and I fight after Doc and Bag. We hit each other a

few times, but mostly we just walk around in circles talking trash and trying to breathe. Boxing is way harder than it looks, and getting punched or punching with the mitten hand sucks!

Levi knocked Nutt out cold. It was really Nutt knocking himself out by leaning into a flailing girlie punch. His eyes glazed over before his knees splayed out to the sides and went out from under him. Andre caught him like a toddler before his head could hit the grass.

The first rule of fight club is, *You do not talk about fight club.* Mostly because it's embarrassing. A few fights ended with guys crying, and even Andre looked like a scared girl during his first rounds. But it's like anything else: once you get whacked a few times it's not so bad. My left eye appears to be swelling shut, and it's definitely throbbing, but I'm having a blast.

We're watching Hormone and J-Low fight when EJ puts his arm around me and says, "You won't get this at some drama school."

"Is that a good or bad thing?" I ask.

He continues, "My dad said I could drive Aunt Jenny to homecoming. Do you want to double-date?"

"Just because we have a car doesn't mean we have dates."

"I'll just take Nicky," he replies. "And I heard you were taking Amber Lee."

"How do you even know about that?"

"Nicky told me that Abby was gonna ask you to ask her, and we all know you'll do anything she says."

"That's kind of rude, dude."

"Are you or are you not planning to ask the pregnant

girl that ditched you at that same dance last year?" he asks.

"Shut up."

He laughs. "I hear pregnant chicks get mad horny."

I give him a disgusted look. "Gross!"

"Don't tell me you haven't thought about it, you sick freak," he says. "Come on, we could have fun at that dance."

"Naw, man, you're hanging out with Nicky because she lets you have sex with her. I, on the other hand, avoid crazy."

He scoffs, but I know he's actually kind of bummed because he doesn't want to be alone with Nicky. I change the subject. "What do you think about the New York thing, seriously?"

But he's still too pissed about the prospect of an evening with Nicky to be objective. He just asks me, "Do you even know how to make mac and cheese?"

"Shut up."

While Hangin' Chad is beating the crap out of TrimSpa, some juniors come walking down the slope of EJ's backyard. They heard about the fight club and they want in . . . until Andre randomly clocks one of them with the boxing glove. He thought it would be funny, and I guess he thought it wouldn't hurt the kid if he was wearing the glove, but it looked like he killed the guy. The junior eventually started twitching and moaning, but it was scary for a second.

My best friend and I never really got the chance to discuss my leaving home early. I fought three more times that day, and I know I got hit a few times, but I don't think I got rocked. I must have, though, because I don't remember riding home. Mom freaked out a little about my haircut, but then she noticed my bike was parked in the guest bedroom instead of the garage. Once she figured out why I was stumbling around the kitchen like a wino, she stopped worrying about the hair.

# 6. FOCUS, DANIEL-SON

EJ passed his driver's test, so we're officially mobile! Eleven dudes pile into Aunt Jenny after football practice on Friday. We go to EJ's for a fight club session and then head to the theater to see the new Fast and the Furious movie. Unfortunately, only a few of us have money, and the penguins busted us trying to sneak everyone else in the side door. EJ only has permission to drive to the movie and the gas station, so we head to QuikTrip to loiter for a few hours.

At the stoplight on Merrian Lane, an old yellow Cutlass pulls up next to us real slow. Everyone stiffens because it's exactly like Scary Terry's car. No one looks at the driver, but eventually J-Low says, "No bass, right?"

"The trunk bolts aren't rattling," Nutt agrees.

We all look over at the older man in the car next to us. We should explain why we seem to be laughing at him, but that would be even weirder. You see, Terry likes his music with a lot of bass. His sound system is probably awesome if you're in the car, but if you're not, all you hear is bolts rattling.

The old dude is gawking at Aunt Jenny like she's wearing a bikini. Eventually he rolls down his window and says, "Nice Swinger!"

I mutter, "Take it easy, buddy," but no one can hear it because EJ has put Aunt Jenny into neutral and revs her huge engine . . . *VVVRRROOOOM, ROOOOHHM, ROOOOHHM!!!*

The whole car shudders like a wild animal shaking water off of its fur. The old guy nods with admiration before revving his own engine.

Nutt says, "I think old boy wants to go!"

"Hell yeah!" Bag yells. "Fast and Furious!"

"Smoke this fool!" Andre barks.

My wuss instinct says, "I don't know, dude, it's the first time—" but my words are drowned out by the roaring engine again. The light turns green and the Cutlass lights up its back tires and rips across the line. I see EJ floor the gas pedal, but the car doesn't move. He seems to have flooded it. We're covered in smoke and defeat . . . until Aunt Jenny shudders again and we're all slammed into our seats. Four hundred and twenty-six cubic inches of American muscle scream like a rocket being launched as the back end fishtails around and the tires start eating pavement.

We chant, "GO, GO, GO!!!" as she easily overtakes the Cutlass and leaves it in the dust.

"Aunt Jenny was just toyin' with him!" I cheer.

EJ yells, "Holy crap, we're going a hundred and ten on Merrian Lane!"

Things look so different when you've crossed that hundred-mile-an-hour mark. We fly right past QuikTrip and almost take out a Mitsubishi Eclipse that's trying to turn ahead of us. EJ whips the massive steering wheel around and skids to the side, plowing through the grass in front of the Econo Lodge. We bounce over a median before getting back to QuikTrip. We crack up and make fun of EJ's driving, but we're all very impressed with Aunt Jenny.

She is suddenly, completely out of gas, so EJ almost nails a gas pump while pulling up to it. We act out a skit where EJ has blown up the station as we get out.

Doc says, "Speaking of explosions, has anyone even seen Scary Terry?"

"I bet he got arrested again," Bag says.

"We would've heard something like that," I say. "I think he heard about our fight club and he's like, 'Screw that! I'm ain't messin' with Will Carter now that he's a badass.'"

Nutt adds, "Or he's in Cambodia, training with Muay Thai monks, so that he can kill you without evidence. . . . Make it look like you just died in your sleep, but when the doctors open you up, all of your organs are mangled."

"Shut up."

EJ pumps gas and adds, "I bet he's in New York City. They love crazy people there. He's just waiting for you in some subway tunnel."

Abby downloaded the application for the New York Drama School for me, and EJ saw it in my backpack yesterday. I haven't filled it out because it's ridiculously long, but he keeps making these negative comments about New York all the time. Before I can call him out, Rusty's LTD pulls up to the pump across from us. Old cars are cool, but they love gas.

Rusty's without Amber again, and hanging with some sketchy dudes instead. They seem drunk when they stumble out of the car, so we keep our distance. He struggles with the gas cap as one of his friends lies down on the hood of that Eclipse we almost smashed into.

Doc quietly observes, "It could be worse, Carter. You could be having a baby with Amber Lee and living with her dad."

"There's always next year," I say. "Have you guys ever been inside her house?"

Bag replies, "Nope, I like my dick right where it is!"

"It's really nice, and her dad isn't so bad. . . . He's kinda funny, actually."

My boys obviously care more about junk food than interior design or the complexities of human nature, because they just walk away from me into the QuikTrip. We enter as a group and find Jeremy waiting in line to pay for some Twizzlers. He's with Bandana Boy, obviously on an awkward first date, so I get right behind them and ask the clerk in a deep voice, "Yo, you guys still keep the Magnums behind the counter?"

Jeremy and Bandana Boy slowly turn around, and I say, "I'm sorry, did you just ask that same question, J?"

Jeremy gasps and says, "Shut up, Carter!" as he swats my shoulder.

"No penis jokes on a first date?"

My boys head for the chips like they're hungry, but I'm pretty sure they just don't want to talk about condoms with gay dudes. They're not bashers or anything; they just haven't spent enough time in the drama department.

Jeremy introduces me to the guy. I think his name is Brad, but it's hard to concentrate on anything except his head wrap.

I tell them about getting kicked out of the movie

theater, but Bandana Boy obviously couldn't care less and heads to the magazine rack. Jeremy rolls his eyes, so I ask, "Is it not going well?"

He sighs. "I don't know. He's kind of annoying. We just talked about gasoline for five minutes. I tried to help fill up his car, and I got a lecture about 'performance engines' and 'octane levels' or something."

"I didn't realize the Eclipse was a high-performance vehicle."

"Nobody did," Jeremy quips.

Rusty and his crew slither through the glass doors and head back toward my boys. Jeremy says, "Poor Rusty. He's an a-hole, but I feel sorry for him now. Hey, can I ditch my date and hang out with you guys?"

"Absolutely."

"Where are you headed after this?" he asks.

"Oh, we've arrived. We're just hangin' out in front of QuikTrip tonight."

He rolls his eyes. "Never mind."

"I thought you liked this dude."

"I do," he explains. "It's just that barf-scarf he's wearing on his head! Yuck. I tried to talk to him about it earlier, and he got snippy."

"Does he have cancer?" I whisper.

"No!" Jeremy laughs. "He may be going bald, though. That's still no excuse for being rude."

"He's probably nervous. Nobody likes criticism . . . especially on a first date, and when the person owns an Eclipse and does show choir—"

Jeremy snaps, "Watch it! I told him the bandana was

cute, but I suggested that he keep it in his pocket or wear it like a sexy cowboy neckerchief."

I prove that I am related to Lynn Carter by rolling my eyes.

Jeremy sighs. "You're right . . . I'm the a-hole." And he goes back to collect his new friend. My boys come up to the counter with Rusty right behind them. Rusty rams his shoulder into Jeremy and says, "Sorry about that, sweetie."

Jeremy straightens himself. "No, it's my fault, my shoulders have gotten so big, lately. I work out a lot."

Rusty looks at Bandana Boy and asks, "Is this like a gay date?"

"It's *just* like a gay date, Rusty. That's very observant. Is Amber home with the kids?"

Rusty is no match for Jeremy's wit, so he turns his attention to Bandana Boy. He touches the guy's head scarf before Bandana Boy knocks his hand away and says, "Don't!"

Rusty puffs out his chest and says, "Take it easy, gangsta."

"There is no need to touch, Rusty," Jeremy scolds. "Did you have some after-work cocktails at the body shop?"

Nutt laughs out loud any time he hears the word *cock*. Rusty seems to think he's being made fun of, because his cheeks flush and he just walks out of the store without paying for his drink. His friends follow, and the cashier picks up the phone like he's going to call the cops.

"No, no . . . I'll pay for their drinks, and all of this crap," I say, like a boss.

I like to complain about paying for stuff, but I love being able to do it. The clerk seems bummed that he doesn't get to bust somebody tonight, but I know the last thing Rusty needs is to get arrested, or get into any stupid fights . . . which he's totally going to do.

"Yo!" EJ yells, and points out the window.

Rusty has just thrown his whole soda onto the hood of the Eclipse. His friends think it's the funniest thing in the world. Bandana Boy does not. He's charging toward his car like an angry little dog, and I rush out the door. I don't want to get beat up defending a Mitsubishi, but Jeremy is one of my best friends, so what are you going to do?

Jeremy is pulling Bandana Boy back, yelling, "Stop! It's so not worth it."

But Rusty kicks the hood of the car and sneers, "Don't want to mess with the homobile!"

"Hey!" Jeremy yells.

I back him up and say, "Rusty, chill out."

He turns his attention to me and says, "You need to learn to mind your own business, boy!"

My heart races, and I can't think of anything to say, so I just glare at him. I should've said, *This* is *my business, fella!* But the moment has passed, so I keep my mouth shut.

Bandana Boy says, "You bastard!" when he notices the scratch on his hood. He has tears in his eyes as he charges Rusty again.

"Step off!" Rusty sneers as he shoves the kid and snatches the bandana off his head. "Do-raggot FAGGOT?!"

For the record, Bandana Boy is losing his hair.

Rusty's friends laugh, and I'm only able to say, "Hey—" before Jeremy has leapt five feet into the air and spun around. I've seen him jump before, so I knew he had some ups . . . but he's not doing jazz hands tonight. His fists are drawn up beside his face, and his right foot swings around with lightning speed just before bitch-slapping Rusty's head with the sole of his Top-Sider. *WHAAAACK!!!*

My boys yell, "OHHH!" and my eyes are wide with shock as I file in behind my best (gay) friend who's secretly a badass.

Bandana Boy reties his head scarf, and Rusty holds his red cheek while debating getting beaten up or punking out in front of his friends. Jeremy asks, "Why would you say something like that?! You know that I'm gay. You can see we're on a date, and you also know I've been in Tae Kwon Do since third grade! Every time I won a tournament or got a higher belt, I brought it in for show-and-tell. You really want to gay-bash a fourth-degree black belt? What's wrong with you?"

Rusty just silently fumes.

Jeremy continues, "I'm sorry I did that in front of your friends, but you need to check yourself, Rusty."

This hate crime was over the moment Jeremy's feet left the ground, but it officially ends when a police car's siren chirps and a cop's voice comes over the loudspeaker: "You fellas need to disperse. This a no-loitering zone."

Gotta love the Merrian P.D. Fighting crime without ever getting out of their car! They broke up a brawl last month and didn't bother to arrest the kid who started it.

Rusty and his friends jump into the LTD and speed away, and Jeremy gives me a nod as he opens the passenger door of the Eclipse. "Thanks for backing me up, Carter. It means more to me than you could know."

"Sure," I reply. "Thanks for not needing any help. I

didn't know you were Bruce Lee! Hey, we're doing this fight club thing at EJ's house. Will you come and teach us some of that?"

Jeremy looks at my friends and smiles before he says, "I'd love to."

# 7. THE LOST ANT

My mom found the New York City Drama School application in my backpack and freaked out like it was a donkey porno. Both of my parents were obviously nervous about the prospect of their retarded son (me) moving to the gnarliest city on earth . . . until they really looked at the application requirements. They don't tell me I can't go to the school; they're too slick for that. They've learned through dealings with my sister that the surest way to light a fire under a kid's ass is to forbid them from doing something, so Dad just mentions how difficult it will be to raise my GPA, and Mom explains that my laundry will not "do itself" in New York. They totally agree with Abby that it would be a great learning experience, though. . . . Sneaky, sneaky. They know how much I hate learning experiences and folding clothes.

Dad went to Manhattan when he was ten, and his family got off of the subway without him. Grandpa went berserk trying to pry the doors back open. He says my dad would still be riding that train if he hadn't rescued him. Dad also got yelled at by a drag queen. He says, "For no reason!" but I bet he was gawking at her.

My folks looked over the huge stack of paperwork the school wanted me to fill out, but they didn't offer to help me with it. I could tell that they didn't believe I'd ever fill it all out on my own. What they don't know (because I can forge my dad's signature like a champ) is that I have my first Saturday School coming up.

So I'm sitting in the school library on a Saturday at 5:59 a.m. I didn't kill anyone, but because I keep showing up to my classes thirty seconds after the agreed-upon time, the attendance Nazis have labeled me a menace. Our school district outlawed caning and corporal punishment a few years ago, so this is what they came up with. Can anyone say cruel and unusual? I can't go to after-school detentions because of football, hence Saturday School. They've forced me to wake up at 5:15 a.m. on a Saturday!

If you show up at 6:01 a.m., the warden/evil attendance lady (Mrs. Trimmer, the wife of my prick health teacher from last year) will send you home and give you two more Saturday Schools (a stoner kid, Clint, just learned that lesson). And if you fall asleep at any point, you get two more (a band girl with a snoring problem found that one out at 7:05 a.m.). You *have* to do schoolwork, but you're not allowed to use a computer. It's a recipe for disaster! A quiet, boring library that's a little bit warm . . . why would someone be sleepy in here, especially when they woke up before dawn after hanging out with their boys on a Friday night?

First thing I do is clean out my backpack. I find the Jolly Rancher I've been looking for since the first day of school, as well as a math worksheet I was supposed to do last year! I whip out the old assignment notebook (the one that I haven't opened for four days) and see that I've got a persuasive essay due on Monday for English, and a midterm in biology on Wednesday. Dang it. I consider what to write "persuasively" and flip through my biology textbook for a second, but I find myself looking around the room at my fellow convicts. They're a motley, tired-looking crew. I don't know a lot of them, and it doesn't seem like we're going to get much time to socialize. I wonder if they have Saturday School at the New York Drama School. I doubt they do. I bet I'd be rehearsing some play on a Saturday morning or shooting a little movie that I wrote with a group of cool kids. That would be so rad—

Mrs. Trimmer is snapping her fingers at me, and points to my papers. "Get to work, Mr. Carter."

I whip out a pen and write my name on the drama school application just for something to do, but the next thing I know, I've knocked out fourteen pages of questions and B.S.ed a whole essay about Method acting and my experiences in both film and theater. I don't know my parents' tax ID numbers or my dance belt size, but most of it is done . . . and I've still got two hours left! Dang it.

As I start the rough draft of my English paper, I realize that I've accidentally written a "persuasive essay" as to why I should be allowed into the New York Drama School. Holla! I'll have to change a few details when I type it up (hopefully my mom will help/force me to actually do that).

I bust out my history and science crap. I'm so ahead of the game that I go ahead and take a break to watch a gang of ants enjoying an apple core on the windowsill. It's kind of like biology. They're taking little pieces of fruit back to their hideout. They have one line to get a chunk and another to lug the pieces away. Everyone's got the system figured out . . . except this one ant, who's just doing his own thing and screwing everyone else up. It's like he's lost or doesn't understand the goal or what the hell the hurry is.

He seems to be saying, "Sorry, my bad. Hey fellas, what are we doing again?"

And all the other ants are like, "Move, dumbass!"

I know this ant because he is me! I'm always going the wrong way in the hall, and when it finally starts to thin out and I'm able to consider where the hell I'm headed, the damn bell rings!

The good news is that detention is great focus time. The bad news is that I think there's a connection between success and getting up at the butt crack of dawn to force yourself to do a bunch of crap you don't want to do. Also not having any distractions (like a computer or food) might be good for focus-challenged individuals like myself. It's just a theory, though. . . . I'm not going to write a persuasive essay about it or anything.

McDougle says that the New York Drama School doesn't accept dummies no matter how talented they are. I'll need at least a B+ average to raise my GPA to a B–. That's the lowest they will take, so that's what I'm shooting for. I thought I was pretty close, but it turns out that just because you got a couple of Bs doesn't make that your average. I wasn't that bummed about my C– average until I found out that EJ has a C+ and Bag's dumbass has a 4.0 (that's all As) and Levi somehow has a 4.2 . . . WTF?! What hope is there for me if I don't even know the grade that's higher than an A?! I'm going to need a lot more of these Saturday School detentions if I really want to go to New York.

Fingers are snapping in front of my view of the ants, and Mrs. Trimmer's deep voice says, "Mr. Carter."

"I'm awake!"

"I know." She laughs. "It's ten. Get out of here."

I've got books and papers strewn all across the table, so it takes me a few minutes to jam it all back into my pack.

Mrs. Trimmer asks, "Did you get a lot done?"

"An insane amount!" I reply. I haven't been allowed to speak all day, so I start rambling: "I read two chapters in biology, and I aced the practice quiz. You always see those practice quizzes, but what kind of nerd actually does them? Turns out, I do . . . in Saturday School! I actually read *ahead* in American History. I didn't mean to; I was just reading about the Battle of Concord and I wanted to know how it turned out. . . . We whipped some ass! I did the bonus questions in this geometry packet too. My teachers are going to freak. It sucked getting up early, but I'm going to make school my bitch this week!"

Mrs. Trimmer squints her eyes like she's pissed all the sudden, but she says, "That is great!" all friendly. Then she adds, "We'll see you next week."

"I don't have a Saturday School next week."

"I think you do, since you just called me a bitch," she says.

"No! I meant 'bitch' like a female dog and I was talking about school, not you! I was just trying to illustrate how I was going to dominate the . . . uh . . . Look, we're both tired here, and not thinking clearly, let's just—"

"Maybe you'll use next week's detention to think about how you could use your language a little more carefully."

This is an abuse of power if I've ever seen one. We walk out of the library together, and I explain, "Did you know the Battle of Concord started with an unjust tax on tea and sugar, Mrs. Trimmer?"

"I did," she replies, and marches off toward the faculty parking lot.

All of the other hoodlums have split, but I have to go straight to football practice. I've got fifteen minutes to be in my pads and on the field. I got that, EASY! I am sooo pissed about the additional detention, but I know it's probably a good thing.

I attempt to save a few seconds by taking a short-cut through the auditorium, but I run into Jeremy, who's onstage singing, "'In Camelot!'" at the top of his lungs. I sit in the front row and wait for him to finish, because the song is awesome and I want to make fun of him since the auditions are more than a month away. We're doing the musical *Camelot* this winter. I really want to audition, but it's during the swimming season, so I can't.

He stops singing and takes a bow before he says, "I love your black eye. The *thug* look really works for you, Carter."

"I can give you a haircut when you come over to EJ's this afternoon."

He seems less into the look all the sudden. "Oh, noooo thanks. Are you sure you want me come to your fight club?"

"Absolutely!"

"You're sweet, but come on," he says. "Your friends don't really want to hang out with me."

"Why, because you're older and not as stylish as us?"

He sits on the stage and says, "Seriously, they don't want a gay boy teaching them how to fight."

"Dude, they watched you bitch-slap a guy with your Top-Sider; we fight like kangaroos! We need you! They're good guys, they just don't know you. Let 'em prove you wrong."

"Okay," he sighs. "I'll be there."

I tell him I've got to go, but he adds, "A little bird told me you were planning to ask Amber Lee to homecoming."

"Really? Did this bird have a nice tail and big—"

"You know she does," he says. "When Abby told me, I totally cried. That is sooo sweet, Carter!"

I start to say, "Well, I still haven't—"

But he interrupts me. "I'm renting a limo so I don't have to ride in that stupid Eclipse. A bunch of drama kids are coming, too. You guys are totally welcome."

"Okay, cool . . . I'll talk to Amber."

He continues, "Brad did not ask me to the Rockford Academy homecoming, but I've decided that I am the bigger man, so he will be allowed to dance next to me in my new fake Prada suit!"

"Play on, playa." I give a fist bump.

"I'm going to get him some Rogaine and make him wear a fedora to the dance," he says.

I cross my arms, and he asks, "Why are you giving me that look?"

"What look?"

"You look just like your sister!" he replies.

"Do I? Sorry, I was just realizing that boyfriends are dicks even when they're with another dude. Jeremy, the guy is obviously insecure. Just buy him a hat that you think is cool, give it to him as a gift, and then he can either figure it out or not. But don't buy him Rogaine. That's like telling a girl to go to the gym."

Now he's the one making a face, so I ask, "You told him he should work out, didn't you?"

"I wanted to make it like a date, but he did seem a little upset," Jeremy replies.

I shake my head in disappointment . . . just like my sister would. "I gotta go. I'll see you at three o'clock at EJ's house for fight club and I'll let you know when I talk to Amber."

He does a sweet jumping spin kick as he gets back to his rehearsal and sings, "'They saaay it never rains, in Caaamelooot!!!'"

As I jog out of the auditorium I say, "Congratulations, you just made karate gay!"

I will probably pay for that at fight club.

Although I've been at school for more than four hours, I'm still going to be late to football practice! Anyplace else, they'd be like, "Ten minutes? That's not late! Who cares?" But football coaches are insane. They blow a gasket if you make the tiniest mistake, and they're always yelling, "Every second counts!" But that's kind of ridiculous. You're a grown man who wears cleats to work. Surely some time was wasted, and a few mistakes were made along your path . . . because here you are on a Saturday morning . . . not out on your yacht with your supermodel wife!

I swear the coaches wouldn't care if I robbed a bank on my way, as long as I was on the field and in my pads at 10:29 a.m. But since I can't make it until 10:41 a.m., I'm the Antichrist. I'll have to do some extra-heinous exercises after practice. I might puke. It will suck for sure, but on the bright side, I'm getting in some mean fighting shape!

Fight club goes up about twenty notches with Jeremy's help. We get better, quick . . . because he hits you when you forget a lesson! We call it "reverse gay bashing," but he says that's how martial arts are taught. His teacher is an old-school

Korean dude, so that's how he learned it. I guess Jeremy's dad enrolled him in Tae Kwon Do when he was nine because he started to suspect that Jeremy's *effeminate phase* wasn't a phase. He says his dad is cool with him being gay, but he knew that there were plenty of a-holes in the world who weren't, so he hooked him up with a *gi* (karate costume) and the skills to bitch-slap homophobic d-bags. At first Jeremy just liked the dance routines called "forms," but then he developed a taste for blood. He can break boards with his fist and pressure-point you to the ground if you lip off. He still trains twice a week, and he fights in tournaments. He says it helps him jump really high and keeps him super flexible for dance.

The biggest thing he tries to teach us is patience. He wants us to keep our hands out in front of our faces at all times and just concentrate on our opponent. He wants me to calm down and not get so worked up when I fight. Staying relaxed seems to be the key to life! If you can just stay on your toes and wait for the other guy to do something stupid, you can land a lot more shots. For a guy with as many wuss instincts as I have, I'm doing pretty well. Jeremy obviously likes me more than anyone else, and he keeps giving me tips on how to beat my friends' asses. I also never get very winded during the bouts because of all of my CrossFit punishments, and I'm the only guy who's got an actual psycho looking for him, so that helps too.

# 8. KICKOFF

No one has seen or heard from Scary Terry since Bag's party, but I'm still preparing for the worst. We had a false alarm in front of the movie theater when we heard trunk bolts rattling, but it turned out to be just another old car with an awful stereo system. I freak out whenever someone yells, "CARTER!!!" I really wish people wouldn't do that, but my boys love to see me flinch. Good thing ADD allows me to forget about Terry most of the time, and the fight club lessons are building up a nice sense of false confidence in me.

We've all got bruised faces and we've reshaved our heads. People have stopped asking to borrow pencils from us. Abby likes to rub my stubbly head, but teachers are kind of thrown off by my hooligan look, almost as much as they are by my sudden class participation. They just keep asking questions that I know the answers to! I got a hundred percent on two different tests. That hasn't happened since kindergarten. Unfortunately, I've been given two tardy slips by Wednesday, so preparation doesn't help with every problem.

On my way down to football, I find Amber Lee sitting on the field house steps. There's only a week and a half until homecoming. I've put off asking her long enough, but I really don't want to be late to practice. . . . I'll just do it quick!

She's not usually alone; she must be waiting for a ride. You can't see her bump from this angle, so she just looks like any other hot girl with nice hair. She's not as intimidating from behind (especially when she's seated) because you can't see her swollen boobs or those green eyes. I've known her forever, but I remember that in sixth grade, even before the boobs showed up, she developed this bewitching stare. Her eyes are sort of clear, and whenever they'd lock on to mine, at least one of my bodily functions would shut down. . . . Usually breathing is the first to go, and then everything else goes haywire from the lack of oxygen. I kind of feel like an a-hole for not being anxious around her anymore, but I can't help it. The baby in her belly seems to have taken away some of her powers. I find that I'm not trying to impress her, so my heart stays out of my throat and I'm able to be myself.

I plop down next to her and say, "What's up, momma?"

She looks over at me with an icy glare before she says, "That's actually funny now."

Her eyes have little effect on me, so I poke her belly and reply, "I know!"

"Ooouuch!" she cries.

"Oh my God, I'm so sorry, I shouldn't have—"

She laughs. "No, it wasn't that. The baby kicked."

"Are you okay?"

"Yeah," Amber says. "She's never kicked that hard before, but it's fine. You touched me and then she just nailed me, like right in the same spot."

"Gross!"

"Shut up, it's not gross!" she says.

"You're definitely having a girl. Chicks want to kick me, even in the fetal stage."

"No they don't," she objects. "'Chicks' think you're adorable."

"You're right. I don't know what I was thinking. Are you sure you don't need to fart? Sometimes I'll get a sharp pain right there and I'll be like, 'Oh no, my appendix is gonna burst!' and then, *Ppfffffrurrrrrt!* Booty burst!"

"I get it," she replies. "But I don't think that's it."

"Well, let me know if you think you're going to shoot off your cannon. You're farting for two now so—"

"Oh my God!" She laughs.

"What're you doing out here by yourself? Where's your entourage?"

She shakes her head. "I don't have an entourage. I'm just waiting for my idiot boyfriend. What are you doing?"

"As an idiot myself, I'm headed to football practice, so I gotta get moving."

Just as I'm about to ask her to the dance, she reaches up and touches my eyebrow. I've got a small cut from when Doc "accidentally" head-butted me. Her touch doesn't hurt, but it sends a lightning bolt through my body all the same. I feel my heart heading up into my windpipe. Dang it, she's still got it! I'm just doing this as a favor to Abby, but here comes the stutter.

"Y-y-yeah, so I w-w-wanted to check in w-w-with you because it seems my girl Abby is headed to New York City next weekend and my mom already had my suit cleaned for the dance . . . because I may have drank too much Mountain Dew at my cousin's wedding in August and started break-dancing and it got all grimy from doing back spins and whatnot. A-a-and Jeremy is getting a limo, so you w-w-wouldn't have to ride on my axle pegs or anything."

I stare into her green eyes until she says, "What are you talking about?"

I'm thinking that Abby didn't check with Amber before asking me to ask her to the damn dance! "Oh, uh, wait . . . I-I-I went in the wrong order. My bad. I'm gonna need a do-over here!"

She's looking at me like I'm burping these words, but I continue anyway. "Uh, d-d-do you want to go to the home-coming dance? There we go! That's what I meant to say."

"Yeah, I totally want to go," she replies.

"Okaaay, I think I need a redo on my do-over! It's like Ms. Holly used to say, 'Carter, you need to be more specific!' Did you have her for freshman English? Never mind. . . . Uh, do *you* w-w-want to go to the dance with *ME*?"

Her sour face bursts into a smile, and she starts laughing. "I've missed you, Carter."

"Did I go somewhere?"

She nudges me with her elbow and says, "I would love to go to the dance with you . . . but you don't have to."

"I know. I want to. I've never really been to a school dance before. I was supposed to go to one last year with the hottest girl at my school, actually. But there was some mis-communication, and even though we rode in the same car, we never actually got to dance or make out or anything."

She touches my leg and says, "I am sorry about that."

I look down at her pink fingernails resting on my jeans. After a few seconds I'm able to breathe again and say,

"I-i-it's okay, but, if you'd like a do-over, I'm offering you the opportunity."

She smiles. "I'd love it. So we're going in a limo?!"

"Yeah. As long as Jeremy and his boyfriend are still together by next weekend."

She says, "Well, I'll wear a short dress just in case I have to ride on your axle pegs."

She's kidding. She wouldn't have gotten on my pegs even before she was pregnant.

"Do that. Are you okay to tango in your condition?"

She laughs. "My condition? Yeah. I'm getting down for two, so you'll have to keep up."

"I'll do my best."

She leans over and gives me a tight sideways half hug. She might be crying, and the top of her head is right in front of my face, so I kiss it. I've never done that before, but it seems like the thing to do. And pregnant or not, her hair smells great.

She lets me go and leaves a little snot souvenir on my shirt.

She wipes at my chest and says, "I am sorry."

"Don't worry about it, it's not a—"

She interrupts. "I'm sorry if I was ever a bitch to you. I regret . . . a lot of things."

Tears fill my eyes too, and I oddly move my hands around as I say, "Naw, naw, don't . . . Everything works out the way it should. You're gonna be great. Maybe being a mom is like *your thing*. Maybe it's the thing you were born to do."

"I just don't feel ready," she says.

"I doubt anyone thinks they're ready, but it's already

made you more compassionate, and you're not so hung up on your looks anymore—"

She pulls away and glares at me. "Are you calling me ugly now or just shallow before?"

"What?! Neither!"

Her icy eyes soften and she laughs. "I'm kidding. I know what you mean." She pats her belly and says, "I'm pretty much awesome now."

I offer up a high five. "That's what I meant."

We both stop smiling when Rusty's LTD rumbles up to the curb. I give him a nod. He totally sees it, but he just looks away because I saw him get bitch-slapped by a drama boy two weeks ago.

I walk over to the car and ask, "S'up, man?"

"Just on a break from work," Rusty replies.

Amber gets into her seat awkwardly.

For some reason, I keep talking. "How's it going? Is the body shop stuff getting easier?"

"It's just work, man," he says like a beaten down fifty-year-old.

"Hey, uh, my girlfriend is gonna be out of town . . . and I heard you don't want to go to the homecoming dance . . . so I was thinking Amber and I could just go together, like friends, you know?"

He looks at Amber for a second, but she doesn't meet his gaze. He asks, "Ya'll friends now?" Then he adds, "Come on, man, you don't want to take a pregnant chick. Everyone can see the bump now, so when you walk into a restaurant or wherever, folks are gonna stare at you like you're the one who did it. . . . They're gonna look at you like a monkey at the zoo. They've got pity for her but disgust for you."

I'm not as moved by his speech as I should be, because in his scenario, people think I've had sex with Amber Lee, so I add, "Yeah, I think we're just going to go to the dance, sooo it should be fine. We got a limo and we're gonna tear up the dance flo'!"

I do some James Brown footwork until Amber starts laughing and Rusty says, "Whatever, I don't care," and they roll out.

I wave at the bumper and say, "Okay, then . . . maybe people are staring at you because you're an a-hole, huh?"

I hear whistles blow in the distance and realize that football practice has started without me again. Dang it. I'm still sore from yesterday's punishments.

# 9. WEDNESDAY, BLOODY WEDNESDAY

After only two Saturday Schools, all of my grades appear to be climbing. I'm still a long way from that B+ average, so Ms. McDougle put two of my latest geometry tests in my application packet to show the New York Drama School people that I'm "turning things around." My teachers are all stoked about my grade spikes. And I guess the news that I'm taking Amber to the dance has been discussed in the faculty lounge as well. Teachers I don't even know are giving me nods in the hall like, "Respect." They still give out mad detentions, though.

McDougle won't let me read her letter of recommendation, probably because it says, "Do not let this idiot into your school! His grades are improving only because he's got Saturday School every weekend!" or something. She's pissed at me right now because I'm planning to do swim team instead of *Camelot*. I can't explain it. I just love swimming back and forth in a pool and hyperventilating.

Abby's leaving for her New York visit tomorrow, so I pop by her house after fight club. I want to say good-bye and tell her how I beat J-Low's ass like a rented mule for three rounds tonight. He caught me with the ski mitten, right in the nose at the start of the fight. It gave me a nosebleed but it totally fired me up. I'm going to describe it to Abby like, "Manny Pacquiao fighting a Girl Scout." She's going to love it (if she knows who Manny Pacquiao is). I also want to wish her luck and maybe have farewell sex (you never know). She's hand-delivering my application to the school, so I'm pretending to make sure she has everything she needs . . . and I've got condoms.

For some reason, I'm not usually allowed in her house, but her mom seems to have lost her mind tonight. She has a weird tension-filled smile on her face when she tells me to, "Go on up."

I can hear the music blasting in Abby's room from down the hall. She usually listens to overly cool old bands like the Smiths or the Clash, but tonight it's a full-on nerd jam: it's the original cast recording of *Camelot*. She's singing along to Guenevere's part of the song, "If Ever I Would Leave You."

She doesn't hear it when I open the door, because she's rolling around on the bed singing, "'Nooo, noooo neeeeveeeer coooouuuld I leeeeave you at AAAAAAALLLL!!!'"

She catches me laughing at her before I notice she's crying. She jumps up and turns off the music.

"I'm sorry. I didn't mean to barge in. I knocked [lie], but you didn't . . . Are you okay?"

She wipes the tears from her face and says, "I was just rehearsing."

"Yeaaah, it's a . . . an emotional song . . . but you won't be able to do the winter musical if you're in New York, right?"

"I know," she replies. "I'm just working on it for fun."

"Obviously. It looks like you're having a blast."

"Shut up," she says. "It's such a good play. I've had this song prepared since August."

"You are a neeerrrd." I come in closer and push some hair out of her eyes. Calling a chick names is not textbook foreplay, but I've seen it work.

She's on to me, though, so she turns away and says, "I know."

"I see that you're all packed. I assume you have your boarding pass printed out."

She shows me the ticket and says, "I have your application right here as well."

"I figured you would." I attempt the hair move again, but she dodges my digits. "Sooo, everything is okay?"

"Yeah," she says. "I'm just nervous."

"Why? You've already been accepted and given a scholarship."

She sighs. "I know."

"That's what this trip is all about," I say as I dive onto her bed. "Just see if you like it. You can't be afraid of new experiences, Abby."

The "new experience" I'm talking about is "sex," but she seems to think I'm referring to skydiving or spicy foods or something. She keeps her distance and nods. "I know."

I continue, "If you decide you hate it, you're already ready to star in the winter musical at Merrian High."

She sits on the bed. I can't see her face, but I take the closeness as a green light. I wrap my arms around her waist and hug her like a confused koala bear. I'm not sure where I'm going with this, but my right wrist is just touching her left boob. She pats my hand and says, "You're right. Thanks, Carter."

I kiss her kidney and try to maneuver myself into some sort of offensive position. She obviously has no idea that I'm being amorous here. I caress her trapezius muscles while she keeps yapping. "My mom is freaking out."

"Yeah, she seemed kind of . . . medicated."

"I think she is," she replies with a laugh, but then she hops back up and flips on the serious switch again. "Carter, what if *you* don't get in?"

"Me? I'll be okay."

"No," she says. "I don't think I can do it without you."

"What?! That's crazy. You don't need me."

"What if I do?" she asks kind of breathlessly.

*What's up, green light? I haven't seen you in a while!*

I jump up from the bed and swoop in on her. I flip some hair out of her eyes . . . real smooth this time. "I'll come visit you," I whisper. "We'll go to the Statue of Liberty and see a Broadway show and get mugged on the subway together, and you'll remember how annoying I am."

She says, "You are annoying—" but I shut her up with my lips before she can continue (pimp). Things are going well. I get some fast boob and she squeezes my back tight. Then *she* takes off my shirt. I don't want to be the only one here with his shirt off, so I lift hers. I try to calm my breathing because it's getting loud. This might actually happen! I start to get a little light-headed all the sudden. *Get focused, playa!* I've just never been this close to sex in a bedroom before. The room has started to spin, and there's a new salty taste in my mouth, and my upper lip is sweating like mad. I better take this action to the bed, or I'm taking it straight down to the floor when I pass out.

I pull away from her so I can breathe for a second, lock the door, and kill the lights. I steal a quick glance at her bra, but I'm distracted by her face . . . and the scene takes a turn.

Instead of the romantic porno I thought I was about to star in . . . I find myself in a vampire horror picture! Abby has a shocked, hungry look in her eyes, and *blood* is smeared all over her mouth and nose. She gasps, "Oh my God!"

A crimson droplet falls from her chin onto her chest. I yell, "What the hell is going on?!"

She wipes her mouth and looks at her hand in shock. "Carter, your nose is gushing blood!"

I look in her mirror and see that this make-out session is over. Blood is not as sexy as they make it seem in those Twilight movies. She leaves the room, and I try to dam the flood with my shirt as I explain, "J-Dow hit me wit da ski gove . . . but I won da fight! I sorry, I dought it uz done daining—"

She reappears and hands me a wet towel. She lowers my head and inspects my face. I ask her, "Do you, by any chance, know who Manny Pacquiao is?"

She just forces me to tilt my head back. "When are you going to stop this stupid fighting?"

"I 'unno."

"I thought Terry joined the navy," she barks.

"At's wha' Nick heard."

"Do you think he's lying?" she asks.

I lower my head to say, "No . . . but fight club is kind of fun. And it's good to know how to protect yourself."

"From what?" she asks. "That's so stupid. This is the stuff I will not miss about Merrian."

"You don't think there's violence in New York City?"

She says, "I really doubt I'll be around a bunch of pea-cock boys who feel like they have to strut around proving themselves all the time."

"Yeah, there won't be any insecure kids at drama school."

She doesn't have anything to say to that, so she puts her shirt back on to punish me. My stupid cock-blocking nose seems to have stopped bleeding, so I try to get us back on track with a few questions. "Um, did you get Mace for your trip?"

"Mace?" she asks.

"Yeah, pepper spray. In case somebody tries to jack you."

She sighs. "God, you sound like my dad. New York is the safest place ever. They have cops everywhere."

"Why would they need cops everywhere if it's the safest place?"

"Why are you being a dick?" she asks.

"It's just conversation, dude. You were just saying you needed me to come with you for protection and—"

"I don't need *you* for protection," she scoffs.

"Easy now. Who's being a dick?"

She gives me the silent treatment for a minute, and it's obvious I'm not going to get anywhere sexually here, so I head for the door. "Okay, I'll let you pack. I need to do homework."

"Why are you mad at me?" she asks.

"No, I actually mean it. I've got homework. Someone is forcing me to apply to some fancy school, and I've got all these people looking at my grades now, so it's embarrassing when I flunk—"

She gasps. "Forcing you?"

"Yeah, I also need to steal a tie and some black socks from my dad so I'm ready for this dance on Saturday. . . . You know, the one that I'm attending with your pregnant friend."

She shakes her head in disgust. "You *are* mad at me! Why?"

"Your shirt was just off!"

"So?" she asks.

"And now it's back on!" I continue, but she's still not seeing a problem. "We're alone in your bedroom and your mom is downstairs hopped up on loopers. How many opportunities like this am I going to get?! I'm in love with you, Abby, and you're leaving. They're not gonna let me into that school, and you're going to be fine without me. The clock is ticking on this thing, so I'm not mad at you, but I am pissed off!"

Her face is totally flushed as she strides toward me. She's all intense and hot. I think we're back on, but she yanks the towel out of my hand and wipes my nose like a toddler. "You're bleeding again."

*Of course I am!* She doesn't return my declaration of love or make any promises. She just tilts my head back and pushes the cloth into my face.

I step away from her and put my shirt back on before saying, "I'm gonna go. Have fun on the trip . . . seriously."

She kisses me on the cheek and I take off. On the way out of the house, I wave to her mom. She looks up from her TV show, and we share a quick moment of sadness before she remembers exactly who I am.

# 10. FRIDAY NIGHT LIGHTS

I wanted to surprise Abby with some flowers at the airport on Thursday to make her feel better about the trip, but I had a sophomore football game. I got to play tight end, and Bag played quarterback and he threw me a pass (I may have dropped it when a punk-ass linebacker nailed me from the blind side). I also played defensive end, and I tackled a bunch of dudes and only got screamed at twice for being in the wrong area of the field at the wrong time. I kicked three extra points too (I made two of them) and we won! Football is way more fun when you're actually involved.

I've been asked to suit up for the varsity homecoming game on Friday. All of the sophomores were asked . . . but it's still an honor! We're playing our oldest rivals, the Nortest Cougars, and we're probably going to lose, but I'd never say that out loud. It's so cool to run out onto the field before the game. All of the drill team (except Abby) and cheerleaders are lined up beside the field as we run through their tunnel of Lycra and crash through the paper sign. You'd think we were about to go cure cancer! Everyone is cheering like crazy and I'm sooo fired up! I head-butt about ten guys before my ears start ringing and I stop. It would be even more fun if I actually had a prayer of playing in the game.

I've watched Merrian High football games since I was

little. I thought all of the players were rich and huge. From my backyard, you could faintly hear the announcer calling out the action over the loudspeaker. I used to think the ominous voice was God talking to me about numbers, but now I know it's just a history teacher with nothing better to do on a Friday night.

The marching band is rocking tonight and I can't help but bob my head around to the drumline's beat . . . until Coach sees me, and I put my game face back on real quick, like, *I don't even hear that music!*

I space off after a while, though, and wave to my sister, who's sitting with Nick Brock in the stands. I realize why they call it "homecoming." There are tons of people who've come back home to watch this game (the JuCo kids are always here). I give a few "S'ups?!" to my friends who are too smart to play football. Eventually, my dad catches my eye and shoots me a look like, *Turn around, dumbass!*

I see we're just about to kick off. . . . Perfect! The varsity kicker, Alan, is a great kicker. He's taught me a bunch of kicking strategies and techniques this year because he thinks I'll be taking over for him when he graduates. He almost always gets the ball past the ten-yard line on a kickoff, but it looks like Coach asked him to do a squib kick, since the ball is bouncing all around the field. The Cougars must have some speedster returning kicks, and Coach doesn't want to give him a chance to be featured on the cable access channel's high school sports report.

I hate it when they ask me for a squib kick; everyone just thinks that I muffed by accident (I've been known to bust an unintentional squib from time to time).

Alan's is absolutely on purpose because he's the first guy

on the tackle. Most teams use the kicker as a safety, but not on a squib; he's the guy who's got the best idea where the ball is headed.

It squirts and bops around for about thirty yards before a big lineman finally scoops it up into his thick arms. As soon as he does, Alan is on him . . . and he's way too fired up. They really shouldn't let kickers listen to the pregame speeches or run through the paper sign. We need to be doing yoga and staying focused. Alan's feet leave the ground and he lowers his head to drop the hammer! I think he's seeing this play on the public access highlight reel. It's probably going to be there, but not for the reasons he's thinking. They also have a blooper reel.

The big Cougar glances up and just stays low for a second. Just as Alan's body is sailing over the guy's helmet, he goes ahead and pops up into Alan's legs. Alan goes from football badass to Special Olympics diver in the blink of an eye. If we were at the pool, his jackknifed front-flip attempt would be fine. Or if the Cougar had hit him a little harder, Alan might have been able to stick the landing like a gymnast . . . but he didn't. Alan dives headfirst into that turf, *WHAAAMMM!!!* I'm no chiropractor, but I know the neck isn't meant to bend back that far.

The crowd gasps, and other Merrian guys wrestle the big guy down. Everybody rushes off the field to start the game, but Alan stays put. The coaches all trot out and kneel by his side. They're trying to figure out if he's really hurt or just embarrassed.

EJ hits me on the shoulder pad and gives me a nod.

I nod back and ask, "S'up?"

"You ready for this, boy?" he asks.

"Hell yeah . . . For what?"

"If Alan's hurt, you're the guy," he replies.

"No, that other senior, Doobie, is the backup kicker."

He's just staring at me, so I say, "He's that skinny stoner with the—"

EJ barks, "Didn't you look at the depth chart before the game?!"

"The what?"

"Doobie got kicked off the team, Carter!" he replies.

"Why?"

"Who gives a— You're the backup!"

"DUDE, I didn't even warm up!"

EJ springs into action and grabs Bag by the face mask. Nutt and Doc snag a few footballs, and the four of us march to the edge of the track, where a net is set up. It's here for the kicker to work out if he gets bored during the game.

Alan eventually gets up and staggers off the field. Everyone claps to celebrate the fact that he didn't break his neck, but he doesn't seem right.

Nutt says, "Either he had a few cocktails before the game or he's jacked."

"You got this, Carter!" EJ yells.

Bag is my holder on the sophomore team, so he pretends like someone has hiked him the balls, and I kick the crap out of them into the net. It feels good to release the nervous energy. I have no idea if these balls are going straight, but they are BOOMING!

Our defense stops the Cougars on three straight plays, and Coach sends his offense out onto the field. In the break he turns around to see who's jacking around with the kicking nets. We lock eyes, and at first he's like, *What the hell are you doing?!* but then he seems to realize I'm his only hope for extra points, field goals, and squib kicks.

He gives me a nod like, *Way to take the initiative, son!*

I doubt I could feel more pride if I kicked a game-winner. Thank God EJ thought of this or I'd be puking right now.

Our team marches straight down the field like they're avenging Alan, and my anxiety grows with every yard. When the running back crosses the goal line and the ref throws up his hands, the crowd goes nuts and I almost fill my football pants with diarrhea. Bag hands me the kicking tee and says, "Piece of cake, Carter!" before he slaps my ass, hard.

I've just stepped onto the field when Coach yells, "Go for TWO, men!" and my heart sinks. I spin around like it's not a big deal and he didn't just rip my heart out by not allowing me to kick the extra point. Maybe he doesn't think I'm warmed up yet, or he doesn't trust me. I don't trust me either, but I like surprising myself. Tonight would be the perfect stage on which to exceed everyone's expectations. I've sometimes thought that kicking could be my thing, but I've never been asked to save the day with a clutch field goal. It's probably like theater, where you have no idea how great you can be until the curtain goes up on opening night and you either freeze or spread your wings.

For the two-point conversion, our quarterback runs a sweep to the right, but the Cougar defense stuffs him on the two-yard line. YES!!! I feel bad for switching sides, but it's just that one play . . . until Coach snatches the kickoff tee out of my hand and gives it to a lineman before instructing him to, "Give me a big squib kick, son!"

We prevent the Cougars from scoring again and march right back down the field, but this drive is stopped on the five-yard line. On fourth down, Coach spins around and looks me in the eye. I take a deep breath and flex my jaw like, *I'm ready!* or possibly, *I will not vomit!* because he spins back around and yells, "Go for it! Get me that touchdown, men!"

The crowd cheers, but my heart sinks even further. I've practiced kicking footballs for countless hours, and he's seen me make kicks from beyond forty yards, but he doesn't have enough faith in me to try a fifteen-yard field goal. I want to scream, "Give me a chance, man! I *will* rise to the occasion." And I'd like to clarify, "Just because I'm late to practice doesn't mean I'm gonna miss a fifteen-yarder in front of all these people!" But you don't change someone's mind with words. He's seen something in me that looks like weakness, and no amount of pleading or reasoning is going to affect his decision.

I thought I couldn't be more disappointed than when Abby put her shirt back on a couple nights ago, but this feels worse. The only thing that keeps me from crying is the fact that our running back got tackled on the three-yard line. Everyone groans and cusses the failure . . . except me, because Coach looks like an asshole for not putting me in again. I have to cover my face because I can't help smiling. I'm a terrible teammate. Sorry.

I take a seat on the bench and wait for the game to end. If only I could've frozen time back when Coach gave me that nod. Back when it seemed like he was proud of me, and that my football career had great potential. I thought the announcer would finish off the night yelling, "Carter does the impossible, folks!" But looking back on it now, that nod was just the cherry on top of a turd sundae. Screw this game.

Coach never let me kick off even though that lineman messed up every one of his kicks. Coach went for two points after all three of our touchdowns and didn't try a single field goal, not even a thirty-two-yarder at the end of the game, when we only needed two points to win. His varsity kicker was injured; I was his only hope, but he still didn't put me in. Maybe I'm the only person (besides my mom) who thought I could make that kick, but I am positive I would have.

I will not forget this hollow, sick feeling. I'm going to try to remember it, actually. When I'm dicking around instead of studying for a test, or right before an audition, or when I do my phone interview with the New York Drama School. And I'll sure as hell break it out next summer if my boys are trying to get me to sign up for football again.

Everyone is going to some party after the game, but I get a ride home with my parents. I'm taking a pregnant girl out tomorrow night, and I've got a Saturday School in eight hours. I've got to get to bed and download the script for the spring musical *RENT*. I've only got four months to prepare, so I'm starting before the sun comes up. The only choice I'm going to give Ms. McDougle is *which* part to give me.

# 11. DANCE WITH THE DEVIL

Nick Brock won't take Lynn to a high school dance, so she's screaming at *me* for not washing the notes-to-self off my arms. Mom is pissed that the limo isn't coming to our house and I won't let her come to Amber's and show off her paparazzi skills.

My dad tries to make her feel better by saying, "Do you really want him and his pregnant date on your Facebook wall?"

Mom's eyes flare, and she snaps, "I am more proud of him for taking Amber Lee to this dance than I would be if he'd kicked the game-winning field goal in that stupid football game." Then she mutters, "He could kick a damn thirty-yarder in his sleep!"

"Mother," Lynn scolds.

My mom may have taken the football game personally, because she keeps bringing it up. She likes to help us, and it kills her when she can't. She's got tears in her eyes, so I give her a hug and say, "It's okay."

"So, I can come over to Amber's?" she asks.

"No."

She pleads, "But I might not get another opportunity—"

"Mother!" Lynn barks.

"I love you, Mom," I say.

This makes her start sobbing. "You're such a good boy. Why do you have to grow up so fast . . . and threaten to leave your poor mother just when you're getting fit to live with?"

"I'm sorry."

"You're not really going to New York City, are you?" she asks. "You're not going to rip my heart out on purpose, are you?"

"Pull yourself together, lady!" Lynn barks.

"They're not going to accept me, Mom."

"Oh, yes they are! They know talent. They've snatched up Abby and they're coming for you next."

She shuts it down because it seems like her daughter is about to slap her across the face.

Dad drops me off at Amber's, and her dad invites me inside to wait. Rusty is playing Mortal Kombat in the living room. His opponent looks a lot like me when I had my flop-do, which makes the awkward situation even more awkward. He doesn't pause the game or look at me until Amber comes down the stairs in a skintight Snooki dress and stripper heels. Just like last year's homecoming, when she broke out this god-awful '90s green dress, she has stepped up her look for this dance, and the results are unfortunate. Once again, a lot of makeup has been applied, and an unbelievable amount of hair product is being asked to do some pretty terrible things. It seems that she's trying to draw attention away from her swollen belly by featuring her bloated boobs more prominently. Her dad is *not* snapping photos. Amber gives me a kiss on the cheek that takes my breath away, but only because her perfume is so strong.

She says, "You look great, Carter! Doesn't he look handsome, Rusty?"

I'm starting to feel a bit used again, but a horn starts honking outside, and I see a long black limo with two dudes standing through the sunroof laughing. One of them is wearing a fedora, and they're singing along to the Black Eyed Peas' "I Gotta Feeling."

The lyrics remind me of something my dad is always saying: *Every situation is as bad or good as you allow it to be.* So I *decide* to make this a good night. I stick out my hand for Amber to grab, and say, "And *you* look amazing! Let's do this, Cinderella."

Rusty's avatar gets pummeled by his flop-do'd opponent when he glances our way. Amber smiles and takes my hand. I give her dad a high five on the way out because . . . why not?!

He adds, "You kids be good!"

I *almost* say, "I'll try not to get her pregnant!" but I'm able to shut it down in time.

When we step out of the house, Jeremy's eyes open wide to fully "appreciate" Amber's dress. I give him a look like, *Be nice.*

So he yells, "Oh my God, girl . . . you are too fierce!"

Amber smiles as I open the door for her, and will.i.am's voice blasts into the neighborhood, "Tonight's gonna be a good-gooood night!" Jeremy and Brad cheer for us like we're crashing through a paper sign that says CARTER AND AMBER! GO FIGHT WIN!

The limo is rad! I thought *Aunt Jenny* was a motel on wheels. *This thing* is designed for illicit acts. It's got a pull-up bar next to the sunroof, just in case anyone wants to work out . . . or maybe have an orgy! We've got multi-colored strobe lights and a bumpin' stereo! All I'm missing is a slutty girl with a giving nature . . . preferably one who's into me and not already *with child*.

I have to yell over Fergie when I tell Jeremy's boyfriend, "Yo, I dig that hat!"

He blushes and says, "Thanks! Jeremy got it for me!"

Jeremy gives me a wink, and I do a few pull-ups. *The student teaches the teacher!*

After two more stops, we've added eight drama kids, and things are getting loud. Amber's instinct would probably be to call them geeks and tell them to "Pipe down!" but she's totally outnumbered tonight, so she keeps it under control. Lady Gaga is blasting, and drama is the rule in this limo. It would be weird if you weren't pumping your fist and singing along at the top of your lungs. Eventually, Amber starts dancing in her seat and belting with the rest of us. Even the stoic driver is yelling, "'I'm on the right track, baby, I was boorrn this waaay!!!'"

We walk into the gym as if we own the place (and not like a bunch of overdressed misfits). It's kind of nice not being interested in your date (sexually). It's way easier to be impressive and funny when you're not trying to be impressive or funny. Plus, she's a great dancer. I wish her belly would stop running into me, though. I really wish Abby were here, but I'm not thinking about that. She didn't call me today. I assumed she would, but she's probably having a great time in New York and has just completely forgotten about me already. No big deal. I need to get used to not having her as my dance partner.

People are kind of staring at Amber and me. They're either thinking I'm a bad dancer or a pregnant chick shouldn't be throwing down like this, but Amber says that it's good for the baby. Who knew?

The same judges are looking at Jeremy and his gender-matching, fedora-wearing friend. I don't see anything but run-of-the-mill jealousy in those glances because Jeremy and Brad are obviously having a blast. Some of my boys are here, and I say hi, but mostly I stick with the drama kids.

When a slow song comes on, we have to stop jumping around. Everyone snuggles in close to their dates. Amber seems uncomfortable for the first time since we left her house, so I just grab her hand. Screw it. I've dreamt of being pressed up against Amber Lee since the second week of sixth grade. It's cool, but kind of weird when her fetus starts kicking at me again. I also can't breathe for a second because her stinky hair is too close to my face, so I spin her away like a swing dancer. I learned a dance called the jitterbug for *Guys and Dolls*. It's a lifesaver when biology class is coming to life right in front of you, and it looks very impressive. I'm able to crack a few jokes, and Amber's laughing like crazy. Next thing I know the DJ says, "Last song!" and the drama kids yell, "NOOOOO!!!"

Call me a dork, but I like school parties way more than house parties. No one is threatening to kill me, and I haven't seen anyone puke yet. We're some of the last people to leave, and we file back into the limo, where Jeremy invites us to an after-party at his house at Grey Goose Lake.

Amber says, "Hell yeah!" and I give Jeremy a suspicious look, because this party doesn't seem spontaneous. It seems like everyone else knew about it, and Amber and I were not on the list until just now. I guess we've proven our coolness.

I always love an excuse to get into Grey Goose Lake, because it's private and riffraff like me are not usually allowed beyond the security checkpoint. But I'm not rolling up on a Redline BMX tonight. I'd like to stick my head out of the limo and ask the guard, "How you like me now, bitch?!" but that would only prove him right, so I don't.

About twenty of us head into Jeremy's house. His mom has made hors d'oeuvres (cheesy crackers and tiny hot dogs). There's a karaoke machine set up and a pinball machine. I sing a Katy Perry song, and that goes great, but then I try to sing one of the numbers from *RENT*, and it's ugly. I need to work on it, but one of the many sucky detention rules is: No singing!

The party is super fun for me, but Amber appears to get bored with the drama talk. I ask if she's feeling okay, and she gives me a thumbs-up and a half smile. Show tunes start to dominate the karaoke playlist, and I can tell that she's annoyed the second time we sing "Seasons of Love" from *RENT*. I nod to the front door and help her off the couch.

"We're going for a walk," I explain.

The drama kids yell, "OKAY!!!" but Jeremy raises an eyebrow like, *Don't do anything you'll regret!*

I return his look with an expression that should say, *Are you crazy? Do you really think I'm going to hook up with a pregnant chick?*

It doesn't help my case when she takes my hand on the

way out the door. But we are friends, and friends are totally allowed to hold hands while they stroll along a lake . . . in the moonlight. It's sooo not a big deal that I swing our fists back and forth as we walk.

She confesses, "Carter . . . I had no idea how cool you were."

"Yeah, sometimes I'm shocked by it myself."

"I've really had fun tonight!" she continues. "I don't think I've ever had so much fun, actually."

"It's the drama kids. They just bring it! They're not even pretending; they really *do not* care, and when that rubs off on you, the good times begin!"

"I was so stressed about tonight," she says. "I thought people would be judging me or thinking that you and I were really together."

"No need to be rude."

She laughs. "You know what I mean. That like, Rusty and I broke up. I'd be proud to be your girlfriend, Carter."

"Well, thank you and ditto . . . or vice versa . . . w-w-whichever one applies."

I just got nervous. *Why did that happen?* I try to regain my cool and change the subject by pointing back to Jeremy's house (with the hand that's not still holding hers). "These guys have some goofy fashion sense, and they may not understand the concept of an 'inside voice,' but they've got *this* right. You can't care what other people think . . . especially now that you're gonna be a mom. You'll have poop on your shirt all the time and have to scream at your kid in the mall when he tries to pull the bikini tops off of the mannequins—"

"What?" she asks.

"Maybe that's just my mom. You shouldn't have that problem with a girl. My point is: there is no such thing as a cool parent. You didn't care what other people thought about you tonight, and it was awesome, right? You don't need to impress anyone anymore."

She makes a face and says, "I don't really like the sound of that. I like it when guys notice me or check out my butt."

"Hold up! How could you possibly know if someone is looking at your butt?"

"Trust me, we know," she scoffs.

"Really? Well, people are still going to do that. You're not going to stop being hot just because you have poop on your shirt. You'll just be a MILF! Tonight was fun because you didn't care what those drama kids thought or what I thought. . . ."

"You're wrong. I do care what you think."

Amber stops talking and just looks at me. *Uh-oh.* I may have accidentally turned on the charm. Was I asking her questions and cracking jokes?! I was. Damn my playa instincts!

She continues, "I think back to last year, and I want to pull my hair out. If I'd just gone to the stupid dance with you . . . maybe I wouldn't be in this mess, and like, how much more fun would we have had?!"

Amber Lee is looking up at me with those eyes, like I'm supposed to say something, so I try a joke. "What could have been more fun than walking home by myself?"

*Stop with the questions!*

She giggles and says, "I'm so sorry I did that to you. I really did feel bad."

"So you've stopped feeling bad?"

*Quit it!*

"I was just so hung up on Rusty that I was blind to what I was doing to everyone else. I was so worried about what he thought."

Oh good, Rusty has greased himself back into the conversation! I'm actually stoked for the first time to be wrong about a girl flirting with me.

"I've come to realize, if he's thinking at all, it's just about sex." She chuckles.

"Well, t-that's annoying."

"It's like our only connection." She sneers. "It's all we ever do. But like, we never laugh!"

"I don't think I'd w-w-want a lot of laughter in the bedroom myself."

That was a dead-serious statement, but Amber Lee finds it hilarious. She stops laughing and turns on her sexy-witch vibe. Dang it. I know a green light when I see one. She wants me to kiss her, but my brain is like, *No, nope, hell noooo!*

The alarm in my eyes must look like a green light to her, because she presses her bump into my stomach and puts her lips against mine. Not long after that, I've got an uninvited tongue in my mouth and her teeth have clacked into mine! This is a nightmare . . . but kind of a dream come true. It would be rude to not kiss someone back, right? I'm a lot of things, but rude is not one of them. Pregnant or not, she's as good a kisser as I always thought she would be.

I guess I'm usually wearing jeans when I get a boner, because these slacks are not disguising anything. Abby pops into my head and gives a disappointed look that helps calm things down. . . . Then Rusty—and Amber's dad's blowtorch—finally lower the mast.

My mind starts racing: What if my boys find out? I'd be

a legend! But I don't want *this* to be the thing I'm known for.

Amber eventually pulls back and says, "Sorry."

I wipe my mouth and say, "No, no . . . it's totally my bad. I w-w-was asking you questions and I a-a-accidentally turned on the charm."

She laughs, and we start walking back to Jeremy's house. She suddenly starts crying, so I put my arm around her and wait for it to stop. Then she cackles, "My hormones are just so jacked up!"

"Ditto! Or vice versa . . . whichever one applies."

We don't talk much after that. The limo drops her off first, and I just offer up a high five and say, "Good game."

She slaps my hand and replies, "Good game, Carter," so I guess we're cool.

# 12. DING-DING

We got an early snowstorm, so Mom wouldn't let me ride my bike on Monday. Lynn drove me to school. I go ahead and tell her about the prenatal make-out session. For the first time ever, she's speechless. Her mouth is gaping and she's just shaking her head as she drives.

"I should just tell Abby, right? She called yesterday, but I didn't pick up and she never called back. I didn't really do anything wrong, but I feel guilty as hell. She's not back in town until tomorrow. I should just tell her to make sure the situation doesn't blow up in my face. Because you know it will!"

Lynn shocks the hell out of me when she says, "Noooo, if Amber doesn't confess, you really can't. Even though Abby made you take that skank to the dance, and she must have known this was a possibility . . . But it's not about you being a sick freak or your relationship with Abby. This secret has to be kept for Amber. You have to swallow it because that girl can't afford any more scandal. She can't lose one of her best friends right now. She clearly doesn't know how to look out for herself, so you have to."

I start to defend Amber. "You know she's dealing with crazy hormones, and I accidentally turned on the— WHOOOAAA, look out!"

Lynn takes the corner into the school parking lot too fast (or furious) and slams the Honda right into a fire hydrant. I was hoping water would shoot all over the place, but the unit didn't break off completely. It just bent back really far. Now it kind of looks like a little man wearing a funny hat, yelling, "AAAHHHHH!!!"

Lynn doesn't have a sense of humor about the wreck because people totally saw her drive right into the fire hydrant, and she hates mistakes, especially public ones. We're fine, but the front of the Accord is mangled.

I tell everyone to check out the hydrant, but I don't breathe a word of the kiss to anyone (not even EJ). I've decided it's not a big deal. I'm going to tell Abby that I had a great time with Amber, and unless she asks, "Did you kiss her?" there is no reason to bring it up.

Because of the snow, football practice is canceled. No workouts, no game film, nothing! The season is almost over, but we have no idea what to do with ourselves. I think it was me who suggested that we go to EJ's for fight club, but the rumor mill got a hold of the info, and suddenly EJ is having a party. At least a hundred new kids are in EJ's backyard, drinking and smoking and betting on the fights. At first we weren't supposed to let anyone in the house, but then some girls needed to pee. Next thing you know, people are having sex in EJ's bed, and some girl is wearing his little sister's pink cowboy hat.

I've led my parents to believe that EJ's dad and Jeremy are supervising our little fight club, so it's a big problem when my dad comes walking down the slope of EJ's backyard. He's smiling as if he remembers what it was like to be a young man and do stupid stuff. But then he sees the ski glove being duct-taped to my left hand, and the "parent mode" washes over his eyes.

There's no supervision for miles. There's snow on the ground and I'm not wearing a shirt. I'm also getting ready to get my brains beaten out by a guy who outweighs me by thirty pounds. I accidentally agreed to fight Andre this afternoon.

I've got my mouthpiece in, so I just give him a nod like, *It's cool, Dad. Everything's under control.*

"Hey, Mr. Carter!" Nutt yells, throwing his beer into the bushes.

Everyone shuts up. Cigarettes and booze fly as if my dad is undercover Merrian P.D.

"You're just in time!" Bag says.

My dad coolly replies, "I see that."

Dang it. If I'd remembered that he was going to pick me up, I'd have tried to fight Nutt or Doc. My father doesn't need to see me get beat up, but I won't let him see me puss out either.

Our matches are supposed to be fun, but it's not like a video game. When you get hit, it hurts like hell, and when you lose, it's embarrassing.

I can see that my dad is thinking about shutting this whole thing down. His phone is out like he's debating if he should call EJ's parents before he calls the police, or the other way around, but then someone starts chanting, "Carter, CARTER, CARTER!" He seems to be swept up in the moment (*Bloodsport* is one of his favorite movies), and he doesn't do anything. I try to block him out and laser in on my opponent.

Bag bangs the pots together and says, "Ding-ding!!!" The crowd roars when Andre and I step over the garden-hose ring and touch gloves. We circle around a few times to see if anyone has a plan. I know I don't have one, and it doesn't seem like he's got—*WHAM, WHAM!* He punches me in the head a couple of times, and I stagger backward. He thinks I'm stunned, but his blows just woke me up. He comes in wild to finish me off, but I pop him with a quick three-punch combination that shocks me almost as much as him. And the crowd goes nuts! He stumbles back and loses his footing in the snow, so I come after him. He makes me pay for my cockiness by nailing me in the stomach with the ski glove hand, hard. I wasn't flexed, so my lunch thinks about making an encore appearance.

Thankfully, it stays down for all three rounds, and we mostly just trade blows and block each other's shots for the rest of the fight. We don't count punches or keep score. If we did, I bet I would have lost the fight, technically, but I didn't get knocked out or quit, and I didn't freak out or cry, either. I can tell my dad is proud. That's about as good as it gets. He's way more familiar with the Will Carter who bawled every single time he fell down or got pinched by his sister, so this a pleasant surprise.

He still makes me put on my coat even though I'm covered in sweat. He grabs my backpack and starts toward the street, so I say good-bye to a few people and follow him. He stops at the top of the slope and turns to yell, "The Merrian Police Department will be here in fifteen minutes!"

EJ looks at my dad in hurt shock, but my dad gives him

a sly wink and continues, "You don't have to go home, but you can't stay here!"

Grumblings abound, and kids call my dad a dick under their breath, but they start rounding up their friends to leave. You can hear EJ shouting, "Get out!" from inside the house as Dad and I approach the mangled Honda.

Dad says, "So that's fight club?"

I just shrug my shoulders. I assume he's going to tell me I'm grounded and not allowed to attend anymore, but he just says, "You did pretty well."

"Thanks."

"I'm not going to tell you what to do, son, but . . ." He really wants to tell me what to do, but EJ's dad isn't the only one trying to allow some healthy failure into his son's life. "Let's get you guys another pair of actual boxing gloves, huh?"

"That would be cool."

"And when did you get so buff?" he asks.

"We have to do all of that CrossFit stuff for football, so I've been hitting it pretty hard lately."

"I can't believe you got into that ring with Andre," he adds.

"It's not much of a ring, and I'm pretty sure I lost."

He wipes some blood off my ear before he replies, "No way. I think you had him."

We both know he's lying, so I give him a nod.

We get into the car, and he continues, "You won when you agreed to fight a guy that you'd probably lose to. The only people who'd do that are crazy, or destined for really big things."

"So you think I'm nuts?" I ask.

"Absolutely." He laughs. "Seriously, though, son, you don't have anything to prove . . . to anyone. If Terry Moss or anyone like that comes after you again . . . just walk away."

"I already did that. I actually ran, and it felt so bad."

"I know," he says. "And on some level, it's smart that you guys are learning how to defend yourselves. But you need to make sure that *your* fights are worth the trouble. Some idiot calling you out at a party doesn't merit what it could cost *you*."

"I guess Terry joined the navy, so I don't really have to worry about that anymore."

Dad continues, "There are going to be other Terrys. Hopefully they won't be quite as bad, but there will always be guys with nothing to lose who'll want to take a guy like you down a few pegs. Because you have a bright future, and guys that don't will always be jealous."

He attempts to start the mangled Honda, to no avail. Kids are driving past us as they make their way out of EJ's neighborhood. On the fourth try, the little engine finally rattles to life. I have to raise my voice over the knocking sound. "I don't know if I can handle New York, Dad."

He sighs. "No one does. But you're capable of anything you put your mind to, son. I'm not talking about New York or acting here, though. I'm telling you that *you* have more control over confrontations than you realize, and if you *look* for trouble . . . that's what you'll find."

I accidentally wink at him because the left side of my face is twitching; he thinks I've understood the point of his lecture and slaps me on the back.

I'm not nearly as beaten up as the Honda, so we squeal our way down Merrian Lane to Lee Auto Body. Dad pumps me for more info about the wreck. "In case I need to talk to the insurance company."

He wants me to tell him that Lynn was driving recklessly, which she was, but I don't focus on that part of the story. Instead, I just stick to how slick the streets were this morning. He's proud that I'm becoming a man but bummed that I've stopped being a tattletale.

Mr. Lee is out today because he took his daughter to the birth doctor. While she is biologically old enough to be a mom, she is not yet of legal age to drive. And Rusty couldn't get the day off of work (from Lee Auto Body).

One greasy guy takes our keys while another types on the computer, one finger at a time. My dad is waiting for the estimate to be calculated while I pretend to read a ten-year-old copy of *Popular Mechanics*. I'm trying not to stare at Rusty through the shop window. There is no way he knows that I kissed his baby mama, but I'm not exactly comfortable here. He's covered in oil, looking miserable, tired, and lost . . . with a blowtorch in his hand. Amber Lee is hot, but this seems like a hard trade for having sex with her.

My dad knows the situation, and he has no shame. He really is watching Rusty as if he's an animal in the zoo. "You really dodged a bullet by striking out with that girl."

"It wasn't a choice, Dad."

He explains, "Sometimes getting lucky . . . isn't lucky, if you know what I mean."

He points at Rusty, so I give him a nod to let him know that his joke landed (and I'm not ten years old).

As if to drive my dad's message home, Rusty is struggling to spark the torch of his welding machine. He keeps clicking this spark box and twisting the knob on the handle. Dad takes a step back from the glass as if he knows something bad is about to happen. "You're using condoms, right?" he asks.

"No . . . but I'm being safe."

He might be under the impression that his son is cooler than he really is, so I clarify. "I only have partnerless sex, Dad."

Rusty's spark box finally flicks a long white flash that shoots a burst of flame all around the garage. The other mechanics hit the deck and yell things like, "Idiot!!!" and "Stupid mother . . ." You can tell they are not happy with their newest employee. Rusty, on the other hand, is so beaten down that he just focuses the wide flame into a sharp point and starts cutting something off of a car.

We get the estimate, and my dad throws a fit because he's going to have to tell the insurance company. I guess our rates have doubled since my sister started driving, and he thinks the sky is going to fall when I turn sixteen. The only positive thing he's ever said about New York City is that I won't need a driver's license and therefore will not be added to their insurance policy. Ms. McDougle lived there for a few years after college, and she says only morons drive cars there.

Dad wants to leave a note for Mr. Lee, to remind him who we are and how I took his daughter to homecoming, twice, but I doubt it's going to get us much of a discount. If Yosemite Sam finds out I made out with his fallen angel, we might get some fresh dents and told to take our *dad-blame* business elsewheres!"

# 13. MOUNTAIN DON'T

I still have trouble falling asleep. I can pass out ten seconds into a biology lecture, but around ten p.m. my mind just starts racing. That assignment notebook is not helping with my sleep. It just stares at me from the dresser and reminds me of all of the crap I didn't get done.

The notebook says I should have been in bed at 10:30, and asleep by 10:45. Unfortunately, it's 11:38. It shows me that I've been tardy to bed twenty-three nights in a row. At least I'm consistent, but that damn alarm clock is going to do its thing at 6:39 a.m. whether I'm rested or not! Seven hours of sleep is my goal, so I've got thirty seconds to fall asleep, but it's unlikely because I drank a can of Mountain Dew after dinner.

I've just got to clear all of these thoughts out of here . . . and I will . . . just as soon as I figure out what's causing that clicking sound in the handlebars of my bike.

I have trouble focusing when I get eight hours of sleep, and somehow it's 12:11 a.m. all the sudden! If I conk out right now, I'm only going to get, like . . . No! It's not time for math . . . it's time for sleep!

What the hell is up with time? I don't get it. I understand that there are sixty seconds in a minute and all of that, but how is it almost one a.m. all the sudden? I could swear I ate dinner about an hour ago. How can time go by so slowly in geometry class and so fast in drama? I swear McDougle takes roll and then it's just over. Don't even get me started with those damn passing periods. Five minutes my ass! I'd like to time the actual break one of these days, to make sure the attendance ladies aren't messing with the clocks. (I wouldn't put it past those Birkenstock-wearing fascists.) But then I'd be even more tardy, and they'd just love that.

Everyone else seems okay with time, so I have to suspect that they have more of it than I do. Like everyone gets twenty-four hours, but somehow I only get about sixteen. If I'm able to get my seven hours of sleep, that only leaves nine hours in the day. School wants their eight no matter what. Rehearsal or practice takes another three, so right off the bat I'm in a deficit! The only thing that catches me up is detention. Vo-Tech. The medicine is bitter, but time *really* slows down in there. It's like a twilight zone where you're forced to concentrate on homework. I know Mrs. Trimmer isn't really armed, but I like to imagine that she is. And she's just waiting for me to start doodling or spacing off so that she can pull out a shotgun and cock it aggressively, like, "Back to work, Carter!"

I attempt to get busy with a few imaginary girls. That usually helps me fall asleep, but no dice tonight. So I strategize a fight with Scary Terry, and then Andre. I know how to beat them if I just stick to the plan. I also know exactly how I'll take down a terrorist if I'm ever on a plane that gets hijacked. Once that's settled, I have an epiphany: I should fake an injury to get out of football! I plan it out for a few minutes but eventually decide that I'll just have to stay in the moment and allow it to happen.

Epiphany #2 comes around two a.m.: we should take our football helmets to fight club! (I should write this down! But I'm sure I'll remember something as important as this.)

At 2:15 I make an important life decision: I want to be a J.Crew model. They dress cool, they hang out with hot chicks in cool locations, and they really seem like they're enjoying their lives. Thank God that's done. Now I can sleep.

But at 2:45 I'm skeptical: I don't know any J.Crew models. I have no idea how to get a hold of those people. Mom tried to call them once when she accidentally ordered my sister an orange sweater and they wouldn't take it back. She thought they sounded foreign.

I slam my head into the pillow to get it to shut off, but that never works. I deepen my breathing and deepen my thoughts. Why do I keep sabotaging myself . . . with Abby . . . with school . . . with success in general? Why am I so afraid of New York City? I've only seen it on TV, but when I imagine Will Carter in the city, I can only see it like Gotham in the Batman movies. I see myself getting kidnapped and murdered ten different ways, but what if New York is the place I'm supposed to be? What if the reason I feel like a misfit in Merrian is because I really don't fit here?! What's the worst thing that could happen? I could get run off the road by a masked villain driving a garbage truck, or someone could drop an acid-filled water balloon from their balcony, or I could get shanked in a dark alley— Stop it!

Where does fear come from? Am I causing it or just reacting to it? What good is it? How does it help me to worry about something that I can't control? I get that immediate fear is good. Like you should avoid dogs that look as if they've just had a cappuccino, but I'm like, scared of everything. I'm terrified probably eighty percent of the time I'm awake.

It's all totally irrational stuff and things I can't do anything about, but I can't stop myself from worrying and then feeling like a loser for stressing about it all. It's a vicious circle. I worry when I'm riding my bike that a car is going to plow into me from behind. I'm petrified of snakes, though I've never been close to one. I've never been bitten or even startled by one. Yet, every time I use a Porta-Potty or move a log, I'm certain that I'm going to wake a king cobra that's miraculously made its way to Merrian and is living in an unsuitable habitat and sustaining itself on species of plants and rodents it's never eaten before, just to rear back and strike my tender, unsuspecting ankle or butt cheek. I can feel the venom draining from its sharp curved fangs into my rushing bloodstream. I have never actually felt this feeling, but it's in my head as if it's happened a hundred times. It seems crazy to worry about past lives at 3:21 a.m., but I must have been a cow at some point, in India. I do like the taste of curry.

Go to sleep!

Abby is going to leave, and I'll never trick another girl into liking me. I suck at flirting with girls, especially ones I don't know. My charm gets lodged in my throat and I can't speak, let alone crack jokes. I believe I'm even more afraid of girls rejecting me than I am of snakes. I haven't tried to go down Abby's pants since last year because I don't want her to tell me no.

When she leaves, I'm going to have to get really comfortable with rejection. Bag says it's a numbers game. He doesn't mind if ten girls tell him to "get lost" because he knows eventually some insecure girl is going to find his B.S. attractive. But I can't handle ten rejections! I'd die after the fourth.

What if I got a girl pregnant? What the hell would I do? The only job I'm qualified to do is lifeguard. How's the kid going to eat during the other nine months of the year? What if I get a venereal disease? My mom would have to take me to Dr. Pajali, and he will be so disappointed in me, and he will judge my mom because her child contracted Portuguese Mountain Herpes from some skank!

What if there is a big war and they reinstate the draft and I have to go fight in the desert or the mountains? There's no way I could fall asleep on the ground, or if I was really cold or really hot. They might give me a cot, but there'd be bombs going off all the time. . . . I can't handle it. Shut up!

My real issue is purpose, I think. I bet I'd be asleep right now if I had a purpose in my life. I would be set if I just knew what my future held. I would be stoked if I could focus on one thing. If I positively knew what I was doing tomorrow and why I was doing it, my body would force me to get the rest it needs.

Mr. Owens, my history teacher, says that really successful guys choose their thing when they're about my age. Bill Gates, Oprah, Obama, they got it figured out early in life and they went after it with a vengeance, and then they became super successful. So what is my thing? The clock is ticking!

Auditions for *Camelot* are coming up and I'd like to sign up, but it's swimming season and Andre's always claiming that the only reason I beat him last year was because he had mono. But my fastest time was exactly the same as his fastest time. Usually I'm okay with a tie, but not with Andre. I don't know if swimming is really my thing or if I'm just scared that I'm not good enough to get cast in another play. I haven't read *Camelot*, but I've watched the movie and it's sooo cheesy, but kind of in an awesome way. If I had a copy of the play, I would bust it out right now! Reading knocks me out like a sledgehammer.

I bet every one of my friends is asleep. They aren't worried about snakes or girls or what I'm doing right now. They are not wondering if football or basketball or whatever is their "path." They're just putting one foot in front of the other and going down the road. None of the drama kids are stressing about whether or not they should audition for *Camelot*. They're just going to read the damn play, work on the scenes, and save the stress for the auditions!

I know that getting busy and staying busy is the best way to solve your problems, but what if I'm so busy that I miss out on the thing that I'm supposed to be doing? Like, I miss my calling because I'm on the other line. That's pretty good. I should write that down. *What was the other thing I was going to write down?*

Go to sleep!

I think I really am desensitized to violence! I honestly don't mind getting hit sometimes.

I hear there's a goth girl at school who sells Ritalin. I may need to buy some from her because my mom won't let me have it. I don't think she understands how hard I'm trying to stay focused. That's why I drank the Mountain Dew after dinner. I was self-medicating! I thought the caffeine would help me concentrate on my biology homework, but I never even opened the book. Sometimes ADD is cool, like when I find money in my pants, but most of the time it sucks. Can you just take the ADD meds every once in a while? Doc told EJ that they shrink your penis, but Doc likes to mess with EJ.

Amber Lee's boobs are definitely bigger, but I think Abby's are shrinking. I wonder if they could just trade bras, like, "Here, Abby, let me help you with that. . . ."

Darkness.

# 14. PRACTICE MAKES ... SOMETHING

I don't see Abby the next day at school. Subconsciously, I may have been avoiding her, but by the end of the day it's just weird. I'm worried that the rumor mill has informed her that I made out with Amber Lee and not explained the whole situation.

I wait for her before drill team practice, but when she finally shows up, she's with a big group of girls, and they stampede past me without a word.

She may not have seen me, but that was odd. I am officially concerned . . . and late for practice. Dang it!

Sophomores only have one football game left. But varsity has at least two more because of the state tournament. If *they* keep winning, *I* have to keep practicing. I will not get to play in any of these games, but I have the honor of suiting up as a backup kicker (that Coach doesn't allow to kick). Some of my boys will be done after Thursday's game, but I could still be practicing in December! I am so over this crap.

As I creep onto the field I see that we're doing blocking drills. No one seems to notice my arrival, so I slip into the formation. I'm stoked but a little nervous that I've somehow become invisible. EJ can definitely see me, because he clobbers me on my first trip through the drill. I go through twice more before we take a water break.

I'm in mid-guzzle when a whistle crashes into my helmet and Coach barks, "You work up a big thirst, Carly?! You're doin' burpees and somersaults after practice until you puke!"

Awesome. How much am I getting paid for this?

We've got open-field tackling drills next, so I decide that I've got to put my acting skills to work and fake a damn injury. I've just got to get hit hard enough to make it believable and then deliver a great performance. I skip ahead a few places to be paired with Andre. In this exercise, I'm playing the part of the ball carrier. I'm supposed to sprint down the sideline, while Andre (the tackler) pursues me on a slant. He is learning how to judge the best angles and most effective way to smash a guy into the dudes hanging out on the sidelines. Those are the best clips on *SportsCenter*, so I totally get why we practice this.

The whistle blows, and Coach tosses me the ball. I take off down the sideline as fast as my feet will carry me. I'm not trying to juke Andre or even look at him; I'm just running in a straight line like a motorized bunny at a dog track. I'm trying to concentrate on my performance, and debating whether or not to scream. I'll probably just lie there in pain.

My eyes are closed, but when the thunderous sound of Andre's feet stops drawing closer, my left eye snaps open to confirm that he's left the ground and his helmet is aimed directly at my left knee. It's perfect! I might have an actual injury here. I could get some crutches out of this. What heartless teacher would give a cripple detention? I might use it to get out of swim team and audition for *Camelot*! But my stupid nervous system gets nervous and my body overrides the brain.

Everything shifts away from my attacker, and my left hand automatically presses into his oncoming helmet. My left knee raises itself out of the line of destruction in a smooth Heisman Trophy pose. I bet I actually look cool for a second . . . until Andre's momentum becomes too much for my arm to bear and his helmet gets up under my left butt cheek and keeps moving until it's finally stopped by my right inner thigh . . . and my balls. My two flat-as-nickels and now-useless testicles! In a flash of painful realization, I'm reminded that in my haste to get to practice, I forgot to put on my nut-cup.

The earth shifts on its axis, and I fly through the air sideways and then upside down until my head collides with the ground and compresses my spine in the weirdest way. I flop onto my face, and my stomach crashes into the football that I just dropped. So all of the wind is knocked out of me, but somehow a noise comes out of my mouth that sounds like a wounded dog. You can't act this kind of pain.

The team lets out an, "OOHHHHHHH!!!" in sympathy.

This is not the injury I was looking for! I really hope I didn't just break my neck. My hands still work, though, because they're grabbing my nuts, as if to protect them from further trauma. I'm probably sterile. At least I can stop worrying about getting girls pregnant (if I ever get to have sex with them). Do you still get horny if your nuts are broken?

My eyes open, and I find Andre standing over me, saying, "I felt your nads through my helmet!"

I stop writhing for a second to give him props. "That's gold, dude!"

Eventually, Coach comes over and yells, "Oh, get up! Maybe this'll teach you to get to practice on time and wear all of your equipment."

A voice in my head (or nut-sack) whispers, *This is not where you're supposed to be!*

My nuts can be so dramatic when they're hurting. I don't take their advice, because I'm an idiot. Eventually I get up and file back into the line.

Practice finally ends and everyone heads back to the locker room, but before I can get very far, a whistle smashes into my helmet and an angry voice asks, "Where do you think you're going?"

You might think that testicular trauma is enough to get you out of punishments, but you'd be wrong.

I have to do a hundred burpees and a hundred yards of somersaults to atone for my crimes. And if I don't get it done in fifteen minutes, I have to start over. And my coach has nothing better to do than watch.

A hundred somersaults scrambles your brain in ways drugs could only dream of goofing you up. But I've officially decided never to be late to another practice ever again. I also really want to go to New York all of a sudden.

## 15. ALCATRAZ

On my way out of the locker room, I see Abby walking out of the gym with her drill team friends, so I limp over and say, "Hey! Hey, what's going on?"

The big girls seem to know something, and they peel off toward the parking lot. Abby says, "Nothing," but she's not looking at me. She obviously knows that I kissed Amber Lee, so I start blabbering, "Cooool. Sooooo, how was NYC? Did you hang out with Jay-Z and Beyoncé? Did you see *The Book of Mormon*? Did you go to Alcatraz?"

"That's in San Francisco," she scoffs.

"So you didn't?"

She finally smiles and says, "No, I did not go to Alcatraz in New York."

"Okay . . . so everything is cool? I thought I'd hear from you and then I didn't."

She sighs. "I know. I just . . . don't even know where to start with you. I am so disappointed."

Dang it, I knew she'd find out!

I clear my throat for the big confession, but before I can speak, she says, "I had a terrible time . . . and I don't want to go anymore, and I don't know what to tell people because I'm so embarrassed."

I try not to look too relieved as she continues. "Carter, it was so scary."

"It's like Gotham City in the Batman movies, isn't it?"

"Everywhere we went, people were yelling at me in a different language. Everything smelled like urine, and I almost got hit by a taxi. A woman pushed my mom on the subway, and the people at the school were rude and pretentious, and I don't know what I'm going to do."

She starts crying, so I instinctively give her a hug before saying, "That's exactly how I picture it. People say how pretty it is in the fall, but isn't every place pretty in the fall?"

She laughs, so I pull back and wipe a tear off the tip of her nose before asking, "Is that everything that's bothering you?"

She shakes her head no, so I go ahead and ask, "Someone told you something . . . that upset you?"

She starts really crying now, and I'm surprised when she gives me a tight hug.

"I'm sorry," I say. "You really deserve better. . . . You know it didn't mean anything."

"It meant everything, Carter." She blubbers. "When she said that to me, my whole life . . . my world just crumbled!"

"Really?"

"Ms. McDougle told you?" she asks.

Okay, that's weird. . . . If I was still a dumb-ass freshman I'd ask, *Told me what?* But I just stay quiet and allow her to talk.

"She really shouldn't have . . . but she was angry too. I asked her not to call the school, but I bet she did."

Okay, detective! We're still talking about New York . . . not Amber. After a long silence I finally say, "Tell me what happened."

She pulls back and says, "They called me fat!"

"What?!"

"Two different teachers," she says. "I sang for their vocal coach and he said I reminded him of Adele!"

I can see how someone would make that comparison, but I can tell that Abby can't, so I keep it zipped.

"Then I got to take a dance class, and it was so awesome. I totally thought of you because they weren't all about technique, but everyone danced from the heart and worked their asses off. And I started to think I could handle New York and so could you, and then I talked to the teacher afterward. She said I was 'too curvy' to be a dancer! She said it all matter-of-fact and explained that I should lose fifteen pounds before next semester. Fifteen pounds in two months!"

Too curvy?! I can't even comprehend that statement. That's like saying you have too much money! I want to go to New York now just to set this hater straight. But I try to keep it positive when I say, "I think these people were giving you compliments, Abby."

"No, they were being rude. You had to be there. They're all professionals and they know their industry."

"They know dick! I know what people find attractive, and Abby, you are it!"

"Now I don't know what to do," she says. "I'll guess I'll try to lose the weight, but all I've wanted to do since I left the school was gorge myself on M&M's and pizza."

"Screw that place."

Tears fall from her eyes as she says, "But I told everyone I was going, and I got you to apply, and I just feel like a fool."

"So? You don't care what people think. . . . I know you don't."

"And what about you?" she asks. "I turned in your application and they were so excited. I guess they saw clips from the *Down Gets Out* movie and they can't wait to meet you."

"They can't?"

"Of course," she says.

"I didn't know anyone had footage from the movie. . . ." *But that's not what we're talking about*, so I say, "Maybe you could sit out this semester and try to . . ." I almost said *lose a few pounds*, but my sister jumped into my throat and strangled the statement before it could escape. I quickly add, "You know, figure things out. Maybe you do *Camelot* and *RENT* here and get even more experience, and then maybe we'll go to NYC together and kick its ass!"

She laughs. "I don't know. You've got to visit that place, Carter. It's pretty intense."

I put my arm around her and walk toward the parking lot like a pimp. "I play football and do fight club, dude. I'll show 'em intensity!"

Abby's mom scowls at me when I wave at her, and everything seems back to normal. I should be having sex very soon . . . right?

# WINTER

# 16. LOU-OWE

Wrong! A cold front rolls into Merrian as well as my relationship with Abby. She decides not to go to New York in January, and falls into a weird depression that I can't snap her out of. She won't eat, and I know why. She knows I don't approve of any plan that reduces the junk in her trunk, and maybe she's pissed at me for not being more supportive, or just because I know this secret, but we are way off. We've been to the movies a couple of times, but we struggle to talk both before and after. I ask her questions, but it's more like a bad interview than a date. We kiss, but she's phoning it in, and we're back to karate chops when I go for boob. My jokes seem to make her mad, so I stop making them, and then it gets really weird. We say hi in the halls, but she makes excuses not to hang out with me. Lynn says I have to give her space, but that's the opposite direction I want to go. By December we've basically broken up (without the breakup).

Auditions for *Camelot* came and went, and I didn't go, so now I'm spending my afternoons in a testicular-crushing banana hammock, swimming back and forth in an over-chlorinated pool. The tiny amount of oxygen that's allowed into my lungs is so tainted with chemicals that it makes me want to barf. On a positive note, it also causes me to forget how much pain my muscles are in, as well as the fact that I'm hanging out with Andre all the time. Of course I didn't want to sing and dance away my precious time and hang out with smart, fun kids and have people clap for me and maybe win Abby back again. Screw that!

Abby and Jeremy got the lead roles in *Camelot*, which caused a lot of drama in the wing because Abby hadn't told anyone that she wasn't going to New York. She just showed up at the auditions and killed it. Drama kids are all "supportive" until audition time, and then a bus accident is great news. The other girls are pissed, to say the least.

I still help build sets and hang lights when I have time. The other day I was talking to Jeremy instead of working when Abby just walks past us without a word. He knows about the fifteen-pound/Adele situation from New York, but he's as perplexed as I am that she's taking it out on me.

He pats me on the back and says, "That's why I don't date girls."

"Yeah, me too."

"No . . . you need that girl," he says. "Unfortunately, she's as stubborn as she is hot. Keep after her, Carter. I know she loves you."

"She won't even talk to me, dude."

"Who told you awesome was easy?" he asks. "You've got to fight for a booty like that!"

He throws a quick punch at my head, and I duck without thinking. He repeats, "Fight for that booty, boy."

My boys and I go to the first basketball game of the year without EJ . . . because he made the varsity squad! We're all super proud of him, but a little jealous. He lettered in football and now basketball! I think swimming is awesome, but it's not much of a spectator sport. In basketball there are only five guys and no one is wearing a helmet, so everyone can see who made the big shot and who missed it. Hundreds of people come to the basketball games. Even Jeremy.

We played our old rivals, the Nortest Cougars, and they beat our asses. Everyone is bummed, but no one more than EJ, because he never got in the game. He didn't even get to take off his Trixxxy warm-up suit.

Basketball sweats were invented either by strippers or busy moms. They have snaps all down the legs so the dude can just yank them off and get in the game (or the mom can extract the diaper, or the stripper can show off her G-string) quickly. The removal of your Trixxxy pants is very important in basketball, so EJ and I have been rehearsing. He wants to look like he's so focused on the game that he doesn't care how his pants fly off . . . but you've got to practice. If you pull too hard, you could smack yourself in the face with one of the metal snaps. But if you don't yank hard enough, you could trip all over yourself in front of everyone, and that's the last thing you want in sports (or on the pole).

After the game, I give him a fist bump and say, "You'll get 'em next week, Trixxx."

We pile into Aunt Jenny and follow the CRX and an old Mustang to some party. We've all got the same paper invitation with a map, but it feels good to travel in packs.

Bag looks at the photocopied paper and says, "Yo, this is really far away! It must be someone's dad's house."

The invite has a Hawaiian motif and the party is titled a "Lou-owe." It's even got a slogan: EVERYONE GETS LEI'D

AT THE LOU-OWE! It also says, PLEASE DON'T REPRINT OR DISTRIBUTE THIS TO ANYONE. THX, LOU ☺

EJ asks, "Who gave you this flyer, Carter?"

"Nutt did."

"Who gave it to you, Nutt?" Bag asks.

"A drill teamer," Nutt replies.

"Which one?" EJ asks, suspiciously.

Nutt mumbles, "Fat Sal, but I thought it was from Abby to give to Carter."

From the backseat, Andre says, "But Abby hates Carter now."

"Shut up. We're just giving each other space," I respond.

Nobody (including me) understands what that means, so they get back to making fun of Nutt. Everyone knows Fat Sal is in love with him, and he's always pretending he doesn't get it.

"Put that girl out of her misery, dude!" Bag suggests.

"Shut up!" Nutt replies. "I'm not hookin' up with that fatty."

I tell EJ that the car next to us wants to race. "That old lady wants to go!"

She obviously doesn't, but I want to take the heat off of Nutt because it's obvious to me that he kind of likes Sally.

We finally rumble into a really nice neighborhood. The houses are way bigger than the ones we usually hang out in, but there's definitely a party in this one. We see a few kids we recognize and a few we don't, so we hop out of the car to check things out. We're wise sophomores, so we know this house is going to be a hotbox. Everyone tosses their coats into Aunt Jenny's trunk, and we extract a cooler that's filled with stolen Milwaukee's Best. There's no ice, so it's less of a "cooler" and more of a plastic container that Bag and Nutt are lugging into a stranger's house. I take one of the warm beers to lessen their load and so I have something to do with my hands. This party seems like every other high school rager I've been to, so we just stroll in through the front door.

The place is packed. There are strings of Christmas lights and tiki decorations. Some of the kids are drinking fruity-looking drinks in Solo cups and others are wearing those flower leis around their necks. EJ points at the neckwear and asks, "Is that what 'lei'd' meant on the flyer?"

"No . . . I'm sure it was a spelling error. They're probably giving out the sex upstairs."

"Who the hell is throwing a Hawaiian party?!" Nutt asks.

Bag reads the banner hanging from the fireplace mantel: "'Welcome to the Lou-owe!'"

A skinny kid is staring at us, so Doc asks him, "Are you Lou?"

The geek replies, "Yeah. Who are you guys? Do you even go to Nortest?"

Everyone stiffens when we realize we're not at a Merrian party. My boys just walk into the guy's kitchen, but I'm afflicted with politeness, so I say, "No, do you?"

He makes a face like I asked, *Do you like hot poop?*

He replies, "Yes, this is a Nortest party, bro."

I raise my eyebrows at him like, *That's what you think.*

It appears that Lou thought he was just having a little get-together. I'm only a sophomore, but I've seen "a little get-together" turn into a rager a few times now.

I shrug and quietly explain, "You could always call the cops."

He nervously surveys the situation as more kids he obviously doesn't know file through the front door. Lou whines, "But they'd call my parents. They're in Florida and they'll kill me."

Something breaks in the next room, and Lou's eyes widen. I say, "I probably wouldn't do it either, but sometimes you've got to cut your losses. I'll try to round up my friends, but I think we're the least of your problems."

I pass though the kitchen and see that Nutt has pushed J-Low into a vase of fake flowers, and that's what broke. So we're definitely not "the least of his problems," but we can't be his worst. My boys won't leave because there's a keg in the garage.

Since I seem to be stuck here, I do a lap around the house. Music is bumping in the basement, and I'm stoked to find Abby and Jeremy dancing with a group of drama kids. They don't care whose house we're at, nor do they want to break stuff; they just want to have a good time. I nod my head to the beat and start to dance over.

Abby kind of dances with me for a second, but then she spins away and starts jamming with some girls I don't know. This goes on for a few songs, so I take off.

I go back up to the kitchen, where Bag tells me, "Duuude, you gotta try the Hawaiian punch!"

I "recycle" a red Solo cup out of the trash and fill it with a mixture of grain alcohol and Kool-Aid powder. It sounds like it would be fruity and delicious, but it tastes more like peroxide that's been mixed with Splenda . . . and fire! I'm not into that taste, so I abandon my cup and do another lap around the party.

I'm just killing time waiting for the cops to show up . . .

or maybe the fire department. The backyard has tiki torches all around the deck, which is really cool, but sooo irresponsible. Some Nortest guys are competing to see who can keep their hands closest to the flame for the longest. I never do very well at those games.

A whole gang of kids come spilling over the back fence. They seem to have been denied entrance in the front, but that's never stopped a resilient party animal and it never will. They're a pack of Merrian freshman. I only know one of them, though.

In a deep voice I say, "Hold it right there . . . young lady!" because I can't remember her name. She's on summer swim team, and she was always kind of a beanpole that I didn't pay attention to. But I've noticed she's been developing, and puberty is friggin' magic.

She laughs like crazy when she recognizes me. "Oh my God, Carter! You are too funny. I drank a wine cooler! SHHHH!!!"

She touches my chest, and I say, "Oh snap!" and give her a high five.

I've got to stop high-fiving girls, especially when they seem to be into me. I've always wanted to be the cool older guy, and she seems to think I am. I like to fantasize that if I dated a freshman, I would just tell her what to do and she'd do it. But Bag has been dating younger chicks, and it doesn't work for very long. They seem to give you the benefit of the doubt for a while, but as soon as you let them know you're just as big a geek as the guys in her grade, your reign is over.

I'm not trying to flirt with this girl; I'm just being nice and asking her questions out of habit. But if Abby and I are really done, I guess I need to start looking around. The problem is, I don't really want to, and the problem with that is: when you're actually not into a girl, they're drawn to you like a cat to a can opener.

"I missed you this summer," she says. "How come you didn't swim?"

"I was busy."

"Oh . . . that's cool," she says before guzzling more wine cooler. "A-a-are you swimming for Merrian?"

"Yep, we had our first meet on Thursday. We suck."

She about dies laughing. I reel her in even further by turning to her friends and explaining, "You girls don't need to sneak into parties. You're hot, so just walk in like you own the place. You might need to ditch your guy friends, though."

The dudes hear me, but they pretend not to because I'm a sophomore football player with a thug hairdo and a cut on my face. They obviously didn't see the tears in my eyes at the basketball game when my best friend ran out onto the court to warm up.

A girl asks, "Hey, um, do you think the police will break up this party?"

"Absolutely."

A freshman guy says, "Seriously?"

"Yeah, they'll be here any minute, but you want to wait until they get here. Running from the cops is the best part."

They all crack up as if I'm Chris Rock, and I start laughing too, because somehow I *am* the cool older guy! Then this swim team girl grabs my shirt and starts talking passionately . . . about algebra. At least I think that's what she's talking about. She's obviously nervous, because she's all over the place. I'm stoked to be the cause of this anxiety, but her intoxication is jacking everything up. EJ says that drinking helps him talk, but all I see is blind courage and bad decisions here.

Her mouth is stained red, and I'm having a lot of trouble following her random categories. "And the combo to my locker is fifteen, too!" she yells like a fourteen-year-old schizophrenic wino.

"Cool," I mutter as I look around the deck.

She grabs my forearm and goes, "That's a polynomial!'"

We both crack up. She thinks she's being funny, but I'm laughing *at* her.

She tells me how buzzed she is for the fourth time, so I reply, "I gotta pee," and just walk away like a pimp. I don't really have to go; that girl is just annoying. And if that's what dating another girl is like, I need to track Abby down and beg her to go out with me again.

I stroll around the side of the house and see that the party is getting even bigger. The front yard is covered in trash, and a girl is puking in the bushes. When I walk back inside, the whole vibe has changed. That kid Lou is sobbing on the stairs, and some Nortest guys are giving me snotty looks. If I still had that flop-do, they probably would've given me some static, but nobody wants to fight a guy who might kick their ass. Only I know how unlikely that scenario is.

I've convinced myself that I really do need to pee. As a sophomore, I know that using an actual bathroom at a party is not a good idea, but at least I'll have a purpose for a few minutes. I walk past Lou on my way upstairs. A Nortest guy and girl are already in line for the toilet, and all of the bedroom doors are closed. People are grunting and moaning inside all the rooms (including the bathroom). I think I know what Lou is upset about. Since I don't have anything better to do, I just hang out and listen.

The guy in front of me is hopping from foot to foot and grabbing his crotch like a little boy. I know the pinching technique works, but you can't just use it in public anymore. If we were friends I'd school him, but we're not, and I can smell the booze on him from here.

The girl in front of him shakes her head and mutters, "I'm just going outside" as she marches down the stairs. The drunk dude starts yelling at the door, which is slightly open. "Whaz takin' so long, brah?!"

The door doesn't answer, so he pounds on it, and it swings open and reveals a Merrian guy getting up from the floor as if he's just waking up. He staggers out with bright red vomit all down his shirt, and the smell is not good.

The kid in front of me yells, "Ohhh, God!" as he tiptoes inside. I want to yell, "Don't go in there!" but whatever he's seeing and smelling is not bad enough to keep him from his duty, so who am I to stop him . . . from pissing all over the room! Daaamn. He doesn't shut the door, so I have to try not to watch him watering the room like an evil sprinkler.

"Nice aim, bro," I say as he passes by. "Maybe go back to diapers until you can control that thing."

I should just go pee outside, but I've really got to go at this point, so I step into the Terror Dome and quickly shut the door with my foot. Wow, I've been in some foul crappers, but this is the worst. There's puke all over the sink and walls. The floor is slimy and somebody dropped a deuce right in front of the toilet! That's why Drunkie was keeping his distance.

I attempt to do what I came in here to do, while standing on one foot and only breathing through my mouth. I'm a better shot than the guy before me, but not by much. I can't wash my hands because the faucet is covered with vomit, and it's making me want to add my own lunch to the mix. I grab the knob, quick, but the door won't open. Dang it! One of my a-hole friends must have somehow locked it from the outside! (To meet them, you might not think they're very bright, but when it comes to torture, they're brilliant.) I pull, in vain, and pound on the door. "You bastards!"

My blurry eyes finally see the Post-it note stuck to the wall: DON'T SHUT THIS DOOR, THE LOCK IS BROKEN. THX, LOU ☺!

I'm sweating buckets and my mouth is watering like crazy. I put my foot against the wall and pull with everything I've got. But the knob rips off of the door and I fall backward. Falling rarely feels good . . . but it's way worse when you know you're about to land in vomit, pee, and poop. I'm able to grab the towel bar on my way down, but it's one of those decorative ones. A handicapped grab-bar might have saved me, but this one just rips out of the wall and whacks me in the face as I'm sliding across the slop.

I spring up fast, but slip right back down. "Son of a—"

*Okay, calm down, but don't take any deep breaths! You can either climb out the window or kick the door down!* A second-story window seems a bit daredevil, and since Lou's dad is already going to have the tools up here to fix the towel bar, I go ahead and draw my leg back to karate out of here. But as I do, the stick where the knob used to be rotates and the door slowly opens. Sweet oxygen drifts into the room. I'm able to drink in some of the air, but unable to recall the kick.

A girl asks, "Is everything okaaa—?" just as my foot

connects with the door, *WHAM!* And it smashes into her head with a *BOOM* and shoots her back into the hall. I should've gone with the damn window!

"I'm so sorry!" I say, sliding out of the bathroom. I attempt to pick the poor girl up, but since I'm covered in fecal matter and regurgitation, my help is not appreciated. A group has gathered to see who was going Tasmanian Devil in the crapper, and more are coming up to see who kicked a door into a chick.

The girl yells, "What's your problem?!" as another guy steps into the bathroom and gasps, "OHHH, NASTY!!!"

He notices the smushed turd on the tile and starts screaming, "This Merrian guy took a dump on the floor!"

"No I didn't!" I try to explain while heading for the stairs. Of course Abby and Jeremy are among the curious people coming up, so I dart into one of the bedrooms before they can see or smell me. Unfortunately, this room is already being "used," and there appears to be a lot of activity happening on a twin-size bed.

A guy yells, "Yo!"

And a girl whisper/yells, "I thought you locked it!"

It couldn't get any weirder, so I say, "The locks in this house suck!" as I flip on the light. I remove my shirt and start rummaging through a dresser, where I find a tiny T-shirt that says, NORTEST STROLLING STRINGS . . . PLUCK YEAH!

I try to find an alternative, but the guy on the bed interrupts my search. "Carter, get the hell out!"

I spin around and find Nutt . . . buck naked, embarrassed, and angry. He's next to what I think is a drill teamer. Fat Sal is attempting to cover her boobs and red face with a pillow. I stammer an apology, grab the shirt, and flip off the light before I dash out of the room and find twenty people . . . still looking at me.

Abby seems shocked to see me. "Carter, what are you doing?"

"And why aren't you wearing a shirt?" Jeremy inquires.

I wedge myself into the shirt as I say, "I'll tell you later . . . but it's not what it looks like."

"What does it look like?" he asks with a smile.

Abby interrupts us to say, "Your stupid friends are about to get into a huge brawl with some Nortest guys."

I shake my head with frustration and finally say, "That's it!"

If the cops around here won't do it, I'm going to have to break up this party myself. I use my theater voice to yell, "Fifteen cop cars just pulled up front!"

A drunk kid yells, "OH, NOOO!!!"

Abby and Jeremy laugh, but the girl I just kicked a door into backs me up like I'm her commanding officer. She screeches, "COPS!!! The police are here!"

I shout, "Everybody out! Run for your lives!"

The dude who accused me of pooping on the floor says, "He's lying! That room doesn't even face the front—"

"What are you, an architect?" I ask him. "Get out!"

Jeremy says, "Jeez, Carter!"

Abby yells, "COPS!!! Five-O!!! It's the po-po!"

We laugh as the bedroom doors open and half-naked teens come flying out like startled bats from a cave. Nutt blasts into the hall with just his BVDs and Nikes on. He's closely followed by a plus-size Victoria's Secret model.

"Sally?" Abby gasps.

Fat Sal looks like she's been caught stealing, and retreats

back into the dark room without a word. Nutt looks like he's been caught hooking up with a girl named "Fat Sal," and he's not sure how he wants to handle it, so I whisper, "The cops aren't really here, dude. You can go back to . . . doing whatever you were doing. I owe you one . . . or two."

"Or, you could just keep this to yourself," he whispers.

I give him a wink and say, "We'll see."

He darts back into the room, and I grab Abby's hand and chase the crowd down the stairs. You can tell that there's a confused tension in the air . . . between me and Abby and this whole dumb party. Andre and some Merrian dudes are still staring down some Nortest guys in the kitchen.

Abby's the best wingman ever, so she slams the front door and yells, "OH, NOOO!!! Everyone out the back!" And then in case anyone hadn't heard, she booms, "COOOPPPPS!!!"

Andre and the rest of my boys have no choice but to back away as panic rips through the herd and people run for the exits. Jeremy flicks the living room lights on and off to add some drama.

Lou looks terrified, so I whisper, "The cops are not really here."

Once he gets what we're doing, he looks up at me with total gratitude. I say, "You're welcome, but I need to borrow this shirt."

He obviously doesn't care about the shirt, so I continue. "There might be some kids having sex in your bed right now, and someone may have ripped a towel rod off of the bathroom wall . . . but I want you to know . . . no matter what you hear . . . that is not a Merrian dookie on the floor, okay?"

"WHAT?!" he gasps.

Abby pulls on my hand and says, "Come on, CARTER!!! If these cops catch you, they'll throw away the key!"

I wish Lou luck, and because I'm a total drama geek, I add, "I ain't goin' back to jail, man!!! They'll never take me alive!"

Abby might still be mad at me, but she loves to improvise. She cries, "Don't talk like that, baby!"

We squeeze out the back door. Everyone is ramming into each other, but we're having a blast. "I'm sorry, sugar! I just love you too much!"

Whoops! I used the "L" word again. I was just jacking around, and I said it in a Southern accent, but you can feel the vibe change for second . . . but then she screeches, "I'll visit you every day, baaaby!"

People are staring at us because they think there's real drama happening in the front yard and they're confused by the Telemundo soap opera going on in the back. Abby throws her arms around me and shoves her tongue in my ear. She's just goofing around, but I'm totally aroused.

I try to keep the scene going. "If I know you's waitin' for me . . . I'll do twenty years, no problem!"

"Twenty years?!" Abby asks. "What did you do?"

That makes me laugh and kind of stops the scene. We step off the deck into the grass when Abby spits in disgust before she asks, "What is in your ear, Carter?"

I don't have the heart to tell her that she may have just licked someone's vomit or poop out of my ear, so I pretend not to hear the question and hop the fence. I help her get down from the other side, and she asks, "Seriously, why do you stink so bad?"

Thank God EJ rushes out of the darkness and motions

for us to follow him past another house and across the street, to a McMansion with all of its lights off.

We creep around back, and I pull my head over a wooden fence and see a hot tub! Bag is removing the cover, and steam shoots into the air. Bitchy Nicky obviously doesn't see me here, because she's taking off her jeans right in front of me. The pale moonlight is making it tough to tell what kind of panties she's rocking. My brain goes ahead and fills in the blanks: they're hot pink hip-huggers (Victoria's Secret, winter catalog, pages 4–5) with black trim, and they say, "Naughty" or "Juicy" or something suggestive right across the—

"What is it?" Abby asks as she pulls herself up next to me.

Abby notices me watching Nicky and gives me a judgmental glare, but I just shrug my shoulders like, *What?*

We can hear Jeremy and a group of drama kids running down the street, screaming and singing. Neither of us make a move to tell them where we are, and it causes us to laugh.

"There's only so much room in the hot tub," I say as I hop over the fence.

Abby jumps down into the yard next to me. We approach the tub as Nicky slowly slides into the water and says, "Why am I the only one in this tub?!" EJ, Bag, Doc, Nutt, and I are admiring the stars with our shirts off, but still wearing our jeans. She doesn't get that nobody wants to rock a boner in a friendly hot tub.

After a minute or two, we finally start ditching our pants. I honestly started wearing boxer briefs just in case something like this happened. I knew whitey tighties would be embarrassing, and they are.

"Are those Underoos, EJ?" Bag asks. "Did your mom lay those out for you this morning?" Nicky chuckles.

EJ's not that embarrassed, because he's had sex with the girl making fun of him, and everyone is too busy gawking at the little scrub tree that Abby is disrobing behind.

I embody my father and say, "Guys . . . come on."

After the bras are submerged, we calm down and start having a great time. They're soaking, but I am actually bathing! I go under for a minute and scrub the crap out of my skin. My friends are mad because they had to ditch their cooler when "The cops burst in!" but I think this hot tub party is just fine without booze. I don't tell them how Abby and I made up the whole thing just to get out of an embarrassing situation. I also keep Nutt's Fat Sal situation to myself . . . at least for a while.

I thought a neighbor would eventually call the cops for real, because we're laughing a lot, but we hang out there for over an hour. The tub is so hot that we have to sit on the edge for a few minutes. Which is no big deal until Abby and Nicky do the same thing . . . and the conversation dies for a while. We splash around and talk about dumb stuff until our skin is prunier than raisins.

We ditch the wet underwear and struggle to put our cold clothes back on. We pile into Aunt Jenny and crank the heat as we roll past Lou's house. A few kids are putting trash bags on the curb, and a few more are picking up the house. They're laughing and you can tell they're having fun. I'm sure this is the original crew he actually invited. I'm glad they're getting to have their "get-together" after all.

We find Nutt and the rest of the boys at QuikTrip. Unfortunately, the cops show up a few minutes after we do, so people start scrambling around and jumping into random cars. Nicky stayed with us, so I didn't realize that Abby was gone until I saw her wet butt squeezing into the back of Jeremy's car. I open my door to follow her, but EJ grabs my arm and says, "Let her go."

I ask Nicky, "What the hell is going on?"

"I honestly don't know," she replies. "Abby hasn't been right since she went to New York."

# 17. WHO CASTS THE FIRST STONE?

I left Abby a couple of messages, but she never called back, and she's continued to blow me off at school, so I've decided that *I* am pissed at *her*. I just wish we could talk for a second so I could bitch her out! I cannot figure out how we've gone from moving to New York together to not speaking.

The last message I left her was the first Friday night of winter break. My boys were partying, but I took the evening off to go to bed early. (It's not quite break yet for Mrs. Trimmer and me. We still have to be at school before six a.m. on Saturday.) I really needed to talk to Abby because the New York Drama School called my mom and told her that I was being "seriously" considered for fall admission, and they were going to send a team of evaluators to my next performance. They explained that if they liked what they saw, I would receive an actual invitation in May. Mom didn't tell them I wasn't interested, because she was kind of crying during their talk. I'm not sure if I am or not, though. I've really been busting my ass at school, and I plan to keep busting it. I've continued to rehearse the songs from *RENT*, and I'm having a blast doing it. Most days I think I would go to the drama school if they invited me . . . but other days I'll find myself in some new hallway at school and get all turned around for few minutes, and I'll think, *You are insane! You can't handle New York City, dude!* I wish I knew if Abby was rethinking her decision. I wish she would just talk to me.

After Saturday School, I feel like a million bucks because most of my break homework is done. I still need to finish reading *Slaughterhouse-Five*, but hopefully I will be able to. It's a good story, but so far it's not as gory as the title suggests.

My boys are too hungover to do fight club, which is fine with me because I'm getting a little burned out. We got a second pair of boxing gloves and everyone is getting really good. It's cool to see the progress, but it sucks to feel the punches. So instead of going to EJ's house, we're headed to the Lord's. A church on Merrian Lane just put in two sand volleyball courts beside their parking lot. We assume they're planning to start a league in the spring, but we're going to break in the courts for them. Nutt stole a volleyball from the equipment locker (he's going to beg forgiveness while we're there).

On his way to basketball practice this morning, EJ got pulled over by the Merrian P.D. for "unlawful display of acceleration." He tried to explain why he'd peeled out into the lane. "I've usually got a thousand pounds of dudes in the car with me!"

But the cop bitched him out for five minutes and made him even later to practice. The guy was cool enough (or lazy enough) to not to give him a ticket, but he said he'd "throw the book at him" if he caught Aunt Jenny doing any more Tokyo drifting. Of course we keep encouraging EJ to burn out and take corners fast. But EJ's taking the warning seriously and driving like Aunt Jenny would want him to (his actual great-aunt, not the car).

Before volleyball we stop at QuikTrip to grab some drinks. When EJ creeps back onto Merrian Lane, I have to ask, "Seriously?"

"You haven't gone over fifteen miles an hour all day!" Bag says.

EJ whines, "That cop's looking for me!"

"Well, you're not hard to find!" Nutt observes as a grandma in a Corolla blows past.

We keep dogging him until Nutt notices something coming up on the right side of the road. It's an eight-foot-tall white tube that's rocking from side to side.

"Oh, snap!" Bag gasps. "It's a new mascot!"

Another unfortunate tradition in Merrian is throwing things at human advertisements. I don't know how it helps profits to stick a clown out in front of your business and make him wave a sign at oncoming traffic, but teenage guys absolutely love to chuck things at them. We've never done it, not because it's horribly mean, but because it's not as effective on a bicycle and the CRX wasn't much better. Aunt Jenny, on the other hand, seems to have been made for suburban terrorism. She's got big windows and a powerful engine. She even has a rain gutter on her roof that you can hang on to while you're crushing a mailbox or picking up trash cans on the go . . . or if you want to throw a Coke at a giant can of Pepsi (or something) and you really want to zing it.

"What the hell is that?" I ask as EJ creeps closer to the curb.

"It's a quart of Pennzoil, made of rubber!" Doc replies.

"Ooohhh, it's brand new!" J-Low giggles.

"You gotta go faster than this, E!" I suggest.

Every roadside mascot must know the horror of a passing car slowing down. All he can do is watch as a skinny punk springs out of the passenger window armed with a Big Gulp and an evil smile. You can't run when you're yoked with a giant costume, and you can't block a liquid no matter how big your sign is. Your only hope is that the cup isn't filled with tobacco spit and you can wipe your eyes in time to see the license number as they speed away.

Nutt rolls down the window and slides out so far that Bag has to hold his legs to keep him from falling.

The mascot isn't facing us. It's just rocking back and forth, lazily waving its fat white hands at oncoming traffic. My heart is pounding as Nutt cocks his arm back like a major league pitcher. The can of oil seems to sense something is up, because it stops waving and starts to waddle around into the path of destruction. Even though I'm just smashed in the backseat, I wish I wasn't here. I could've sat this tradition out. Some poor bastard is freezing his ass off to make a few bucks, and then he has to suffer this kind of embarrassment at the hands of pricks who barely know how to drive the car they're terrorizing you with. It's too sad to bear . . . even before we recognize the face in the middle of the "O" in the Pennzoil can. My eyes open as wide as Rusty Dollingsworth's do when I realize that Mr. Lee has really outdone himself this time. He's spared no expense in his quest to humiliate the boy who knocked up his daughter.

Doc quietly asks, "Is that——?"

"Don't throw it——" I yell just as Bag whizzes his soda. The lid comes off in mid-flight, but Rusty keeps waddling toward it. He flinches when he sees the flying beverage, but relaxes just before it smashes into his "O" and splatters all over his costume. His jaw flexes in proud defiance as the cup rolls down his chest.

We don't cheer or laugh. Rusty has totally ruined it.

Doc yells, "Punch it, E!"

But EJ screws up his pedals and smashes down on the brake. Everyone hits whatever is in front of him, but none of us stops gawking at Rusty.

We're waiting for him to start kicking out the windows, but he seems too confused. He squats down and of course he makes eye contact with me, so I try to explain. "Sorry, Rusty, we didn't realize . . . that it was you in there."

As defeated as I have ever heard a human voice, he mutters, "It's okay."

EJ finds the gas pedal and we shoot dirt and sand all over him as we tear down Merrian Lane. At this point, I'd like to go home, but no one is saying anything, so we just drive. It totally sucks because we all know Rusty's situation. He's missing his senior year of high school so he can rock around Merrian Lane with "LUBE!" written up his back, and he's going to be eating this brand of crap for the rest of his life for having sex with a girl who none of us were qualified to get with. And here we are, throwing fountain-drink stones and judging him like Judy because he didn't use a condom or it broke or she wouldn't get on the pill or she forgot to take it or whatever.

We pull into the empty church parking lot, in need of forgiveness, but volleyball is a really fun game . . . until someone spikes a ball in your face when you're not paying attention and you burst into tears. Everyone seems to feel better after that. It feels good to laugh even when you're the butt of the joke. I wish the feeling would come back to my face, but my boys do a pretty great impression of the spike. Slow motion is comedy gold.

# 18. SUITING UP

I watch *Camelot* rehearsals after detention on Fridays. We have swim practice at six a.m. because apparently my coach hates Fridays. Sometimes I read lines with Jeremy and the other cast members. Abby doesn't need any help, though. She really doesn't. She knows her lines and she's so good in every scene she's in. Her voice makes people cry all the time, and not just me. I've heard others compare her voice to Adele's, but I tell them to keep it to themselves. I swear they're just talking about the sound coming out of her face, and maybe her hair when she swoops it to the side just right. I know she misunderstood the voice coach, but I still want to punch that Jenny Craig dance teacher in her leotard.

Our production of *Camelot* is way better than the movie. Jeremy is King Arthur, and he's awesome. He leaps and swings and swoops all over the place. Abby plays his wife, Guenevere, and she's super in love with him but kind of suspects he's into one of his knights, Sir Lancelot. She tries to sniff out the trouble but winds up hooking up with ol' Lance, and all hell breaks loose in the kingdom.

This stoner/band geek Clint is playing Sir Lancelot, but I know McDougle wanted me to do it, and I'm so mad I want to punch myself in the face every time he comes onstage.

Our school is getting all kinds of press because the gay angle hasn't been explored in any other productions of *Camelot*. Theater folk think it's awesome, but some parents and school administrators are not so into it. It seemed like McDougle was going to have to give in to Principal Banks's request to do it straight until an article came out in *Stage Magazine* (online). The title was "Censorship in King Arthur's Court," and it has been reposted all over the place. I guess newspapers and TV shows called to interview Principal Banks, but magically, there wasn't much of a story to tell. Banks claimed the whole thing was a "misunderstanding" and he "fully supports Ms. McDougle and her freedom of expression."

I really shouldn't come to these rehearsals, but it motivates me to keep working on *RENT*. Kids with smaller parts in *Camelot* are already preparing for the spring musical auditions, too. You can usually find a kid to play the piano, and people are always down to sing in the drama department. I've read the Roger scenes with this girl Kathy playing the role of Mimi so many times that I kind of know all of the lines. I've been working on them in detention a little bit too. You can't sing while you're incarcerated, but Mrs. Trimmer doesn't seem to mind if I talk to myself. She may be frightened of me and think that I am out of my mind, but I'm just mumbling lines of dialogue over and over again.

I watched the movie version of *RENT* with my boys. When they realized it was a musical, they were like, "Carter, what the—?" but they didn't make me turn it off because it's an awesome story and Rosario Dawson plays a stripper and sings about having the best ass below 14th Street. They're kind of supportive, in their own way.

I really want to play Roger. He's a sexy rocker dude

who wears skintight plaid pants. He's also dying of AIDS. I can't grow out my hair because of swimming, so I'm going to have to wow Ms. McDougle with my acting, singing, and guitar work. McDougle told me that the guy who plays Roger *has* to play the guitar onstage.

I was bummed until I realized that I finally have an excuse to talk to Abby. She learned to play one for *A Piece of My Heart*, so maybe she'll teach me or at least lend me her "ax" (that's what Clint calls his guitar). I wait for the right moment to talk to her, and finally catch her coming out of the dressing room one evening.

"Hey, rock star!"

She just raises her eyebrows like, *What?*

So I reply, "Uhhh, s'up? I w-w-was just wondering if I could borrow y-your ax?"

Of course she doesn't get that reference because I didn't set it up right. So I explain it to her and I feel like she thinks that I'm being a dick, but I'm just clarifying a simple pop culture reference. She gets kind of aggressive when she says, "If you ever paid attention, you'd know that McDougle lent me that guitar. I'm sure she'll check it out to you if you ask her."

"Okay, great," I reply. And then I actually become the dick that she thought I was being earlier: "Thank you for your helpful, yet kind of bitchy advice."

She cocks her head like she's finally going to let me have it, but she just sighs. "What do you want? I don't own a guitar."

"I guess I thought you could show me some—"

"I only know the beginning chords to one Janis Joplin song," she says.

"Why are you being so mean to me?"

"I can't help you; how is that mean?" she asks. "It would be a waste of your time. Clint is in a band; maybe he'll show you some stuff."

I'm too flustered to say anything clever. All I can come up with is: "Clint is auditioning to play Roger, too."

"Yep," she replies.

"Well, he wouldn't want to teach his competition how to defeat him, would he?"

Abby snaps, "Not everyone sees the world as a battle-field, Carter. Not everyone has little scores to settle or conquests to make all the time."

"Whoa, what are you talking about?"

She shuts her eyes tight and says, "Nothing. I have to go—"

"Wait, please. I just asked you—"

"I'm in rehearsal right now; I really have to go," she says, and marches back into the auditorium.

I head to the drama classroom, stunned. Kathy's ironing costumes with someone's mom, and yells, "Carter! Do you want to work on the candle song?! Are you okay?"

I tell her I'm fine, and I really try to be, but I'm so confused and pissed off, I don't even know how to deal with myself. We go ahead and rehearse the scene, and it goes really well. Roger is kind of an angry dude, so I just let it all out.

Kathy always says nice things about my acting work, but she really gushes tonight. "Carter, you gave me chills!"

"Thanks, dude. You were really great too."

Kathy is kind of cute, and she's very nice and she doesn't have a boyfriend. I know this because she's told me a few times. I think she's done this because she likes me. I know

I could ask her out, but I'm not sure I like her like *that*. I might just be using her to make Abby jealous, and to practice my skills. But I seem to break girls' hearts by accident all the time, and that sucks bad enough; I'd hate to see the fallout if I actually did it on purpose, and my sister would murder me if she found out I was even thinking about using a girl like that.

On New Year's Day she learned that Nick Brock was cheating on her with a cheerleader/sorority girl. I guess this girl showed up at his dorm room while Lynn was there, and it got ugly. Nick tried to say that she was just a friend, but my sister is pretty sharp. I've seen a lot of cheerleader/sorority girl videos on the Internet. I know how sexy and persuasive those chicks can be, but I'm still pissed at Nick. I'm not going to fight him or anything, because violence doesn't solve anything and I don't want to rock a wheelchair for the rest of my life. My whole family has been walking on eggshells for weeks. Football is like a four-letter word all of a sudden.

# 19. YAHOO

So it's mid-January and it's cold as hell in Merrian. You'd think my boys and I would be stoked to finally have the use of an awesome car like Aunt Jenny so we don't have to ride our bikes in a blizzard and we don't have to show up places with icy snot all over our faces, but you would be wrong. I'm on the front bitch-seat, in between EJ and Andre. Mucus is draining from my trembling red nose and hardening in the breeze because all of Aunt Jenny's windows are rolled down for a game of Freeze-out. The first guy to complain loses. I just shaved my head again for a swim meet, so I have no insulation on my melon, but I will not protest!

I guess we're headed to some party. I can see that drugs and alcohol are the keys to having fun at lame gatherings, but I'm not ready to throw away my years of D.A.R.E. training (I won't let you down, Deputy Dan!). I get that booze lowers your inhibitions and numbs your sense of pain and therefore makes you unstoppable in a game of Freeze-out, but I hate the taste of it, and I'm terrified of vomiting. I honestly think if I smoked or snorted anything out of the ordinary, my body would just freak out and I'd die instantly. Everyone would be like, "I knew he was a space-case, but I never suspected Will Carter was a druggie!" I can't do that to my mom.

My teeth are chattering uncontrollably, but I'm laughing with everyone else. I know that this will be the best part of the night, so I'm trying to enjoy it. The loser of tonight's game of Freeze-out has to "yahoo" beer for everybody. Losing would be especially disappointing if you don't drink and also because "yahooing" is super illegal. It has nothing to do with the Web site; it's a tradition in Merrian that predates computers. If you don't have a fake ID or money, you gotta "yahoo" (walk into the liquor store and grab a case of beer before running out the door yelling "YAHOOOO!!!") it.

I look around the car to see who's going to break, but everyone looks pretty damn focused. I've lost the feeling in my lips, and my feet may need to be amputated to stop the spread of frostbite. I can't believe I'm doing this, but I finally have to cry out, "'or da 'ove a Gah! R-r-roll 'em up!!!"

Everyone cheers, "Yaaahooo!" and "Carter, Carter, Carter!" as they happily crank the windows and heat. Told you they were supportive.

The problem with yahooing in Merrian is that it *is* a "tradition," so when a young guy walks into a liquor store, the clerks are ready to tackle his ass as soon as they hear "Ya!" Some dudes never even get the "hooo" out before they're slammed into a display case or something. We're too smart for that, so we're headed to Hy-Vee! They sell beer, and it won't be weird to see a fifteen-year-old guy walk in. I could be buying chips or bananas. They won't know what hit 'em when I run out the door screaming.

We wrap a towel around Aunt Jenny's license plate so no one can get her digits (gangsta).

"Yeah, no way anyone will be able to identify this huge old car filled with high school dudes!" Doc laughs.

Everyone tells him to keep his negativity/common sense to himself.

To my surprise, Andre and J-Low are joining me on the mission. I believe they're part wingmen, part enforcers. They want to give me courage but also confirm that I yell "Yahoo!" loud enough.

We stroll into the bright store as innocently as possible, but I bet we look like terrorists headed into an airport. We bypass the bananas and march straight back to the beer. Each of us grabs a case of Bud Light. I guess they don't want me to have all the fun, and I assume we all choose Bud Light because they advertise most effectively to teens. I start to giggle, but Andre punches me in the ribs and I get it under control. We try not to make eye contact with anyone as we stride toward the checkout lanes. I never noticed how many security cameras they have at Hy-Vee, but I've never attempted to rob them before. It also occurs to me that I will never get to buy groceries here again, so that kind of sucks.

We're hustling down the chip aisle, and J-Low grabs a family-size bag of Doritos.

I say, "Nice!" as a pudgy dude in a white short-sleeved shirt cruises around the endcap. He's wearing a red tie and a name tag that says CHUCK—ASSISTANT MANAGER.

Chuck's looking right at us, but no one meets his eyes as we walk past. "You fellas finding everything okay?" he asks.

Oh man, we are toast! It suddenly occurs to me that we're not the first geniuses to think of Hy-Vee as a liquor store/yahoo alternative.

He swings around and says, "Hold up a second, fellas."

I glance in Chuck's direction as he hikes up his khakis as if he's about to make a goal-like stand. Ol' boy thinks he's got us . . . but he is mistaken. We play football and do CrossFit and fight club together. We're trained like Seal Team Six for this!

Andre looks over his shoulder just as the big man lunges for him. J-Low instinctively tosses the Doritos into the air, and Chuck makes the mistake of looking up when the bag crashes into a light fixture. Andre dives under the man's arm tackle as I press my case of Bud Light into Chuck's ribs. He was already off balance, so I wouldn't say I "pushed" him exactly. I'd say I "guided" him into the Pringles display. But he really nails it, and tops pop on about twenty cans.

"Yard sale!" J-Low chuckles.

Andre adds, "Cleanup on aisle four!" I attempt to pat him on the back because that's the funniest mean thing he's ever said. He's too fast, though. We're hauling ass for the door.

The whole store appears to be looking at us as we charge the checkout lanes. I scream, "YAAAHOOOOO!!!" as I hurdle the "Lane Closed" sign on register three. Hy-Vee is aghast at the laughing punks running out the door.

We almost get nailed by a minivan as we sprint across the parking lot without looking both ways (sorry, Mom). And Chuck is still in hot pursuit, yelling, "You bastards get back here!"

I guess larceny and wiping out a Pringles display has changed us from "fellas" to "bastards." No one follows Chuck's instructions. J-Low and Andre get to the car before me because they're fast as hell. But they seem to have forgotten that Aunt Jenny's back doors have been sticking ever since EJ backed into a light pole going thirty miles an hour. So while Andre and J-Low struggle to open the door and yell at each other, I dive into the open passenger window like Superman (rescuing a case of Bud Light) and yell, "Punch it, E!"

The tires burn out and Aunt Jenny does what she was made to do! Gangsta getaway! We barrel across the parking lot, with Andre and J-Low clinging to a door handle. Their feet drag along the asphalt and they scream, "STOP!!!"

J-Low uses Andre's face for leverage as he worms through the window, but just as his torso makes it inside, EJ realizes what's going on and locks up the brakes. J-Low is ejected from the car like a stunt man in a Jackie Chan movie; he tumbles along the parking lot for ten or fifteen feet. He doesn't seem to be hurt, though . . . until Andre starts punching him in the face. J-Low cries for help while we all jump out of the car and try to pull Andre off. Chuck stops his pursuit because it's obvious we're lunatics. Once Andre is under control, my boys scramble around the lot collecting a few runaway beers, and we finally make our actual getaway.

After J-Low's nose stops bleeding, Andre apologizes for hitting him. I consider making fun of Andre because I think he was crying during the chaos, but I go ahead and leave it alone.

We're the heroes of tonight's lame field party. We share our beer booty and retell the "yahoo" story to anyone who'll listen. It's a pretty fun night, but I don't think we'll try to repeat it anytime soon.

# 20. COUGAR FIGHT

The battle in the pool continues between Andre and me. I'm going to the state championships in three events. Of course that butt-hole is going in four. The standoff with Abby is still at a standstill. *Camelot* was such a success that they added three performances to accommodate all the ticket sales. I got all As (and two Bs) on my report card, and I basically know every line and song from *RENT*.

It's another Friday night, and I can't stay out late because I've got to be back at school before six a.m. (shocker). But tonight's the final basketball game of the regular season and we're facing off against the Nortest Cougars again. Merrian is hoping for a miracle and some redemption. I've never enjoyed playing basketball because I suck, but I really enjoy watching the games. Especially now that EJ is getting to play. He's even scored a few times!

The Nortest mascot is a tan-colored, furry, pissed-off jungle cat, but everyone jokes that it's actually the slutty old-lady type of cougar. Some senior dudes got the idea that a bunch of us should dress up like desperate housewives to mess with the other team's concentration. That sounded like a great idea at the time, so I'm not wearing my usual jeans and T-shirt uniform this evening. Instead, I'm rocking an extra-large sparkly turquoise bridesmaid's dress that I found at Goodwill. We had to cut out the back so I could fit into it, and a shoestring is holding the whole thing together. I've paired it with a blond Dolly Parton wig. Bag and my sister helped us with our makeup. I won't say it out loud, but I am pretty hot.

Satin isn't as warm as you'd think, however. We realize what a poor choice it is for late January weather when we step out of the CRX. Another concern that's growing is that the game's about to start and we can't find those seniors who came up with this whole cross-dressing scheme. Doc thinks we've been set up. I really hope he's wrong, because we've gone *full-retard* with their cougar idea.

Andre is the only one of my boys that refused to do it, but Bag, Nutt, Doc, Levi, J-Low, Hormone, Timberlake, The Ding-Dong, Coot, Lt. Dangle, Sloth, Hangin' Chad, The Devil, TrimSpa, and I are all dressed up with nowhere to go.

Hormone is the first to say it out loud: "I don't know about this, you guys."

"It'll be fine," I say.

"Why does lipstick have to taste so foul?!" Nutt asks.

"You're not supposed to eat it," Doc explains.

Everyone is adjusting their dresses in the reflections of car windows and feeling insecure, but I can hear the Merrian marching band starting to play our fight song, and it fills me with enough courage. I start to dance a little. "Come on, this is gonna be great!" I jump up and down a few times, and they seem on board again, so I say, "Let's do this!" and start clomping toward the field house in my high heels. I'm feeling good until some softball chicks spot us and one of them yells, "OH MY GOD!!!" and the others start pointing and laughing.

Nutt is wearing a very short, fitted white cocktail dress. You can see his whitey tighties peeking out from the bottom of his skirt. He was so proud of himself at Bag's house, but he's the first guy to really freak out. He doubles over and yells, "I can't do it! Everybody can see my junk in this thing!"

"That's the funniest part of the outfit!" I say.

Bag adds, "Naw man, I'm out too! Screw this!"

"Oh, come on!" I protest. "The game's about to begin, and EJ might get to start tonight. We've got to get in there!"

"Let's just wait for the seniors," Hormone whines. "If they show up, we can walk in as a unit and it'll be better."

I shake my head in disgust and embody my football coach when I yell, "Screw that! *We* are the unit! And we're not following anyone or walking in there with our heads down. This is funny! We don't need to apologize to anyone. If it goes bad . . . so what? Who cares?! We went down swinging. But let's rock this, you bitches!"

They don't nod or say anything, but I think I've got them. I hope . . . I pray they're following me as I lumber toward the gym and fling the doors open. I toss my platinum hair back and flash my student ID to a shocked Spanish teacher as I blow past her. The bright lights of the basketball court are blinding, and my high heels get heavier with every step. The band starts playing "We Are the Champions" by Queen, and I know it's a sign (it's also one of only three songs our band knows). My heart is pounding as I scan the crowd. I do not see the seniors, but a few people have noticed me and they're pointing.

I mutter, "You are the Champion!" to myself when both basketball teams stop doing their layup drills to gawk at me.

EJ yells, "Oh no you di-in't!?" and I notice that my boys are standing right beside me. We're lined up like the proudest, ugliest Rockettes ever. A rush of drama department adrenaline washes over me, and I take off running around the court. I clomp around and blow kisses to the Nortest players and coaches. I grab my padded bra and put on my cougar voice (think Miss Piggy) and yell, "I'm looking for a stuuud!"

I chase EJ around the court for a second and shout, "I'm gonna make a man outta you, boy!" Then I jump into the stands and start molesting a freshman dude I know from swim team.

My boys are being a bit obvious. They feel the need to yell, "We're cougars!" and "We've come to root for the Cougars!" as if our brand of humor is too subtle. The crowd is cracking up, though. My parents are here and obviously a bit embarrassed, but maybe kind of proud too. I catch Principal Banks chuckling as we dance around to the drum line's beat.

Our football coach is sitting high in the stands. I see him say something to his wife before smiling and giving us a sly thumbs-up. My friends have never felt this drama triumph before, and they're digging it.

Just before tipoff, the seniors walk in. They're wearing dresses, but no wigs or makeup, and they're pretty drunk. Not that it's a competition, but we kicked the crap out of them. They're still funny, but we totally stole their thunder.

We all heckle the Nortest players together and ask why they never call us anymore. They try not to look at us or laugh, but I think we're affecting their game. Merrian jumps to an early lead in spite of some bad shots by our point guards. A few minutes into the first half, the coach gives EJ a nod. He gets up and rips off his pants (perfectly), and we all go nuts. EJ tries not to smile.

They feed him the inbound pass, and no one from Nortest bothers to cover the lanky sophomore, so he pulls up for a ten-foot jumper and drains it! We freak out like he won the state championship. A few plays later he nails a three-pointer, and it's pandemonium in the cougar den!

Everything is awesome until halftime, when Abby and the drill team take the floor. My boys and I are dancing along in the bleachers to Rihanna's "Only Girl (In the World)" while the senior cougars go over to the Nortest side of the gym. They call their cheerleaders "ugly fatties" because they think it's funny (but what a drunk finds funny almost never is). Some Nortest guys decide to talk to them about it, and punch them in their faces. It is a shock to no one, except the guys getting hit.

Abby's too busy busting a move to notice the brawl exploding behind her. She doesn't see Principal Banks race-walking around the court, until the violence spills onto the hardwood and a gang of Merrian dudes breaks through her chorus line and she's forced to stop dancing. Unfortunately, I am one of the reasons her dance was ruined, so she's glaring at me as I run past her . . . as if there aren't a hundred other people involved!

I'll apologize later, but I need to stay focused right now. We reach the Nortest side of the gym and I'm not really sure what to do. Fortunately, a guy I don't know shoves me from the side and calls me a tranny.

I try to stay on my feet and locate the guy who pushed me so that I can explain that I am an ironic cross-dresser, not a transsexual! But Andre is punching the dude's lights out, so I'll have to save the lesson. It's a tornado of chaos and yelling. Another guy swings his fist at me from the other side, but I'm able to duck just in time. Thank you, fight club! I don't swing back because I am a LADY (and I didn't react fast enough). Somebody runs into me, hard, so I give the guy a shove that sends him flying . . . before I realize it was a very small girl. Someone clocks me in the side of the head and it stuns me, and really pisses me off! All I can see is blond hair, but I swing my right fist in the direction the punch originated, and I connect with something really hard. I flip the wig out of my eyes just in time to see Principal Banks collapsing to the floor like a wet noodle. In horror, I look around to see if anyone saw me pummel my principal, but everyone is too busy fighting.

A Nortest guy almost steps on Principal Banks, but I push him off. The guy shoves me back and I tag him in the cheek. He stumbles and disappears into the fracas. I protect Principal Banks until five Merrian police officers come running over. They're pissed (because they had to run), but all they do is toss guys around and yell, "Knock it off!" and "Get outta here!"

I stay with the principal until his eyes flutter, and he asks, "What the—? Did I black out?"

"I guess so."

When he seems okay, I casually walk back across the court, but I accidentally meet eyes with my dad. He looks super pissed and disappointed. I'm not sure if it's the dress I'm wearing or the fact that I just knocked out an administrator, but I am ashamed of myself. The cops stand around the court for a while and talk to some teachers and the coaches. Eventually the Merrian band begins to play "We Are the Champions" for the fifth time, and the players retake the court.

I try to just watch the rest of the game in peace, but Nortest guys keep flipping us off and making a bunch of other gestures that I don't entirely understand. It seems like they're threatening some sort of sexual violence. I'm sure we'll find out after the game.

# 21. THE OTHER QUIKTRIP

EJ scored eight points in the game, and we beat Nortest by six. I think he deserves MVP. But before I can congratulate him, I have to go out to the parking lot and try to look tough with my friends, which is difficult in this dress. Thank God there are twenty police cars out front, so all of us cougars are free to have fun again. We wave at the Nortest guys as they pass, and use our cougar voices to say, "Better luck next time, y'all!" and "If you want to talk about anything, just call!"

All of my confidence drops when I hear trunk bolts rattling, but it's not Terry's Cutlass. It's an old Corsica or something with a trunk full of speakers. I realize it's a Nortest car when it pulls up to the curb and a drunk guy leans out of the passenger window. He's pointing at me when he yells, "Meet us at QuikTrip in fifteen minutes! I'm gonna mess you up, tranny!"

My heart rate has skyrocketed, but I'm able to keep my wits. In my own voice, I reply, "I'm not sure all of the cops heard you, tough guy."

Even some Nortest guys chuckle at my joke. Usually I think of my comebacks a couple of hours late, but that just came right out! Then I get cocky and say, "Just 'cause a guy's wearing a dress doesn't make him a tranny, dumbass!"

EJ isn't here to rein me in, so my dad does it for him. He wraps his hand around the back of my neck and says, "Quit while you're ahead, son."

The Corsica rattles away as Dad guides me around the side of the building, where my mom is waiting with her arms crossed. I might be in for a beat-down after all. She says, "Your behavior is unacceptable, young man!"

If I wasn't over six feet tall now, I'd think I was in for a spanking, but Dad shifts us into an adult conversation when he says, "This is what I was talking about in front of EJ's house."

"Ummm . . ." I say.

"When we talked about the fight club," he clarifies.

"Oh, yeah . . . yeah, remind me again . . . like, paraphrase what it was we were . . ."

"You're out here looking for trouble," he scolds.

"Naw, we're just having fun."

"It was 'fun' when you ran around the court before the game, but these Nortest guys aren't having fun anymore. They just lost, and you're out here taunting them."

Mom adds, "Not cool."

"I didn't start it."

"You're smarter than that, too," she scolds.

"You're right, I'm sorry."

"When you led your friends out onto that court in this getup, I don't think I've ever been more proud of you," Dad says.

"Seriously?" I ask. "Of all the crap I do to impress you?"

"You're a talented kid," he continues. "You're a leader,

and people love you, but there will always be guys who will want to take somebody like you down a few pegs. It sucks, but it's what men do sometimes."

Mom finishes his thought. "Don't give anyone the chance to ruin *your* future, Will."

I nod that I understand. I know they want to say more. They want to remind me not to stay out too late and to put on a coat and look both ways before I cross the parking lot, but they shut it down and hope I'll do the right things with what they've given me. As I walk away, though, my dad can't help being a father for another second. "Damn it, what did you do to that dress?! Your mother has been saving that thing for—"

"*That* is not one of my dresses!" she says. "It's from the Salvation Army or something, right? Please tell me I don't own something that terrible."

I assure her it isn't hers, and they go back to their car while I go stand with my friends. I don't taunt anyone else, and neither do they.

I see Abby coming out of the gym with her duffel bag over her shoulder. She looks a little cranky, but I go ahead and approach. She's stopped to talk to some drama kids, who seem to be consoling her about the ruined routine. They're being all huggy and dramatic, so I go ahead and bust into their conversation to say, "Hey, I'm really sorry . . . about . . . what happened."

She glares at me, but before she can say anything, Kathy says, "That dress is fierce, Carter!"

"You like it?! I got this baby for ten bucks!"

"Why don't you get lost?" Abby says.

The drama kids gasp.

"I'm trying to apologize to you," I say.

She scoffs. "Oh, it seemed like you were talking about yourself when you barged into a conversa—"

Kathy tries to defend me. "No he didn't!"

But Abby continues, "We worked very hard on that routine, and you guys just—"

"That fight was not Carter's fault!" Kathy says.

"Nooo . . . nothing is ever Carter's fault!" Abby adds.

"What the hell is your problem?" I ask. "I haven't done anything to you . . . lately."

She rolls her eyes, so I say, "I've never hurt you on purpose, Abby. I've done everything you've ever asked me to do. You made me apply to that school, and then you came back from your trip and just dropped off the planet. We hung out at that Nortest party and it seemed like things were good, but then we go back to just nothing for no reason. Why?!"

It may be my outfit, or that my voice is kind of whiny, but people are staring at us. My boys sense a catfight and gather around.

Abby replies, "I've never 'made' you do anything! I *suggested* that you apply to the New York Drama School because I *know* that it would be great for you—"

"And you're scared of going by yourself," I add.

She nods. "Maybe that *was* true. . . . Maybe I was under the impression that you were someone that you're not. I wouldn't go to QuikTrip with you now that I've seen the real you!"

"The real me? How did you see that?"

She's so pissed that she can't respond, and I don't have

anything else clever to say. Everyone is waiting for something big to happen, but they're in for a long night if they think it's going to come from me.

Abby finally asks, "You really don't know? You're that stupid?"

"No! Yes . . . Shut up, what the hell did I do?"

She says, "What is the other thing I 'made' you do?"

"The skinny jeans? God, I told you, they crushed my—"

"Amber Lee!" she barks.

I feel the eye shadow crinkle as my eyes widen. *Ohhh, that!* "Can we please talk about this in private?"

Bag asks, "What did he do to Amber Lee?"

"It *is* your baby!" Nutt yells. "You son of a—"

"Shut up, dude!"

"Tell them!" she shouts. "Tell *your boys* what you did with Amber Lee after homecoming!"

I look down at my size-twelve heels and really wish I wasn't wearing them right now.

Abby continues, "Tell them that you took advantage of a pregnant girl!"

Everyone gasps, and Nutt says, "Wooow! So unexpected!"

"Hold up. I did not 'take advantage' of her! When you say it like that, they're picturing me having sex with her."

"Why shouldn't they?" she asks.

"I guess I would rather they not . . . because it didn't happen."

"Carter!" Abby barks. "She told me!"

"Told you what?"

"That you guys 'hooked up' on the banks of Grey Goose Lake."

J-Low asks, "What is it with you and that lake, Carter?"

"Whoa, whoa! We did not 'hook up'! We just made out a little bit."

Abby seems taken aback by this.

"Still, dude!" Bag says with a disgusted face.

I try to explain. "Oh come on, I didn't . . . It w-w-wasn't like I was . . . like—"

"So, *whatever* it was wasn't your fault, is that correct?" Abby asks, still angry.

I put up my hand and glare at her to shut her up, but she knocks my hand down. It seems like she's about to slap me or say something mean, so I ask, "Why didn't you talk to me about this? Or at least get some clarification from Amber. I mean 'hooked up' can mean a lot of—"

"Oh my God! You can't take *any* responsibility? You lied to me, Carter!" she barks.

"I did not! I just *didn't tell you* because my . . ." (I really want to blame my sister here, but I don't, because it was *my* decision.) I quietly say, "*I . . . I* didn't want to hurt Amber. She's got it hard enough, and I didn't want to cost her a friend because of an insignificant mistake."

Abby's anger seems to be waning, but I can tell that she's been mad about this for so long that she doesn't know how to let it go. She says, "I just thought you would tell me eventually."

"I'm sorry that I didn't, but I believe I did it for the right reasons. Amber is my friend, and my friends are ridiculously important to me; if you can't deal with that, then I don't want anything to do with *you*. You're the asshole here for dragging this out in front of everyone just because you're pissed at me. Amber deserves better."

Someone says, "Preach it, Dolly!" which reminds me

what I'm wearing, and I feel like a fool, so I just walk away. I have no idea where I'm headed, but I know my cougars are right behind me. I'm cutting through the first row of cars in the parking lot when I hear their footsteps getting closer. A firm hand touches my shoulder and spins me around, hard. I instantly remember that I was almost in a fistfight a few minutes ago, so I draw up my hands to protect my face, but it's Abby. And while she's coming at me aggressively, I don't think she's going to hit me. "You don't get to call me an asshole and then just walk away."

"I'm sorry."

"I didn't mean to have that conversation in public. I just wanted to ignore it forever, but you are so annoying. And I honestly love you. Nicky says I'm passive-aggressive."

"I know. And I love you too."

*WHAM!* She rams her lips into mine. Well, that was easy! She's a great kisser, and really strong! I totally thought that was a dude spinning me around, but I will not share that thought with Abby.

We're able to make out for a few seconds before people start clapping behind us, and we start giggling.

"I'm also sorry that I wrecked your routine," I say.

Abby says, "It wasn't your fault."

"Now you're getting it."

She punches my shoulder (ouch) and I kiss her again. Once the second round is over, I say, "I've missed that. What are you doing tonight?"

Abby replies, "There's a party at Christy Shauper's house."

"Oooh, the Chopper. Uh, do you think I could join?"

"Really?" she asks sarcastically. "Don't you have to go fight those Nortest guys?"

"Naw. Trouble seems to find me pretty easily. I don't need to be looking for it."

Round three of the kissing continues until people start cheering again. We look up as the Merrian basketball team is coming out of the gym. I yell, "Yeeeaaaayyy EEEJaaaay!!!"

He's smiling from ear to ear as he slaps a few hands and tries to get his mom to stop hugging him in front of everyone. He worked really hard to perform so well, and I know he's proud, but I can also tell that he's a little bit jealous that he's not wearing a dress and he didn't get to be in a brawl during halftime.

Once the crowd separates a bit, I whisper in his ear, "I may or may not have knocked out Principal Banks."

"Nooo," he gasps. "That was you?!"

"Shhh! I'd get kicked out of school for something like that, wouldn't I? *If* I did it."

"I would think so!" he replies. "I'm not sure if I want a degenerate like you going to my school!"

"You wanna get knocked out too?"

We start laughing, and guys want to know what's so funny. We tell them to mind their own business, and I add, "I gotta go."

They obviously want to go to QuikTrip and put our fight club training to use, but I tell them I'd rather go to the Chopper's party. They don't call me a pussy and I don't beg them not to get into a dumb fight. I feel bad ditching them, especially when EJ squeals Aunt Jenny's tires as he tears out of the parking lot. The whole Merrian P.D. is here, so EJ looks like a total badass (I bet he just got caught up in the moment and forgot they were here).

I'm the only guy in drag at the drill team/drama party, but it's not weird at all and a total blast. Except when the Chopper accuses me of stealing her shoes, and I explain that I got mine at Goodwill, and she takes it the wrong way and wants to fight me. I'm just walking out when Nutt comes in the front door, looking like a disaster survivor. His white cocktail dress has been torn to shreds and he's covered in dirt and semi-dried blood.

Drama kids scream in horror. Fat Sal rushes over to him, and I ask, "What the hell happened?"

I guess my boys found the trouble they were looking for, (almost) right where they were told they'd find it. While I was dancing to Rihanna songs with the drill team, they were getting the crap kicked out of them by thirty guys. The Nortest guys were a no-show at QuikTrip, and the cops showed up and ran off all the Merrian kids, so my boys joined a caravan of cars prowling the streets, looking for someone to fight. But they had to fall out of line because Aunt Jenny needed gas and EJ had to pee. They pulled into a hornets' nest when they turned into *the other* QuikTrip, the one right next to Nortest High School . . . the one that the Nortest guys meant when they told us to meet them at QuikTrip. They'd been waiting for more than an hour behind the convenience store. My boys didn't even notice all the dudes waiting to beat their asses until that Corsica with the awful stereo boxed Aunt Jenny in. A little guy popped out of the backseat with a baseball bat and smashed out her windshield.

Nutt says they put up a good fight despite being so

outnumbered. The fight club training must have helped them to an extent, because they knew how to cover up, but EJ, Bag, Doc, Levi, J-Low, and Andre are in the hospital.

Jeremy takes me up to the hospital, and it's super depressing because it's a hospital, but also because EJ's mom is crying. His arm is broken, so he's not going to get to play in the state basketball tournament. Everyone's got a concussion. Bag broke his coccyx (it's pronounced "cock-siks" so we manage to have some fun with that despite the somber mood). Andre's nose is broken and he looks awesome. Their injuries will heal, but apparently Aunt Jenny's a different story. All of her lights and windows were smashed out. EJ's dad says she's totaled.

I feel sooo bad that I wasn't there, but I feel even worse that I'm so *glad* I wasn't there.


Lee Auto Body wants two grand to fix Aunt Jenny's glass . . . and since that's two thousand times what she cost, Mr. Lee suggested that EJ's dad sell her to the crash-up derby. They have to remove a car's windows and lights before the competition, and with Aunt Jenny's big engine, she will be the toast of the derby . . . until she gets too smashed up to continue and finally has to be dragged out of the arena or wherever they do crash-up derbies.

I can't handle the thought of Aunt Jenny being crashed for sport. I actually had a nightmare where the old Dodge could talk and she was begging me for help just before a Corsica and a Cutlass rammed her. Unfortunately I had this dream the morning after the brawl and I was in Saturday School detention at the time. So Mrs. Trimmer gave me two more.

My boys have these big, nasty welts on their heads, and cuts and scrapes all over their bodies. Nutt lost a tooth . . . which is odd because I don't remember him missing any teeth when he limped into the Chopper's house. I'm not going to call him out, but I think Fat Sal may have knocked it out a few hours after the fight.

Andre's broken nose is going to keep him from swimming in the state championships, so he's assisting Coach Barker. I thought Andre was an annoying teammate, but he's an a-hole of a coach! He yells at me for breathing and for resting more than two seconds.

"Come on, Carter!" he's always screaming. "This is the only chance you'll ever have to beat me! Don't waste it!"

Despite all efforts to the contrary, I am kind of friends with Andre now. I've learned that his dad lives in another state and has a new wife and other kids, and he didn't call Andre on his sixteenth birthday. I can kind of see that being disrespectful to women and weaker people runs in his family. I get that he's messed up, but it doesn't stop me from cringing every time he says something rude to a girl and then claims to have "made her day."

EJ is super bummed he can't play basketball anymore, but he's really heartbroken about the car. Aunt Jenny was his pride and joy. Everyone knew it by sight, and you could hear her rumbling down the street from a block away. I know he regrets never getting to hook up with anyone in her back-seat too. We think alike, so I know how frustrating it can be to not reach a goal. He told me that he'd gotten drunk by himself on a Tuesday night. He said it like a joke, but it really bummed me out.

I don't have practice the Thursday before the state swim

championships. Coach wants me to rest, but I ride my bike down to Lee Auto Body after school to visit Aunt Jenny. I see her parked out front looking like she got hit by a bomb. Rusty is sitting on her dented hood smoking a cigarette and looking equally miserable.

I haven't seen him since we were throwing a huge soda at him, and that was before Abby broke the news that I kissed his pregnant girlfriend.

I squeeze my brakes, but he spots me. "S'up, Carter?"

I slowly pedal toward him. "Nothin' much. I just came down to pay my respects to Aunt Jenny."

He flicks his cig and says, "Yeah, she won't be helping anyone throw no more sodas. Those Nortest boys really jacked her up."

"I was supposed to have been there."

"From what I heard, it wouldn't have made any difference," he replies. "You can't do much against a baseball bat."

"I just loved this car."

He smiles . . . and I see why he doesn't do it very often. "Yeah, she was a beauty. His parents can't come up with the cash to get it fixed?"

"His mom kind of hates this car, and Mr. Lee wants like, two grand to fix it."

He shakes his head and says, "He's an asshole, and *females* always be hatin', am I right?"

I go ahead and nod.

He continues, "Amber wants me to sell the LTD and get a Honda or somethin'."

I don't say anything because I don't really see the problem.

"I got my eye on a little Civic Si," he says. "I can get a

chip that gives it an extra eighty horsepower. Make a pretty sweet drift car."

"You could go on really fast diaper runs."

"That's what I'm talkin' about!" He laughs as he slides off the hood and looks Aunt Jenny over. "We could probably find all this glass and stuff at a junkyard. I'd install it as a favor to you, Carter."

I didn't even know Rusty knew my name, so I ask, "Why a favor to me?"

"Amber told me about that homecoming kiss. She said she threw herself at you but you didn't take advantage, and I know you got a crush on her."

I don't feel the need to mention that if she wasn't pregnant I would have been all over it.

He continues, "Nobody else found out about it until Abby blabbed. I respect that you didn't tell anyone, and maybe I owe you something for last year's dance as well."

"You don't owe me anything, man. But it would be awesome if we could fix this car. How much would the glass cost?"

He fires up another cig and says, "A few hundred, maybe." But he tosses it quickly when Yosemite Sam comes waddling out of the shop with a welder's mask perched on his head.

"What in tarnation is a-goin' on out here?" Mr. Lee asks. "Nobody is a paying you to gab, boy!"

I swear he used the word *tarnation*!

Rusty sticks out a greasy hand, so I shake it. He says, "Get at me about fixing this car."

Awesome.

## 22. FULL VOICE

The state championships were great. I didn't win any of my events, but I didn't disqualify, either. Once the final relay race was over, I shifted my thoughts and actions back into acting mode. For the past week and a half I've eaten, drunk, and slept *RENT*!

Auditions are tomorrow. That's why I'm singing at the top of my lungs as I ride my bike down Merrian Lane. Baseball tryouts started today, so I have to pick up Aunt Jenny by myself. It was hard to keep the secret from EJ, but I think we managed it. We talked his dad into buying the car back from the crash-up derby guys, and we scrounged around three junkyards and found replacements for almost all of Aunt Jenny's glass (some windows fit better than others). Rusty stole a windshield off a minivan or something, and it's way off, but it was free so I'm not going to complain.

Mr. Lee hands over the keys and asks, "You got a driver's license, right?"

"Just about!" I assure him.

I drive Aunt Jenny back to school and avoid the athletic fields so the baseball team can't see or hear her. I pull up next to the bike racks beside the field house and wait. I put my headphones on and crank the original cast recording of *RENT*. I know I'm making an ass of myself, but I want this part!

*RENT* is so good. The play follows this group of young artists living the bohemian life in the late eighties in a scuzzy part of New York City (Abby says this area is gentrified [really nice] now). The characters are filmmakers, dancers, writers, political activists, and drag queens, but they're all friends struggling to pay "the rent." It's not just what they owe to their landlord, but more like the toll of life and how much you have to give the world in order to make a living or just get through the day. The characters are all outcasts. Some are addicts or in recovery and some of them are dying of AIDS. The show is so amazing that the guy who wrote it . . . his heart exploded the night before its Off-Broadway debut (seriously)! It's about living your life to the fullest and trying not to waste a second because you never know when it's all going to end. The show covers one year in the characters' lives. Some of them don't make it, so it's really sad in spots . . . especially when you think about the writer's heart exploding.

Clint has tried to teach me how to play the guitar, but my fingers will not do what they're told. I totally see why rock stars are always smashing these things. I got a CD of the original Broadway recording, and I love it (even though it's really hard to sing)! My sister won't let me listen to it in public. She thinks that show tunes are unacceptable even when they're awesome. I use headphones, but I can't stop myself from breaking into song all the time. The best place to sing is on the bicycle, after dark.

I used to love to lip sync in front of the mirror in my room, but singing out loud is the greatest. I think the difference between lip syncing and singing with your full voice is like jerking off and making love. I hope to find out for sure someday, but I'm pretty sure I've got this one right.

*RENT* is not like *Guys and Dolls,* where I played Sky Masterson and I could get away with just talk/singing. The character I want to play, Roger, SINGS! Like, full-on, Baptist choir, sell-it-to-the-back-row belting.

My favorite song from *RENT* is called "Seasons of Love." The drama geeks are always singing it (I join them when no one else is around). The song talks about how a year is only, "five hundred twenty-five thousand, six hundred minutes." That's it. And it asks how you measure a year of your life. Is it the "sunsets" that you've watched, or is it the "cups of coffee" you've drunk? I don't understand how those are units of measurement, but I've obviously never grasped the whole idea of time anyway. This song wants you to measure your life in "love," and that's even crazier than using cups of coffee, but I kind of get it. Sometimes my life is not great, and it's usually my fault, but I've got these people around me all the time who are perfectly willing to make fun of me and pick me up (sometimes they're the bastards who knocked me down in the first place), but if you step back far just far enough to get some perspective, you can see that we really love each other (in our own sick and twisted way).

By five o'clock, Abby, Jeremy, Nicky, and twenty other kids are gathered around for Aunt Jenny's big reveal. We see my boys come out of the field house locker rooms, and EJ doesn't seem to suspect a thing. He's holding a bag of ice on his broken arm. Although they took the cast off, he's not supposed to be using it yet. The coach is forcing him to try out for the team again even though he's one of the best players. I guess he's trying to prove a point that "fighting is wrong," but his message is really, "I'm an a-hole who doesn't understand that broken bones need to fully heal."

EJ walks around the building and immediately drops his ice and backpack to the ground before falling to his knees. He hasn't seen the car yet; he's just rummaging around his bag saying, "Ahhh, farts! I don't have the key to my bike lock!"

Thirty people are laughing at him, so I have to yell, "I've got 'em!"

He looks up at the crowd of people gawking at him. "What? How?"

"I stole them out of your locker."

"Why?" he asks.

"So I could pick up Aunt Jenny from the hospital."

He says, "Huh?!" just as Doc fires up the loud engine and revs her a few times. EJ's jaw drops when the gang of drama kids parts like the Red Sea (they don't call them drama kids for nothing) and reveals his awesome old car. EJ instantly starts sobbing like a little girl.

Bag pats his head like a dog and explains, "Rusty put it back together. Carter paid for it with his movie money."

EJ looks up at me and starts crying even harder. Nobody wants to humiliate the guy, so a bunch of us just pile into the car like nothing's wrong and we're ready to go. The other kids peel off, and EJ pulls himself together and climbs into the driver's seat. We slowly roll out of the parking lot, but then EJ guns it like someone's chasing us. The seals on the glass are absolutely terrible, so when we get above thirty miles per hour you can't hear a thing. Guys have to shout to make fun of Rusty's handiwork, but we all appreciate getting to ride in this car again. I imagine this is the best three hundred bucks I'll ever spend.

# 23. RING OF FIRE

I kicked ass at the *RENT* auditions. I was ready. I played all of my chords on the guitar without stopping! I knew every line and I sang every note almost exactly like I wanted to. McDougle actually clapped when I finished singing "One Song Glory." But I didn't get the part.

Clint got the role of Roger. So instead of playing the sexy rocker, I will portray Mark, the geeky filmmaker/narrator of the show. McDougle calls him "the witness" and tries to tell me that he's actually the better part . . . even after she called him a "lovable loser." One cool thing is I'm getting a video camera from the AV department so I can film some of the rehearsals and have people act out situations from the show; my little movies will play during parts of the show. Watch out, Spielberg!

Clint says that he'll continue to teach me how to play the guitar, but I'm not sure if I'm going to be friends with him or not. I like to sing with him, but he and Abby kiss in the show, and that kind of sucks.

Shockingly, there's all kinds of drama in the department because Abby is playing Mimi. The character is supposed to be Latina, and Abby isn't. Maybe I'm biased, but I think everyone is too hung up on hair color. It says right in the script that Mimi has an amazing ass, and Abby's easily got the best butt in our school. Of course the drama chicks won't listen to my logic.

I've yet to see her booty without clothes on, but I'm confident that day is nearing. We've made out a bunch, but I'm taking my time. I'm not trying to steal any bases this year. If I keep getting up to the plate, I *will* hit a home run.

My boys knew I was bummed about not getting the part of Roger, so I'm missing a Saturday night make-out session with Abby to go camping with them. They think sleeping on the ground will take my mind off of it. I'm kind of stoked, actually! The Carters are not a hunting/fishing kind of family. I've never spent the night in the woods or seen a gun that wasn't attached to a police officer. The only fishing pole I've ever held had SpongeBob on the side of it. We don't have a Jeep or a cabin, and we sure as hell don't pack up our stuff and live in the woods for a few days and call it a vacation.

Aunt Jenny is jam-packed with dudes, and the trunk is filled with sleeping bags and tents. We're headed to a woodsy area behind Grey Goose Lake. Jeremy told us about the spot, but said he'd rather "pull my friggin' eyelashes out than spend a night in the forest with your friends." He says some developers are going to bulldoze all of the trees in June to build a neighborhood of McMansions.

I'm ready to become one with nature, but I accidentally start mumbling one of Mark's songs from *RENT*. EJ reaches over and slaps my neck before saying, "Space Cadet Carter!"

"Ow!"

"What is Aunt Jenny's position on show tunes?" he asks.

"She's not into them."

"That is correct!" he says. "Now, tell me where the hell we're going."

"How should I know?! Jeremy just said it was behind the lake. Anywhere in here should work." I point to an open field on the other side of a drainage ditch.

He replies, "There's no road there."

"I'm sorry," I say. "They haven't gotten around to paving the great outdoors for you yet, pussy."

"It'll mess up Aunt Jenny's paint!" he exclaims.

"The doors don't close and the windows won't roll down anymore," Bag interjects. "You're worried about the finish?"

"If anything's in danger, it's the field!" Nutt adds.

"What would Bear Grylls say if he knew a guy like you existed in his world?" Doc asks.

EJ flips the turn signal. He doesn't even slow down before flying off the road. We all scream as the car blasts through a ditch and dirt flies over the windshield. We cackle as Aunt Jenny bounces across the field and tosses us like salad. I laugh even harder when I see Hormone's CRX bopping around behind us. You can see Hormone and J-Low yelling at each other like an old married couple as camping gear (s'mores, beer, and hot dogs) flies around the little car.

EJ's family used to own a camper, and Bag's mom's ex-boyfriend, Carl, took Bag to Jellystone Park a couple of years ago, so he and EJ are going to show the rest of us how to set up a camp properly. Carl bought Bag a three-hundred-dollar North Face sleeping pod (not to be confused with a sleeping bag . . . it's a pod!). His mom dumped Carl, but he got to keep the pod.

The trees eventually become too thick to drive around (or over) so EJ parks Aunt Jenny in a little clearing and we grab the gear. We trudge a couple hundred yards deeper into the woods, where it's creepy quiet but very cool. There are no houses in sight or dogs barking in the distance. You can see a bit of Grey Goose Lake, but it really seems like we're roughing it in the middle of nowhere.

I see why people stopped sitting on the ground and living in tents, though. I also know why my dad never got me into this stuff. The tents stink like butt-crack, and it hasn't rained around here in months, so these plastic stakes won't break the earth's crust without snapping in half. The support poles make great swords, but we can't figure out how else to use them.

We give up on the shelter part of camping and concentrate on the fire, because it's freezing and no one is wearing a shirt. I just peed right out in the open! Camping is hella-good male bonding. If we kill something tonight, it'll be perfect (not for the squirrel or whatever, but for the experience).

We undo some metal hangers to cook the marshmallows and hot dogs. There is no shortage of wiener jokes, but we don't have buns or condiments because our moms didn't plan this cookout. We also have stale Corn Nuts, warm Mountain Dew, and stolen beer. I understand why there are no camping-themed restaurants.

I've heard old people say, "Where there's smoke, there's fire." But they're mistaken, because no matter how much smoke we produce, there is no fire. We've got a bunch of wood, but our notebook paper will only start little fires that put themselves right out. We find out that textbooks don't burn (sneaky teachers), but progress takes a turn for the better (or worse if you're a squirrel living in the area) when EJ discovers an old greasy metal can inside Aunt Jenny's trunk. It's not labeled, but the contents smell very flammable. We don't see the harm in using a few sprinkles to get things going (because our moms are not here to say, "Absolutely NOT!").

Bag sniffs the can and gags. "Whooaahh!!!"

"Aunt Jenny may have been a moonshiner!" Doc adds.

J-Low offers twenty bucks to the guy who takes a drink of the stuff, but we may actually be getting a little wiser in our old age. We also know that J-Low doesn't have that kind of money.

We decide it's gasoline, so EJ drips a drop of it onto the smoking mound of logs and dry leaves. A shot of flame leaps into the air, and we all gasp, "Woooow!!!"

A few more drops get things rolling. When the fire evens out, it's kind of amazing. We cook our food like cavemen and eat it without ketchup, like savages. The fire seems to tap into a primal part of my soul, and I start running around the blaze and howling at the moon. My boys make fun of me at first, but before you know it, they're jumping over the fire and screaming like wild animals too.

It's all good until I notice Andre bending one of the hot dog cookers into a little circle at the end. I'm thinking that he's making an old-fashioned bubble blower, but I'm waaaay off.

He slides the rod into the fire and says, "Yo, we should brand each other!"

Everyone gets quiet and just stares at the fire for a second. The male bonding just came to a grinding halt. Nobody is drunk enough to think that's a good idea, or confident enough to be the first guy to say, "Hell NO!!!"

I know he means "brand" like cow ID, but I say, "You mean like marketing-type branding? Like I'll be KFC and you be FedEx?"

I thought that was clever, but no one laughs because Andre is twisting the hanger in the bottom of the coals.

"No, gay-wad," he says. "I mean we hold each other down and jam this red-hot circle into each other's shoulders! My cousin's in a frat that does it."

He's hoping we'll all yell, "YEAH!!!" and fight to see who goes first, but we just keep looking at the fire until Bag says, "Or maybe the back of the calf? That would look cool."

A few guys nod like, *It would.* It seems as if they might actually be considering this terrible idea! I, on the other hand, had an epiphany last year: my friends are awesome, but I don't have to do everything they do, and I don't *need* their approval. And what good is an epiphany if you don't break it out in situations where people are about to permanently scar themselves?

Andre pulls out the bright orange hanger and asks, "Who's going first?!"

Everyone looks around the camp, giggling, hoping someone will volunteer, when I say, "Stop. Shut up! This isn't like lifting weights or shaving our heads. This is gonna hurt!"

Andre wraps his T-shirt around the end of the hanger because it's too hot to hold. "That's right," he sneers. "It is gonna hurt like a bitch. But sometimes you gotta man up!"

"Is that what I gotta do, Andre?"

He's glaring at me when EJ drains an entire beer, burps, and says, "I'll go!"

"What?!" I gasp.

"Really?" Andre asks.

EJ nods, and everyone stops giggling.

"Dude, you don't have to do this," I say.

"I know!" EJ barks as he rolls up his left pant leg.

"So we're doing the leg?" Andre asks.

EJ doesn't say anything. He starts breathing really hard and fast, like he's about to lift a heavy barbell. He looks like a real-deal caveman as he lies facedown in the leaves.

Andre quickly says, "Hold him down!" and shoves the rod deeper into the coals. I should push everyone away from my best friend, but it's like a raging fire of testosterone has swept through our campsite, and there is no controlling it.

About ten of us pin him tightly to the earth. "Are you sure, EJ?!" I ask as I clamp down on the back of his foot.

He nods, so Andre pulls the branding iron/hanger from the blaze. It glows even brighter as he blows on it. EJ's foot trembles beneath my hand. Either that or I'm shaking. I think everyone is quivering . . . including Andre.

"I'm gonna hold it down for three seconds!" Andre yells. "Don't move or we won't get a good stick!"

He's never branded anyone before, and he's trying to sound like an expert. I'm even more pissed off because it occurs to me that Andre's probably going to be successful in life. He's come up with a crazy idea here and has tricked others into thinking it's a good one. That's like the definition of an entrepreneur! We all know that he's full of crap, but we've got one of our friends pinned to the earth so he can be branded. That's about as legit as it gets!

Without hesitation, Andre presses the circle into EJ's leg. The flesh sizzles like an Outback steak. EJ's body flexes so violently that every one of us is jolted into the air from the force. I've never felt anything as powerful as his foot kicking into my hand . . . until Andre pushes the iron back into EJ's leg in a slightly different spot and EJ kicks up again, even harder. My best friend lets out this primal scream that causes everyone to jump back. We just watch him squirm in agony. His skin is actually smoking! I doubt either touch of the circle made it the prescribed three seconds, but he is definitely branded. His leg is twitching and swelling with every beat of his heart.

He's still breathing really hard when he quietly asks, "How's it look?"

Everyone relaxes when Bag replies, "Pretty friggin' gnarly, man!"

Nutt shines a flashlight on it and says, "It's purple."

"What?" EJ asks.

Andre assures him, "That's a good sign. It means the scarring is deep."

"Is that what it means?" I ask, like a dick.

Bag puts his face closer to EJ's leg. "It stinks! And it kind of looks like a figure eight on its side."

"Like the symbol for infinity," J-Low adds.

We all look closer and nod. "Oh yeah!"

EJ asks, "Like infinity the math term or like, Infiniti the car company?"

"Uh, both, right?" Nutt replies.

Doc says, "No, my stepmom has an Infiniti. It's like—"

"Yeeaah," Levi says. "That's a nice ride. Did she get fake boobs or not?!"

We're all pretty sure she did, but Doc won't confirm it. "How the hell should I know?!" he says.

"Sounds like you do," Bag says.

"That butt-hole claimed he didn't have the money to get me braces, but his new wife's blowin' out her bra all the sudden and no one's allowed to give her hugs anymore," Doc grumbles.

EJ gets us back on topic. "What about the logo on her car?"

"Probably can't touch that either, huh, Doc?" I ask.

"Nope," he says. "I think their emblem is more like a pyramid with a circle around it."

"Naw," Bag says, pointing at EJ's growing scar. "*That's* the Infiniti sign, right?"

Levi is a math nerd, so he says, "It's definitely the *symbol* for infinity."

EJ finally jerks around to look at his new scar. He says, "Why do I have *two* circles?!"

Andre replies, "You jumped like a little bitch, so I had to hit you twice, and then you scooted."

"Way to go, E!" I say.

Doc continues, "The speedometer on that Infiniti says it'll do a hundred and forty."

"You should get her to drive you to the pool next summer," Bag says. "And then get her to go off the diving board."

"Isn't an Infiniti just like a nice Nissan?" J-Low asks.

"We should send a pic of your leg to their marketing people!" Nutt suggests. "You could get paid off of this!"

EJ has no intention of going corporate with his brand. He also has no memory of the branding, which I find fascinating. We try to do an impression of the scream he let out, but he says his brain just deleted it. Eventually he hobbles to his feet and asks, "So, who's going next?"

I have to admit it looks pretty cool and I am slightly jealous, but I will not be getting branded tonight, and neither will any of the other guys.

Everyone says some version of "Sorry, dude" or "No way!"

Even Andre shakes his head like, *That was too heinous.*

EJ has the right to call us pussies, but he's not mad. No one actually said they would do it with him. He just thought we'd follow him off the cliff, but we really seem to be maturing. It's cool, but also a little sad.

After a while the fire dies down, so a few of us go out in search of wood. Some are willing to go farther than others because it's dark and there might be snakes out there! I am certain there's a cobra underneath every log, but somehow my boys have rounded up another huge pile of wood without incident. Lucky is what they are!

Bag is just about to sprinkle more gasoline onto the new logs when a rustling in the bushes stops him. I jump to my feet and say, "What the hell was that?!"

Everyone seems freaked because something is definitely growling out there. Twigs start cracking as the thing charges toward our campsite! Even though there probably isn't a bear within a thousand miles of Merrian, I am positive that's what it is. A real-life Smokey the Bear coming to maul us for using gas on a fire.

I take a fighting stance. I'm ready . . . to throw one of my boys into the beast's path before I run for my life. I never get the chance because Nutt sprints out of the darkness buck naked with a tree branch in his hands. He jumps over the small fire, yelling, "I found wood, boys!"

We all groan and tell him to put his pants on, but he's having too much fun. He uses the branch like a stripper pole and does the helicopter dance for a while. Then he starts leaning on people and asking, "Have you ever seen a moon this gorgeous?"

We're trying to ignore him, but he grabs a hot dog and wedges it between his butt cheeks. "Look who found buns!" he cackles, and waddles around the camp.

I have to laugh, but then he crosses the line by squatting down and grunting, "Who wants chili on their dog?!"

He backs himself over the fire pit and declares, "I like my buns toasted, don't you?!"

EJ is still in a lot of pain, but he's always quick with the improv. He snatches up the can of gas and dumps it on the fire. Only about a cup of liquid erupts out of the lid, but everyone runs for cover like a bomb is about to go off. The only guy who doesn't realize a massive fireball is about to shoot into the air is Nutt.

People tell you to "Pour it on!" in swimming, but I never really got what that meant until I saw gasoline poured directly onto a fire.

Everyone yells, "WHOOOAAAH!!!" except Nutt. He's too busy screaming and rolling around in the leaves.

He thinks his ass is on fire because Doc told him, "Dude, your ass is on fire!"

It's not, but the real Smokey the Bear would be proud of Nutt's fire-safety skills.

"Stop, drop, and rolll!" Hormone yells.

The rest of us are just marveling at the flames as they reach higher and higher above our heads.

Andre kicks the charred hot dog and laughs. "I think you burned your wiener, Nutt!"

"I smell burnt pubes!" I say.

Of course they want to know why I know what burnt pubes smell like, but their burn session dies down when we notice our fire is getting bigger. A lot bigger! I suddenly recall the drought Merrian has been in, and realize that we've built this fire *under* a bunch of dried-out trees. It didn't seem like a big deal at the time, but it seems more significant as the flames lick the low branches and they begin smoking like insecure girls in eighth grade.

Andre thinks fast and throws a sleeping bag onto the blaze. Part of the fire dies down for a second but then eats right through the dusty cotton to burn even higher and hotter.

"Are you trying to make it worse?" I ask.

Doc grabs Bag's North Face sleeping pod but gets tackled by its owner.

"Get off!" Doc barks. "It's polyester—it won't burn!"

"You are not smart!" Bag grunts. "Your nickname is meant to be ironic!"

Doc eventually overpowers him and throws the three-hundred-dollar blanket onto the blaze. It really does subdue the flame . . . until Bag yanks it away. When the fire gets a fresh hit of oxygen, it jumps like a rocket into the trees. My mouth is wide open as the whole forest seems to ignite, and I get really hot, really quick. Bag's sleeping pod is totally ablaze (polyester does burn) and he's swinging it around like a madman. I know he's trying to save his overpriced *blankie*, but it seems like he's trying to start a forest fire as quickly and evenly as possible. We try to stamp out the smoldering leaves, but there's a reason firemen don't wear Nikes! My shoes are melting to my feet as I yell, "Bag! Stop, you idiot!"

Bag is crying and can't hear me. The flames have climbed up to his hands, and he's finally forced to drop the pod. The rest of us are squawking like chickens and running for our lives. We just keep running into each other and spinning around in circles because there is no way out!

Hormone is looking up when he yells, "The fire is headed toward the cars!"

After hearing that statement, EJ just runs right though a wall of flames and disappears. Seeing one penguin jump off the iceberg sends everyone else right after him . . . all except one pussy-assed penguin still debating his options. *I can hear my boys screaming in pain on the other side of the flames, like they regret their decision to run directly into an inferno, but then the only sound is roaring fire. I yell, "You guys?!" but no one responds.

I'm totally alone and frozen with fear. The fire seems to be closing in on me. My eyes are burning and I'm struggling to breathe, but I can't think of anything except, *I will not run into a wall of fire!*

I wish my football coach were here to hit me with his whistle and yell, "MOVE, you dad-burn guckin foose!!!"

Or that my swimming coach would materialize to scream, "Go! Go! GOOOO!!!"

I try yelling at myself, but it just causes a coughing fit. Somehow it works, though, and I find myself running toward the area my boys exited. But just as I'm about to flame-broil myself, I notice a whole area of fire that's died out. The scrub plants are just smoking in this one little spot, like a mirage in the desert. I hit the brakes and dash into the little flame-free corridor.

I jog around the blaze and see that it is spreading fast, right toward Aunt Jenny and the CRX. My boys are all kinds of burned, and there are no cool logos imprinted in their welts. Their clothes are actually smoking. They really seem to be in a lot of pain. I've got an annoying tickle in my throat, but I decide not to complain about it.

EJ can't get Aunt Jenny to start because he's using the wrong key. "Scoot over, drunkie!" I yell, and slam the correct key into the ignition. As the only sober actor in this horror movie, it's up to me to save us!

The fire is rushing toward us like it's pissed. I smash down on the gas and rip the big old steering wheel around as Aunt Jenny hauls us to safety and shoots crap all over the CRX.

The little car is right behind us when we jump the ditch and blast back up onto the main road. We haul ass toward QuikTrip and make an anonymous call to the Merrian Fire Department on the old pay phone.

Everyone is too wrapped up in their own issues to notice that I'm an awesome stunt driver and not burned at all. I won't share the details of my escape for a few weeks, until it's less obvious that my wuss instincts served me so well.

My boys' skin is gross, and EJ's leg gets nasty quick. Our parents are suspicious, but nobody's folks can afford to pay for a forest fire, so all punishments are enforced vaguely and internally. Before the fire department got it under control, our "connection with nature" torched over a hundred acres of scrub forest. This area will no longer need to be cleared. You're welcome, McMansion developers (sorry, squirrels)!

The blaze made the newspaper and local TV news because the firemen found a bunch of marijuana plants growing back there. You're welcome, Merrian P.D. (sorry, potheads)!

I expect the cops to show up at my house any time,

because the rumor mill has spread the story faster than the fire gobbled up that forest.

And this part of Grey Goose Lake is technically in Nortest High's territory, so when they heard it was set by Merrian dudes, they assumed we did it on purpose to screw with them. So a gang of Nortest guys came over and tagged the brick wall behind the art wing: BURN THIS! COUGAR POWER! They used house paint and one of those rollers to make block letters. The janitors couldn't wash it off of the brick, so they used a belt sander. The paint came off, but BURN THIS! COUGAR POWER! is now permanently etched into the side of the building. Retaliations are being planned.

Great.

# 24. THE TRANSITION

February is almost over and I'm spacing off in geometry class (shocker). Mrs. Wang is demonstrating a problem at the front of the room, so I'm looking in that direction, but my problem is snakes and mice today. Bart and a bunch of senior guys broke into the biology department at Nortest High last night and released thirty snakes and over a hundred mice (they've only located half of them). If I went to Nortest, I'd transfer. I can barely concentrate *without* snakes in the vents and light fixtures and toilets! My daydreams eventually flow to lunch plans and then on to the sexual progress that Abby and I made on Valentine's Day (let's just say I needed both hands!) and then I think about what Mrs. Wang looked like as a teenager.

I'm sure she was a nerd, but I bet she was a cute one. Somewhere along the way she definitely stopped trying, though, and the nerd side took over. Being hot is probably a bad thing in math circles, so she rocks the semi-mullet and sensible sandals with socks these days. She keeps her slacks high on the hip to show off her camel-toe and announce to the world that it's closed for business. I hope my wife never breaks out "slacks" on me. I think that's a bad sign. Like she made an investment in *not* being sexy.

I really can't afford to space off in this class. I got an A on the last test, but I had a detention *and* a Saturday School to help me prepare. I can't get cocky! Wang is reviewing the old material before she adds to it. I just have to hook back into the lesson before she makes the transition.

Clint, the guy playing Roger in *RENT*, is in my class. This is his second try at sophomore geometry. I've decided I like him, but Wang hates his ass because he doesn't just *look* like a stoner/slacker—he's the real thing. I feel bad because usually I'd be deflecting some of her rage, but I'm selfishly kicking ass in all of my classes right now.

Today's lesson is on equilateral polygons, so Clint is battling the Grim Sleeper. His long hair is covering his face and his breathing is all heavy. His shoulders are drooping lower with every breath, and his neck seems to be looking for something to take over the job of holding up his head. His locks flop as his muscles go into spasm and try to jump-start him back into this class. Unfortunately, Mrs. Wang's soft voice is lulling him to sleep.

Once he's totally out, he's not as fun to watch, and I feel kind of creepy for doing it. So I look back at the board to see what's happening and . . . Dang it! I missed the friggin' transition! Math sucks. If you miss one piece of the puzzle, you're screwed. Everything builds off of the step that comes before the one you're working on. Now I have to go to the Meth Lab and try to sort this crap out (someone switched the "a" in our math lab sign back in October and no one has changed it back).

I'm writing "METH" on my arm when I feel a hand touch me. It's the girl with the lazy eye who sits next to me. She's gesturing toward the hall. I'm so glad she pointed because I can never tell where she's looking.

Abby's out there laughing at me. I hope she hasn't been watching for very long, and I really hope I wasn't talking to myself. She's motioning for me to join her in the hall. She's the type of nerd who can just get up in a class and go pee or run to the library if she wants to; she doesn't realize how difficult it is for students like me and Clint to leave a room (especially when you've earned a reputation as a "dawdler").

She doesn't get why I'm shaking my head. She obviously wants me to get the toilet pass, because she's miming a guy peeing. It's funny, and kind of hot when she does the zipper gesture. I mouth the words, "Yeah, go for it!"

She shakes her head and whispers, "Stop it! I need you."

I grab my chest, and mouth, "I need you too!"

She flips me off, so I make a bunch of sex faces and gestures. "Oooh, it's like that, huh?"

Abby whispers, "Focus!" and points at Mrs. Wang . . . who seems to have been scowling at me for a while. Actually, the whole class (except for Clint) is looking at me.

"Hey. Any chance I could use the restroom, Mrs. Dub?" I ask.

She sets down her marker and picks up the bathroom pass. "I don't see why not. . . . Take your time."

Uh-oh. She used a sarcastic tone, as if she doesn't care what I do. How did we get here? It's not okay for a math teacher to give up on me. I get away with a lot more now because teachers are under the impression I'm a hard worker. If she realizes I'm a good-for-nothing . . . I'm screwed.

In spite of Wang's snarkiness, I grab the pass and split. Abby gives me a hug and says, "Amber went into labor in gym!"

"Ewww, gross!"

She whacks me on the shoulder and says, "It's not gross."

"Did she have it in the locker room?"

"Nooo," she explains. "It's not like TV. It takes hours to give birth. Her dad and Rusty came and picked her up. Can you come to the hospital after rehearsal?"

"Uhhh, sure. I was going to go to the Meth Lab, and fight club is tonight, but I can blow that junk off."

I know she's responding to my statements, but her shirt is gaping open at the boob and I've got a little view of a turquoise bra. I don't have a record of a turquoise bra. It must be new. Have her boobs grown? I don't think they've shrunk. She's still eating salad all the time. I wonder what kind of clasp that sucker has? I doubt it's a front lock; that would be too easy. Like Mrs. Wang, Abby likes everything so damn complicat—

She stops talking and blocks my view by crossing her arms. "Okay?" she asks suspiciously.

"Yeah. I'm . . . uh, taking you to the hospital?"

She seems frustrated. "No. Jeremy and I are going there now, but your scenes are up at tonight's rehearsal."

"So I'll meet you later." I start to write on my arm, but I see "METH" and "FC" already written on it. "Oh no, I have fight clu—"

Abby's glare suggests that we've already covered this subject. "I mean, I am skipping that and uh . . . am I going to the math lab?"

Abby looks worried that she's been making out with a retarded boy all this time. She says, "You're going to the math lab before rehearsal because McDougle is starting with Kathy and Clair's duet. What happened to your assignment notebook?"

"This is easier. Can't lose my arms. Unless I get into a horrible accident, and then I probably wouldn't have as many activities."

Abby can't help laughing. No way I'm actually retarded. She's way too polite to laugh at a handicapped guy. She says, "Seriously, you need to stop fighting. You're getting brain damaged."

"Brain damaged? You're wearing a new, scalloped, demi-cup, underwire bra with a racer back. It's got reinforced shoulder bracing and triple hooks in the back. Who's brain damaged?"

She rolls her eyes. "You are. It's only double hooks, by the way."

"Slut."

She smiles. "I also got a haircut."

"And it looks great."

She gives me a kiss before jogging down the hall toward the parking lot. I watch her go and then hustle back into geometry.

# 25. BABY WING

My boys are waiting for me after rehearsal, but I tell them I can't do fight club tonight. Of course they want details; they're like detectives. They'll trip you up if you try to lie, and they don't mind beating a confession out of a guy.

"I am going to the hospital to see Amber and her baby."

"You mean to see *your* baby?!" Nutt asks.

"Shut up."

They've all heard about Amber Lee going into labor. Bag heard that she was screaming and cussing up a storm. Doc heard that Ms. Van Dyke (the gym teacher/softball coach, whose real name is Van Dam) fainted when Amber's water broke. EJ heard that some drill team chicks carried her to the nurse's office like a wounded soldier, and the janitor took forever to clean up Amber's water, and some Vo-Tech kid slipped in the mess on his way to the parking lot. When people told him he had birthing fluid all over his jean jacket he started puking, and the tardy janitor yelled at him in front of everyone, and the Vo-Tech kid started crying, and then the janitor started weeping too, but not because he felt bad about what he said, more for poor decisions he'd made earlier in life that resulted in him mopping up puke and birthing fluid. Who the hell knows what really happened?

You'd think that my boys wouldn't want anything to do with something like this. They're all covered in dirt, and still wearing their stinky baseball gear, but they have this fascination with horror movies and gross stuff. They just love trauma.

Nutt says, "Let's go see this kid. I bet it looks just like Carter!"

We've all been to the Emergency Room a bunch of times, so we just head for that area of the labyrinth that is Merrian Med Center.

As Nutt climbs out the passenger window he yells, "We have come for your babies!"

We appear to have the only '69 Dodge. The parking lot is filled with Mercedes and BMWs, so we shove each other into them and set off their alarms. I doubt we look like future medical students.

We walk through the sliding glass doors and start wandering the halls like a pack of stray dogs. Nobody is excited to be here anymore. Death is in the air, and not the dangerous, fun kind. Everyone seems to be waiting for something bad to happen. People are seriously depressed around here: the nurses, the doctors, the visitors, and especially the sad sacks lying in those wheelie beds! You know you're in trouble when they put wheels on your bed.

My boys are wearing either floppy Adidas sandals or baseball cleats, so we're making quite a racket. Especially when Nutt says, "If you can't go pee by yourself, they shove a tube in your dick!" And we all scream in horror.

A young nurse marches up to us with a scowl on her face. "Can I help you guys?"

Bag replies, "Sure, honey, we're looking for the section with babies?"

Her scowl gets more intense when she says, "'Honey'?"

Doc slaps Bag on the back of his neck and says, "Sorry about that, miss. It's called a ward, right?"

"I think she understood what I meant," Bag says. "She's obviously an intelligent young woman."

"We've got a girlfriend in here who's 'with child'!" Nutt adds.

The nurse glares at us while we giggle. She's cute, and there's no shortage of dirty nurse pornos on the Internet. She shakes her head as if we're not the first teen guys she's encountered recently. She points down the long hall and says, "Just go through oncology and you'll find the baby section."

"Oncology means cancer, right?" Doc asks.

She nods, and J-Low asks, "Uhhh, is there any way around the cancer area?"

"You're not going to catch cancer, dude!" Doc says.

Bag yells, "No one thinks you're smart, Doc! His nickname is supposed to be ironic, miss!"

The nurse seems nervous when she asks, "Are one of you boys the father of this baby?"

In unison we say, "Nooo," "Nope," and "Hell no!"

I'm not sure why everyone is laughing until I see that Nutt is pointing at me.

I shove him into a wall as the nurse is saying, "Just head down that hall, quietly, and ask for your friend at the desk."

She walks away, but we stay put because her pants don't have back pockets and you can totally see the outline of a tiny triangle at the top of her butt cheeks.

"G-string theory," Levi whispers.

After the fantasy scenarios have played out, we head toward the cancer section.

There is nothing sexy about an oncology ward. Yikes!

Andre says, "It smells like death!"

"Shhh!" I scold, but I was thinking the same thing. It's just so quiet and sad . . . because everyone has cancer! I look into a room and make eye contact with a guy about my age who's bald. His eyebrows are gone too, but it's not funny like it was when we shaved Bag's off. He looks sick and doesn't seem to care that I'm gawking at him. It takes everything in my power not to just burst into tears.

We press on, and everything gets better when we cross into the maternity ward. It seems brighter, and there are flowers and balloons and cake! Everyone is happy. There's even a T-Pain song playing. . . . Never mind that it's just Bag's ring tone. It seems weird that they'd put these two wards next to each other. One is bringing them in and one is checking them out. I guess it's been about fifteen years since I've been in a maternity ward. I don't remember it. It stinks like a hospital, but it's way better than the rest of it.

The nurses are giving us dirty looks. I'm guessing they don't love having a fifteen-year-old chick here to begin with, and then here *we* come . . . the actual cause of teen pregnancy . . . the true enemy of Planned Parenthood clomping right down their hall: teen boys! We avoid their glares.

I look into a few rooms and find Rusty sitting in a rocking chair holding a little baby in his arms like it's a football he doesn't want to fumble. Rusty's talking softly to the thing, so he doesn't notice us staring at him. When he finally looks up, he's not a bit embarrassed. It's like the guy with cancer; he's got more important things to worry about. He's smiling like a goof when he whispers, "Hiii."

We've mostly heard Rusty grunt in the past, and I'm the only one who's seen his jacked-up grille before. I can tell that EJ's not a hundred percent sure it's even him until Amber's dad waddles around the end of a wheelie bed. He draws a curtain and says, "Hey! Look who's here! Movie Star, how you doin', boy?!"

My boys all look at me, so I say, "Good . . . um . . . congratulations, Grandpa!"

He laughs. "That's the first time I've heard that! Good one."

"Hi, Carter!" Amber says from behind the curtain.

Her dad slaps my back and says, "Look at ol' Rusty holding that kid like a pro. Little girl was howling like a hyena until her papa picked her up, and she shut right up. Rusty's got the touch!"

Rusty smiles again (yikes) and gives his baby-daddy-in-law a nod. Wow, the maternity ward is magic. Some people are coming to life, and others are changing shape!

A two-hundred-pound mother-hen-type nurse busts into the room and asks, "What're you boys doing back here? How did you get in here?"

The only thing we can come up with is "Uhhhh," so she motions for us to follow her. We trail behind and try not to look at her granny-panty line and crinkle butt. Sometimes thicker pants are a good thing. As we come around a corner we hear the distinct sounds of a high school party in full effect. About thirty kids are being obnoxious in the waiting room. There are sodas and pizza. It's like any other Merrian

High party except no one is smoking or drunk. It makes me feel better that our welcome was worn out before my boys and I even arrived. Abby gives me a hug, and asks, "What are you guys doing?"

My friends are saying hi to Jeremy when I say, "Sorry, they really wanted to come."

"No, it's fine," she replies. "Amber will be excited that so many people came. I meant, why didn't you come through the main doors?"

"Oh, we decided it would be better to cut through the cancer wing."

"Didn't you see the huge sign out front that says OB-GYN?" Jeremy asks.

We're supposed to magically know that means "maternity ward"? Hospitals suck. Abby tells us that Amber had her little girl about an hour ago. She mumbles, "Her name is Cinnamon, but she's totally healthy."

"Cinnamon?!" Bag gasps.

"Shhh!!!" Abby scolds.

EJ whispers, "I was worried this kid was going to have an easy life."

Normally, Abby wouldn't put up with Amber-bashing, but I can tell she's not on board with the name Cinnamon, either.

"Is her middle name Toast?" I ask.

She laughs. "No."

Bag asks, "Crisp?"

"No," she replies.

"Twist?" Nutt inquires.

"How about Churro?" J-Low says.

"Stick?" EJ adds.

"Shut up. . . . Her middle name . . . is—" She fights to even say it. "Starshine."

We fall all over the waiting room, dying of laughter. "Cinnamon Starshine Dollingsworth!?" I say. "That sounds like a racehorse!"

Even Abby is cracking up until Rusty comes in and says, "Hiiii!" again.

"Hey, dude! We're just laughing about . . . good times," I explain.

He replies, "Awesome! If a few people want to come back and see little Cinnamon, it's cool."

We fight the laughter, but no one can look Rusty in the eye. He continues, "Amber was trying to feed her, but the little thing keeps falling asleep, so we're going to let her rest for a while, I guess. She's awesome to look at even when she's sleeping."

Rusty goes to talk to some other kids, so I tell Abby, "You go ahead."

"Yeah, we already saw it," Nutt adds.

Abby looks slightly annoyed that he just called the baby "it," and that we just strolled in and saw the thing when she's been waiting around here all day.

I say, "Yeah, sorry, we noticed Rusty in the room. He was holding little . . . Cin . . . Cinnamon—sorry." I laugh for a second before I'm able to continue. "Mr. Lee was being nice to Rusty. He gave him a compliment and everything!"

Abby grabs my hand, so I join her when she goes back to the room. The curtain is open now and Amber's sitting up. She looks tired but happy. She's holding the spice-baby to her chest. . . . Nope, she's feeding it . . . with her BOOB! Oh God!

I try not to look, and fight to think about anything other than, *Amber Lee's boob is out, and there's a kid hooked up to it!*

I haven't seen Amber without makeup since fifth grade. She's still pretty. She gives me a nod and squeals at the sight of Abby.

"You did it, girl!" Abby cheers.

Amber says, "I'm breast-feeding right now! It's so weird!"

*AAAAHHHHHHHHHHHHH!!!*

I don't remember anything until we're back out in the lobby and more pizza arrives. Nicky and all the other cheerleaders take turns holding the kid, but none of the guys even touches it. My opinion of hospitals has changed dramatically. Along with all the death and bad smells, people are fighting for their lives in here. Some people are being cured and others are getting a wake-up call. Yeah, some people are having their worst day, but others are having their first day, and some are having their best day. This party is the best one I've been to in a long time . . . especially when Amber whips out her boob again. She's kind of showing off, but it's hilarious the way everyone shuts up at once. I could tell EJ wanted to jump out the window.

# 26. STALLED STALL

So, Amber and Rusty's baby is a little over a week old, and she's living at her grandpa's house. She has her own pink room and hasn't been dropped yet. Things are looking pretty good for little Cinnamon, especially since Abby gave her the nickname "Cinna," and everyone backed her up. Even Amber calls the kid Cinna after Abby explains that it's the name of the stylist in the Hunger Games books.

It's Saturday night, and I'm driving Aunt Jenny again because everyone else is already drunk. All the windows are rolled down because I used some of my dad's cologne and the guys are saying how bad it stinks. I think it's nice, but they can crow on anything! Luckily, it's March and the weather is warming up, so it's not that big a deal that one of the back windows won't go up. I'm not so much "driving" as I am "following," so it doesn't require my full attention . . . which is usually a problem. Especially when I'm tired. I got up before dawn this morning to be at Saturday School, and then I had rehearsal all day because we're less than two weeks away from *RENT*'s opening night. I didn't have time to do fight club or take a nap.

I didn't feel like coming out tonight, but my boys conned me into it. They said they missed me, but what they really miss is making fun of me and having a sober guy to pilot Aunt Jenny when they get tanked. I kind of need a break from the drama kids anyway. And McDougle has been all over my ass lately, as if she's been trained by my football coach. And as if there isn't enough pressure doing the lead part in this huge Broadway musical, the recruiters from the New York Drama School *are* coming to see if I'm worth the "academic risk." That same woman called my mom again, and somehow she already knew I was playing Mark, and she explained that they've done the show twice. So if I start saying lines from the end of the show at the beginning, or singing the song lyrics in the wrong order (which I keep doing), they will totally know it. Or if I fall into that orchestra pit again, I assume I'd render myself "not worth the risk." I'm still not even sure if I actually want to go to New York, but I'll be so pissed if they don't want me! The girl playing Maureen has also applied to the school, as well as the guy playing Tom Collins. They are both awesome, and nerds to boot. Abby's still eligible for her scholarship in the fall, so they'll be looking at all of us. McDougle is the one who encouraged everyone to apply, but it seems like she's regretting it all the sudden. She's been super bitchy lately.

Abby says her mood is related to a battle she's having with Principal Banks over the show's "content." Apparently he dropped in on a rehearsal and totally freaked when he realized *RENT* was about death, being gay, drug addiction, and AIDS. The techies heard him moaning in the audience after Tom Collins and Angel (Jeremy's character) started kissing. Then, in the next scene, Abby dropped her stash of heroin and sang about having the best ass below 14th

Street. Her "stash" is just a Ziploc bag with some baby powder in it, but Banks freaked out like he was working with the DEA. McDougle was called into his office and told to change the show or he'd pull the plug. She broke out the release form *that he signed* last year and reminded him that he said he "loved the play." I'm thinking someone *said* he did his homework when he *didn't*.

"CARTER!!!" EJ yells, after I plow into a trash can on the side of the road.

"Yeeeaaah!!!" my boys shout as garbage flies all over the place. "Nice driving, Danica!!!"

"How about you yell at me *before* I run into it?!" I say to EJ.

"You're the designated driver!" he replies. "I'm the drunk kid. Do your part!"

"Fair enough."

We just left QuikTrip because the cops told us we had to. I can't believe I'm doing this again! I can't believe this year is almost over. Sophomore year has been like a roller coaster: slow chugging up the hill the first weeks, but then New York came into the picture and it went into a free fall before it started jerking and thrashing me all over the place. One minute I'm upside down in a geometry twist, and the next thing I know I'm flailing through a dance rehearsal. You can't stop the ride once you're strapped in, and a roller coaster doesn't care if you're enjoying yourself or not; it's just going to do its thing. I feel like I've just got to hold on and get through the next few seconds, and everything will chill out. . . . But nothing is cooling off and I can't see when it's going to, especially if I go to New York City. I'm not even sure if I'm having a blast right now, or if I'm horribly miserable. I guess I'll find out later.

"CARTER!!!" my boys yell, and I swerve before narrowly missing a tree and driving through someone's front yard. I'm not sure why I'm the designated driver. My passengers seem to have their doubts too.

We drive past QuikTrip again, and I realize that Aunt Jenny is almost out of gas, so I whip around and pull up to a pump. All of the cars that were behind us in the caravan blindly follow us back into the parking lot. We head inside to pay for the gas and get a little high-fructose corn syrup fuel. All eleven of us walk in together. The clerk says, "You gotta be kidding!"

We pretend not to hear him or acknowledge that we're the cause of the second party in his parking lot in fifteen minutes. We head toward the soda fountain, and my boys glance out the windows as we go. They got the crap kicked out of them in a QuikTrip parking lot, so they're always scanning for trouble.

After filling, drinking, and refilling our cups with crack (Mountain Dew Code Red), I pay and we start to head back outside. Bag shoves the door open, and I hear the dreaded bass/rattle/thumping in the parking lot. My heart stops when I see none other than Scary Terry leaning against his yellow Cutlass! We all scamper back into the store to gawk over the snack foods.

Doc whispers, "What the hell are we gonna do?"

"Just stay put," I say. "He obviously hasn't seen us."

"Does he know my car?" EJ asks. "He's gonna smash it up!"

"And we'll fix it again," I assure him. "Be cool."

Terry is by himself (shocker), but he's looking around the crowd uneasily. His head is shaved and he's got a new tattoo of an anchor on his forearm (kind of awesome). He's smoking a cigarette and fiddling with a stick that looks kind of like a . . .

"Is that a switchblade?" I ask.

"Nah," EJ says.

"It is!" Bag gasps.

But Doc says, "Shut up, that's a pen or a comb or something, dude!"

"His head is shaved! What's he need a comb for? And what's that psycho got to write about?" I ask.

Levi tries to calm me down. "Are we in a gangster movie? A switchblade is not even a real thing."

But Nutt won't have it. "I've been stabbed by a switchblade three times! Bart got one at the army-navy store for ten bucks."

"Looks like he's beefed up, huh?" Andre observes.

I glare at him, but he's right. Terry does look pretty badass out there. We look like turkeys on Thanksgiving morning in here.

The clerk eventually asks us, "Is everything all right?"

I nod and whisper, "Yeah, we just need to hang out in here until that guy leaves, please. Is that okay?"

"Sure," he replies. "The cops should be here in a few minutes."

I give him a thumbs-up, but our plan needs to be quickly adjusted when Terry flicks his butt into the lot and starts toward the doors. We bum-rush the men's room, and all eleven of us jam into the handicapped stall. Nutt and Doc are standing on the toilet. My heart is pounding and I've just nervously consumed forty ounces of Code Red in two minutes, so my stomach is churning, too.

"We're trapped in here!" Bag whispers.

It's too late for a new strategy, so I say, "We'll be okay!" and latch the little lock.

Andre chuckles. "That'll stop him, Carter."

Everyone laughs until the main door to the bathroom opens, and we all stop breathing. It could be anyone, but I'm certain it's Scary Terry. Whoever it is doesn't seem to notice the nine pairs of shoes under the stall. Someone attempts to open the door I'm smashed up against. The latch holds, and I say, "Occupied!" in a deep voice.

A guy says, "Sorry" and heads for the urinals. I try to flip Andre off, but it's too crowded, so I just make a face.

We listen to the dude pee and squeak out a little fart. I have to keep my eyes closed because if I make eye contact with anyone I'll start laughing for sure. The guy leaves without flushing or washing his hands. It must have been Terry . . . dirtbag. We allow ourselves to start breathing again, but we don't venture out of the cramped stall until the clerk comes in and tells us, "That guy is gone and the cops have arrived."

I have to stay behind and give some Code Red back to QuikTrip. Everyone is in the car when I creep outside. The cops are totally looking at me, and of course the only seat available is the driver's seat.

Nutt yells, "This boy doesn't have his license!" Luckily, the massive engine drowns out his attempt at humor, and everyone punches him. Seeing Terry makes me want to drive straight to EJ's house for a fight club session. I'll start with Nutt. But they want to keep driving around, and I'm outnumbered, so that's what we do.

We catch up to the caravan and make a left turn into the Merrian High circle drive. I suddenly realize: "We're at school!"

"Ah, man!" EJ cries. "I hate this place."

"You think the lead driver was spacing off and his auto-pilot took him to school? Do you guys ever find yourself at the pool in October?" I ask.

No one says anything, so I reply to myself, "Yeah, me neither."

We snake around the school until we get to the faculty parking lot behind the art wing. It's kind of hidden because the lot slopes down from the building to the baseball fields.

"This a bad idea!" I say. "We'll be trapped back here. We're on school property with beer in the trunk! AND Scary Terry is back on the scene! The only way out of here is back through the circle drive . . . and it's gonna get really crowded when the cops show up." Which is sure to happen now that some seniors are building a huge bonfire out of old pallets and gasoline.

We climb out of Aunt Jenny's windows and see Nutt's brother, Bart, light a whole pack of matches (because one wouldn't do the trick). Everyone (except my boys and me) roars with excitement as the fireball rises into the sky.

"They've never seen one go bad," I say to EJ.

Nutt yells, "Get your sleeping pod, Baggie!"

I try to laugh, but I'm listening for rattling trunk bolts and looking over my shoulder for signs of a yellow Cutlass. My hunter instincts take a break after a few minutes, and

I find myself wondering what the kids at the New York Drama School are doing on a Saturday night. I doubt it's anything like this, and that sounds pretty great.

Abby, Jeremy, and some other drama kids show up, and I go talk to them for a while. I have to break off, though, when Kathy starts singing. Some guys found more pallets beside the Dumpsters, so I go and help bring them over.

I chat with Clint for a while. Two more times he asks me if I smoke weed even though I tell him at least once a week that I don't. Clint and I talk to some art farts for a while until I see my sister roll up with some senior girls. I go say hello, because Lynn's friends like to mess with her by flirting with me, and I don't care what their intentions are, I like it! Also, despite years of bitter warfare, my sister and I have become friends.

Her friend Sonya says, "Hiii, Carter!"

"Ladies."

Lynn rolls her eyes and says, "Did you hear that Terry was at QuikTrip?" I nod, and she continues. "He could show up here, you know."

"I know."

"You're not scared?"

"Of course I am, but what am I gonna do? Unless he breaks out a switchblade or something, I think I'm done running."

Lynn gives me a smile that almost seems like respect. Clint and some band guys come up, and Clint whispers, "Yo, we're gonna go smoke. You in?"

"I'm good, man; thanks, though."

Lynn's face has changed. She's back to glaring at me. "Do you smoke weed?"

"No, he just thinks I do because I space off and I'm on the swim team. That Michael Phelps video really gave us all a bad name."

She shakes her head and chuckles. "I guess you'll be all right without me. It's kind of cool that you're friends with all of these different people. . . . I never did that. I thought it would make me an outcast, but it actually makes *you* cooler."

"Wow."

"Yeah, I'm pretty great." She smirks. "Those New York recruiters are really coming to see you in *RENT*, huh?"

"Me and a few others."

This is a weird situation because Lynn's my mentor, but she's obviously jealous of New York. She was accepted to all the colleges she applied to, but they're all in the Midwest. I know she wanted to apply to the Fashion Institute in New York City, but she didn't. She claimed it was "too impractical," but there's probably nothing less practical than a performing arts school, and everyone is sooo excited at the possibility of my going. It doesn't seem like people get very fired up for practical things.

She asks, "Have you thought about how this is going to affect Mom and Dad?"

"No."

"Both of their children leaving the nest in the same year? We are their whole lives. Mom's heart is going to break."

"Yeah, but Dad's always threatening me with military school."

"He's kidding. That man will cry himself to sleep every night if you leave."

"So, why don't you stay around for a few years and go to JuCo? You could keep your job at The Limited."

She scoffs. "You're the one who was supposed to do that. With your ADD and C-minus grade point average! I'm the one with transcripts to die for. I'm the one who was accepted to top-tier schools. But aaall anyone talks about is whether or not my idiot brother is *really* going to New York."

"It does sound cool, right? Like bold . . . hard-core."

She rolls her eyes. "Please. Talk to me after you've been there six months, tough guy. You think Dad's gonna cry . . ."

"You could come visit me. Maybe we could go to that fashion school and look around."

She glares at me and says, "I cannot believe you're already snotty about a place you've never even been."

"How is that—"

"Inviting *me* to come visit *you*?" she demands. "As if I need your permission to go to New York? You need more black clothes."

"Wait," I say. "Are you being bitchy or are you giving me fashion advice?"

She sighs. "Both. We really have to transition your look for New York. T-shirts and jeans are fine, but you'll need more expensive ones and better shoes."

"Okay. We'll work on it *if* they let me in."

She barks, "And that better be the last time I hear crap like that!"

"What?"

"If you *want* to go, you *will*," she says. "That's it. I've been beside you your entire life and I've seen you blow off opportunities right and left, but I've also watched you go after stuff like a pit bull when you really wanted it. You don't even know that the counselors in junior high recommended you for all remedial classes in high school, and now you're practically on the honors track!"

"They did? Those bitches. Why am I the last to know everything?"

"Nobody wants you to get cocky," she explains. "And you know Mom didn't want you to feel bad about the remedial stuff. She just enrolled you in regular classes because we all knew that you'd rise to the occasion. And you will again and again. And I *will* come and visit you. I'll probably have to be there all the time, bailing you out of trouble. It might actually make sense for me to transfer to a school out there just to save time."

I roll my eyes at her and she rolls hers right back to mock me. I ask, "You really think I'm ready?"

"Absolutely not," she replies. "But anybody who says they're ready to leave home is full of crap. How do you know until you actually go? You'd have to be delusional not to be scared."

The mention of *fear* seems to conjure Scary Terry back to Merrian High. My sister and I turn toward the circle drive, where trunk bolts are rattling and the headlights of an old car loom a hundred yards away at the top of the hill. Everyone seems to have heard about Terry's return. We're all wondering if we're about to die (that could be just me). I look at EJ and, with my eyes, try to ask him if we should run for it, but he's obviously not getting it, because he starts rooting around in Aunt Jenny's trunk.

I tell my sister, "I bet that psycho got kicked out of the navy."

She replies, "No, he would have told me. He's just on leave."

I look away from the car to glare at her.

"What?" she asks. "He sends me e-mails."

"And you read them?!"

"I don't respond . . . very often," she assures me.

I sound like I'm doing an impression of my dad when I say, "You *reply* to Scary Terry's messages?"

She doesn't say anything because EJ has just thrown a bottle of beer at the thumping car and yells, "Come on down, you pussies!!!"

EJ's got a great arm. The bottle smashes right in front of the bumper and sends suds spraying into the high beams.

I yell, "What are you doing?! Don't antagonize that nut ball!"

"That's not a Cutlass!" EJ replies. "It's a friggin' Corsica! Those Nortest d-bags are coming to jack with our school again!"

Two other cars that no one recognizes approach and are almost hit by the rattling and retreating Corsica. They are way outnumbered tonight, so the three of them drive away, fast. We argue whether or not to give chase, but as long as I've got Aunt Jenny's keys, she's not taking part in any vigilante justice. Thankfully, the debate goes on for too long, and it becomes obvious that they've gotten away.

I tell my boys I'm going to park Aunt Jenny in the student lot. No one will come with me, so I pretend to run them over as I whip the old boat around. I almost nail Abby by accident, though. She's making a face when I lean out the window and say, "Sorry about that. This ol' ship is hard to keep on course."

"Do you need a first mate to help you navigate, Captain?" she asks.

"I believe I do!"

"What's your destination?" she asks.

"I'm gonna dock in the student lot so we aren't trapped back here when those Nortest guys come back or the cops show up."

Abby climbs in through the passenger window and slides right up next to me. She kisses me on the cheek and says, "Don't forget about Scary Terry."

"I almost did; thank you for reminding me."

Abby yells out the window to her friends, "Anybody else wanna come?"

The drill teamers don't move, and Jeremy replies, "No, thank you, my mother warned me about getting into sketchy cars like that."

"No, it's okay, your mom won't find out," I assure him. "I've got a puppy under my seat . . . and I've got candy too!"

"Candy?" Jeremy asks.

I nod. "Snickers . . . king-size."

He smiles. "That's not what I heard!"

Abby snort-laughs, but the rest of the girls scowl because they don't get the "child molester in a van" improv that Jeremy and I are doing. They seem to think I'm making fun of them and their love of candy bars. I put my arm around Abby like an old-time pimp. I don't know who decided that bench seats were uncool. They obviously never had a girl like Abby snuggled up next to them while they drove. I suddenly understand why they call that middle section the "bitch seat," but I don't share the revelation with Abby.

I wink at EJ as we rumble past him, and make a sex face (eyes closed, biting my lower lip while nodding). He yells, "Carter, no, wait—" as I hit the gas and squeal Aunt Jenny's tires.

Abby asks, "What's his problem?" because he's chasing us around the parking lot.

I keep speeding up and slowing down to mess with him while I explain, "He hasn't had sex in this car yet, and he's worried we're about to beat him to it."

"Sure he has," Abby says.

"What?" I ask, looking in the rearview mirror.

"He and Nicky have definitely *used* this backseat," she says.

"He didn't tell me that."

"Maybe he's a gentleman, Carter," she adds.

EJ is still running after us when I say, "Maybe Nicky is just pretending to be a slut. You should pretend to make out with me to freak him ouuuu—"

Abby grabs my head and passionately cleans out my right ear. She may be goofing around, but the hairs on the back of my neck are dead serious, and so is my Snickers. I almost ram into the school, but turn the wheel just in time and step on the gas. Aunt Jenny fishtails onto the circle drive, and EJ gives up his chase.

I reduce my speed as we cruise around the building. I'm kind of looking out for cops and Nortest cars and an old Cutlass, but then I realize, *This may be my pimpest move yet!* It happened by accident, but I've separated a girl from the herd and am driving her toward a dark empty parking lot, in a motel on wheels. I try to keep my cool and chat about school and *RENT* and how little Cinna is doing . . . something. . . . I'm not actually listening until Abby asks, "Are you wearing cologne?"

"Oh . . . yeah. D-d-do you like it?"

She gets in close to my neck and a sniffs me like a sexy Labrador. "Yeah, it's nice. I know that scent. It's very manly."

I am such a pimp I want to slap myself.

"What is it?" she asks.

"It's uh, Drakur, Dracken, something Noir?"

She stiffens. "Drakkar?"

"Yeah, that's it. You don't like it?"

"No," she replies. "I love it . . . but . . . that's what my dad wears."

"WHAT??!! Ahh, dang it!"

She laughs. "He only puts it on like three times a year, but that's definitely his brand. We buy it for him for Father's Day. My mom says it was what everyone wore in the eighties."

I quickly park Aunt Jenny right in the middle of the lot and say, "Excuse me," as I jump out and grab what's left of my soda. I pop the trunk and frantically pour red ice onto a pair of EJ's basketball shorts. I choose to believe that they are clean. Hopefully I'm not rubbing my neck and wrists raw with my best friend's ball sweat. But the last thing I want in Abby's mind right now is her FATHER!

Once I'm disinfected, I toss the cup and soppy trunks back into the messy trunk. And I realize why EJ was chasing us. He doesn't care if Abby and I hook up in his car. There is a whole case of Bud Light back here. Oh, well.

I return to the car, where Abby is listening to NPR on the old AM radio. The dome light tries to reveal my red skin, so I shut the door quick. She touches my frozen neck and chuckles. "It's not a big deal."

"Oh, I know. Is the smell gone?"

She nuzzles in and sniffs me seductively. "Pretty much. It's still musky, but the Code Red really rounds it out."

I hate myself for possibly forcing this beautiful young woman to kiss EJ's gym shorts residue. I want to be a white knight and push her off of me, but if there is a time for chivalry . . . this is not it!

NPR isn't the most romantic channel, but it'll have to do. I take a deep breath and lift Abby's chin with my left hand as I brush some hair out of her eyes with my right. The DJ tries to tell me about a heated Congressional debate. But there's a hot girl touching my leg, so I am not listening. There is no debating it, this is happening!

We make out intensely. I get right up her shirt, but I don't just attack. How often do you get to touch a girl's stomach and lower back? Not often enough! I'm not trying to rush, but eventually I'm drawn north. My elbow pushes into the steering wheel and Aunt Jenny blasts a time-out. *HOOOONNNKKK!!!*

We laugh, but I'm still focused, so I ask, "Have you ever been in the backseat of a '69 Dodge Dart? It's pretty cool."

Abby warily turns to look at the enormous sofa and says, "I've heard of a lot of people using this backseat lately."

"What? Who? I haven't. I think your friends are making stuff up to impress you, Abby."

"Yeah, that's usually what girls do," she says.

"Really?"

"No. Shouldn't we get back to the party?" she asks.

"To do what? We don't drink. The cops won't show up for a while. I'd rather hang out here with you."

She smiles. Debate over! I know at this critical point

in a make-out session, saying anything is just going to talk her out of it. Action is the only way forward, so I flop myself into the backseat like a scuba diver. She giggles and follows me over the wall! We wrestle around and kiss. I have to fight like hell not to giggle.

I've dreamt of getting busy back here since EJ first told me his great-aunt was in the hospital. He said if she didn't pull through we were going to inherit one hell of a car. But the geometry of the backseat is trickier than I'd imagined. The seat is kind of angled, so my abs have to be engaged the whole time, and it's tough to not shake. This sucks because one of my goals is to not seem nervous. We're in one of the largest backseats in the history of the automobile, but it's still confining. My feet keep getting tangled under the front seats. Who knew you used your feet so much? Abby stops kissing me for a second and throws one of her legs over my waist.

"Wow!" accidentally slips out of my mouth. An actual girl is straddling my lap! And I lie back a bit. The trembling in my stomach doesn't shut off, however. I pull myself together enough to unclasp her bra on the first try! She gives a smile of surprise. She has no idea how much I've practiced. The windows are fogging up because we're breathing so heavy. That's some old-school privacy tint right there!

The kissing is great. Her boobs are amazing, but I am programmed to try for more. My hands cautiously drop onto the waistband of her jeans. I wait for the karate chop . . . that doesn't come. She just keeps kissing me. Am I being too sneaky or is this a green light? I go ahead and unbutton the top one. Still no defense. I tug down on the zipper and try to stop the trembling in my hands. My knuckles brush against lace.

I should be allowed to celebrate this enormous victory, but there's no time . . . and I seem to be stuck. Her straddle is damning all forward progress. There really is no casual way to remove someone's clothing; everyone has to be on board. I start kissing her neck to give my poor tongue a break and try to figure out what to do while I build up some saliva. She pets my stubbly head like a dog. It's obvious she's thinking too. I'm pretty sure I shouldn't allow her to think very much here, so I just pull down on the back pockets of the jeans. I've successfully given her hip-hop butt, but unfortunately, this is as low as *I* can go. The ball is in her court. I've made my intentions clear (for the past year and a half), so I stop kissing and look into the area where her eyeballs should be. I'm actually glad she can't see me in the dark, because I bet I look like one of those dogs in a Humane Society ad, and that's not sexy.

I stop breathing when she rocks her weight to the side and dismounts. She does a hair flip as her hands drop to her waist. I'm not sure if she's shutting things down or throwing gas on the fire, because just as she's about to pull her pants down—or up—our love den is filled with blinding light.

I cry, "Noooo!!!" as she puts her bra back together with ninja speed.

I'm angrier than I've ever been in my life. My boys have crossed the line! They think they're having fun with flashlights, but they just wrecked years of hard work. I roll down the window that works and stick my neck out, yelling, "We're gonna fight! You ass-ho-ooo— Howdy officers!"

"Are you kidding?" Abby asks.

"'Fraid not."

Red and blue lights begin to swirl around Aunt Jenny's interior.

Abby gasps. "Oh God."

A cop's deep voice comes over the loudspeaker. "Step out of the car, please."

After a few deep breaths and some clothing adjustment, Abby pushes me out. Two Merrian cops are waiting beside their cruiser. For *this* they get out of the car! They obviously know what sort of business they just wrecked, because they're smirking.

Cop #1 says, "Pretty sweet ol' Dodge."

"Thanks," I say. "We were enjoying it." Abby pinches my arm. "Ow!"

Cop #2 smooths his mustache before saying, "Let me get your license and registration, kid."

"Ohhh, um, I'm sorry. I don't have either one."

"You're sorry?" he says. "You lose your wallet?"

"No . . . no . . . I've got it, I-I-I just don't have a driver's license yet and this isn't my car."

Cop #1 asks, "So, how did you get here?"

I run a few lies over in my mind, but they all suck and I don't think we're really in trouble here, so I go ahead and confess, "I drove it."

"Where did you 'drive' it from?" he asks.

I point to the faculty parking lot. "Just around the school."

Cop #2 asks, "What's going on in the faculty parking lot?"

Dang it. I decide to keep rolling with the truth. "Uhhhh, it's like, a sort of gathering?"

"Like a party?" he says.

"I don't know if I'd call it that. . . . It's just like, people standing around."

"Is alcohol present?" he asks.

"You know . . . we took off so—"

"So there are about how many kids trespassing back there?" Cop #2 says.

Abby jumps in. "We go to school here, so I don't think it's tres—"

"At eleven o'clock on a Saturday, I'm pretty sure you're trespassing, young lady," he says. "The school district doesn't even own these parking lots. . . . They're city property."

"Really?" I say. "Is that so the school doesn't have to pay for snow removal?"

Cop #2 says, "Yeah, and our street sweepers clean up your messes, and the Merrian P.D. has to patrol the lots."

"Ohhh." I'd love to make fun of these guys for all of the vandalism and parties they have not stopped, but I don't.

Cop #1 gets us back on track when he says, "What's your name, son?"

"EJ."

Abby laughs because I said it without even thinking.

Cop #2 asks, "Have you two been drinking?"

Abby replies, "No. We just came down here to talk."

Cop #1 raises his eyebrows, and I give him a nod like, *That's right, playa.*

Cop #2 replies to my look by saying, "Put your hands against the car, EJ."

"Wait, no. I wasn't saying that we were—"

I'm pushed against Aunt Jenny's trunk as he pats me down for weapons. Good thing that boner relaxed. I am not a fan of man hands on my junk.

Cop #2 continues, "You know I put cuffs on a kid named EJ last year? A kid that looked *a lot* like you, but he ran away from the scene on me."

"E-E-EJ is a pretty common name," I mutter.

Abby adds, "I know another EJ."

Cop #2 pulls my wallet out of my pocket and says, "Save it."

Dang it. My student ID is in there!

"Mind if we look in the trunk, EJ?" Cop #1 asks.

I say, "No . . . the keys are in the car."

He pulls them out of the ignition, and I suddenly remember what's back there.

All hope is not lost, because Cop #2 is seriously not very good at his job. He hasn't even opened my wallet. He's too busy looking over Cop #1's shoulder as he shines a flashlight around the trunk, sniffing out clues. He says, "No dead bodies . . . that's good. We got a hundred Taco Bell wrappers, wet clothing; that is disgusting."

Cop #2 picks up the investigation. "I see baseball gear, footballs, boxing gloves . . . and a case of Bud Light!"

"What?!" I ask, as surprised as I can.

"Uh-oh, EJ!" Cop #1 says.

Abby gasps. "That's not ours!" But I know it doesn't matter. If a kid is even in the same neighborhood as a beer, the

Merrian P.D. will nail them for being a minor in possession, and here we are—actual minors—in actual possession—of actual alcohol.

I say, "She had no idea there was beer—" just as their radios crackle to life and a woman's voice says, "We've got a six-forty-seven at Merrian High. What's your twenty?"

Cop #2 says to the dispatcher, "We're at the high school."

The lady replies, "Neighbors are reporting a fire and a large group of kids. The fire department and two other units are en route."

Cop #1 says, "Ten-four. Send them to the west parking lot. I repeat, the faculty parking lot."

I smell the fire for the first time and hear sirens wailing in the distance.

Cop #2 barks, "Hands behind your back, EJ."

Dang it. I do as I'm told, and cold steel pinches my left wrist. But Cop #1 says, "Come on, these kids are fine. Let's get over to that back lot before the idiots burn the school down." He grabs the beer out of the trunk and says, "This is your lucky night, EJ."

Seems like it's his lucky night.

The cuff comes off my wrist, and it feels almost as good as when Abby threw her leg over me. As he gets into his squad car, Cop #2 tosses me my wallet and says, "I'll remember this Dodge, EJ."

"I'm really a pretty good guy."

"We'll see," he replies.

I grab Abby's hand and watch the cops tear across the parking lot. She says, "I can't believe they just let us go . . . EJ!"

"Bart says they prefer it when we run because then they don't have to do paperwork. Speaking of runners . . ."

About thirty kids sprint around the back side of the building. Most of them cut across the football field and climb the fence that leads to QuikTrip, but about ten of them hurdle the fence that leads to the student lot.

I start the car as EJ yells, "COPS!"

"Carter, you're our hero!" Doc shouts.

"Aunt Jenny to the rescue!" Bag says while sliding across the hood like Bo Duke.

Nutt tries to dive over the roof, but belly flops it and rams his face, hard. Everyone is more or less inside the car when I slam on the gas, and we race toward QuikTrip. Abby is sitting next to me, and everyone is laughing and recounting their "near death" experiences. Abby explains why there's no beer and why EJ needs to be super careful for a while.

"Quit using my name!" he yells.

"It just comes out—I can't help it!"

This part of the night is always fun. But tonight the good times come to an end when we pull into QuikTrip and see Scary Terry leaning against his car. He's talking to Bart and my sister, *Benedict Arnold*. My instinct is to hit the gas and drive straight to New York, but I pull into the spot right next to them.

"Is this happening?!" EJ gasps.

I say, "I don't know" as I turn the car off and try to fling the door open. Of course it's stuck, so I have to climb out the friggin' window. I'd like to keep climbing onto the roof and sing at the top of my lungs, " 'No daaay but toooodaaaay!' " if that wouldn't seem like the gayest thing you could possibly do before a fight.

My sister shoots me a look and shakes her head like, *Don't*, but I keep marching around the car.

Terry sees me coming and slowly turns away from Bart to lower his head in an ominous way. He obviously feels threatened and is choosing to watch me through the protection of his eyebrow hairs. I'm not sure if there is an actual advantage to this look, but it's very intimidating.

Abby shouts, "Carter, don't!"

Bart is unaware that anything has changed, so he keeps talking. "Remember that girl Kathy I used be down with?"

Terry must not. He's just staring at me. Bart has never been "down" with anyone that I know of. If I live through this I need to remember to ask Kathy if she even knows Bart.

"I tried to tell her I'm not the boyfriend type, baby," Bart continues.

Most of the party chatter has died down when I stop about three feet in front of Terry. Bart finally shuts up, so the only sound is the Cutlass speakers softly rattling out a beat.

My sister says, "Terry, please!" just as Abby shouts, "Carter!" again.

Terry decides the standoff isn't quite dramatic enough, so he pulls a cigarette from behind his ear and lights it up. "You steppin' to me, son?"

I take a deep breath of secondhand smoke before replying, "I don't think so. I'm just . . . stepping to-*ward* you, to see what's going on."

"Oh, are we friends?" he asks. "I don't remember you comin' to visit me in juvie or seeing me off to boot camp."

"No. The last time I saw you, you were pissed at me, so I just wanted to see—"

Terry asks Bart, "Why would I have been pissed at this boy? Just because he sucker punched me with a book and I had to get locked up over it?"

"Terry!" Lynn barks.

I say, "I'm sorry that happened, but I didn't want to fight you that day, and I don't want to fight you now, but I'm not going to run from you again. You hear me?"

Terry looks over my shoulder and says, "So you got your boys all rounded up to take me on?"

I glance around and find EJ, Bag, Nutt, Doc, J-Low, Hormone, Levi, Andre, Timberlake, Lt. Dangle, Hangin' Chad, The Devil, and TrimSpa backing me up.

I shake my head. "No, Terry. This is about me and you, but they'll stop you if things get out of hand."

"They could try," he says.

I give EJ a look that says, *Please try!*

EJ gives me a nod of assurance.

When I look back, Terry's got that crazy smile on his face. He says, "So the little boy's all grown up?"

"I'm getting there."

He chuckles. "Look at you, even standin' like a fighter, all bladed off to the side."

"Am I? We've been working on that."

He nods. "Cool . . . me too. I'm on the navy boxing team."

Dang it.

He continues, "Ain't nothin' else to do on a ship but work out. I train every day."

"Cool."

"Yeah, I got third place in a tournament. My unit ships out again next week, so I'm home for a minute . . . say hi to my moms and tie up some old business."

"Am I part of that old business?"

He nods and says, "Yeah, you are."

My hands are just about to draw up to protect my face when Terry reaches into his back pocket and pulls out that switchblade . . . which turns out to be a kind of thick ball-point pen. He says, "I wanted to give you my e-mail 'cause your sister wouldn't give me yours. I basically wanted to tell you that I was sorry . . . I overreacted last time I saw you, and I know that you didn't want to fight me in the hall and I was bein' a dickhead, so I had it comin'. The navy's got me seeing a therapist, and the boxing is keeping my head right. That's all I was gonna say. I guess I don't need to send no e-mail. Tell your boy EJ I'm sorry too, when you see him."

"Tell him yourself. He's right there."

EJ's whole body flexes with betrayal. Terry gasps. "Jeez, you got BIG! I really am sorry, dog!"

EJ laughs nervously even though he really is way bigger than Terry now. Everyone seems to relax when we shake hands and Terry pulls me in for a hug/back slap. He whispers in my ear, "I'm gonna ask your sister to marry me."

I pull back and look him in the eye before I start laughing. "You really are crazy, dude!"

"Yeah, dog, I'm crazy in love!" he says.

"That's exactly what I meant." Everyone is cracking up

because I'm laughing my ass off. All of this has really been about my *friggin' sister*! The fight with Nick Brock wasn't even about me! Lynn likes to help people, but she made a mistake when she took this pit bull home from the pound. She's not an idiot, however. She's not going to lose her mind and get married to this Froot Loop.

I give Lynn an ornery smile as Bag explains, "We started this badass fight club, man. We're getting pretty good now that we got a second pair of gloves."

We all stiffen back up when Terry says, "Cool, I'll stop by."

"Oh darn," I gasp. "I won't be there this week. I've got a dress rehearsal for a play I'm doing."

"That's right, you do drama," Terry says. "I always liked that stuff, but I was too pussy to ever try out."

Our cheesy after-school special, *The Misunderstood Bully*, is interrupted when a bottle of beer smashes on the ground and suds splash all over Terry. An old Corsica leads about ten other cars stuffed with Nortest dudes. Trunk bolts are rattling all over the place as this cavalry of cheap used cars screeches to a stop.

Terry says, "What the hell?"

"We've been beefin' with these Nortest pricks all year," I explain.

Terry lets out an evil laugh and lowers his head again. "Cool . . . I always hated those Cougar d-bags."

I don't want him to join my family, but I'm sooo glad he's on my team right now! I almost feel bad for the Nortest kids until this long-haired dude jumps out of the back of an SUV with a golf club in his hand. There is no doubt they have come to fight, and it's absolutely the worst night they could have picked! Terry jogs toward the kid without any fear. He leaps into the air for one of his famous jumping roundhouse kicks. It doesn't even come close to hitting the guy, but I don't think he meant it to. He just wants everyone to know that he knows karate. I can see the fear in all of the Nortest guys' eyes. Terry takes the 5-iron out of the kid's hands and flings it into the grass beside the Econo Lodge.

The girls are smart enough to go inside QuikTrip, but all of the boys are tornadoing around the parking lot trying to figure out what to do. Bart is actually the first to action. He punches the Corsica owner right in the face when the guy gets out of the car. Bart is so impressed with himself that he doesn't see the other dude coming at him from the opposite side . . . until he gets popped in the side of the head. Nutt is all over the guy's ass like a rabid dog before the guy can hit his brother again.

A few dudes are coming toward me, but EJ steps in front of me and they slow up. Without a word, he slides to the left and clocks a guy in his stomach with a hard right. *OUCH!!!* Nobody was expecting him to go for the body, especially the guy who's now wheezing on the ground.

EJ tries to yell, "That was for Aunt Jen—" but another guy cuts him off with a punch to the cheek. I want to remember to ask him what he was going to say, because it looked like he had a sweet monologue ready.

Bag and Doc take out the guy that hit EJ, and then they're overpowered by some other guys. I'm too busy shuffling around, checking my blind sides, and trying not to poop myself to be of much use. But the fight finally comes to me when two guys come at me straight on. The formation is a lot like Oklahoma Road, so I'm not that scared. The smaller guy has a flop-do. He yells, "Where's your dress tonight, tranny?"

"I gave it back to your mom, Floppio."

Awesome! The two guys smile in admiration of my comeback. It's almost like we're not going to fight . . . until the flop-do throws a wild punch at me. I can see it coming. . . . I know right where it's headed and that I should at least try to get out of the way or block it, but unfortunately, I am frozen.

EJ yells, "Duck!" but I don't. Maybe I need more training, or maybe I am, in fact, retarded. Maybe I have the reflexes of a sloth, or maybe I just can't believe that someone I've never met is going to punch me in the face for no reason. But he sure does. *WHAAAM!!!* I stagger back and touch my throbbing cheek. That was way worse than the ski glove! Doc jumps on the guy's back before he can hit me again, and EJ tags the taller dude. I ball up my fist and swing at Flop-do's bangs, but he spins quickly and I punch Doc in the neck, hard. To the casual observer it might look like I switched sides all the sudden.

Doc cries out, "Damn it, Carter!" as he slides to the ground. Flop-do thinks he's out of the woods, and tosses the hair out of his eyes . . . just as my left fist drives into his nose. *POP!!!* Awesome. His hair snaps back from my knuckles like it's spring-loaded. That really hurt my hand, but it looked so cool. He doubles over and grabs his beak as I shake out my hand. His buddy must have gotten free of EJ, because he's lunging toward me. I swing at him way before I should, and totally whiff. The move hurts my shoulder more than the punch would have hurt his face. I fall into him and we snuggle for a second before he starts punching me in the back of the head. I know from fight club that punching someone in their skull only injures the fist doing the hitting. He figures it out pretty quickly and stops doing it, so I drive into his stomach with my shoulder and we fall to the pavement like angry Siamese twins. I "accidentally" knee him in the balls, and he chills out for a second. But some other kid, who is wearing wing tip dress shoes, kicks me in the ribs.

I groan, "Uugghhhh!!!" but I'm such a badass now that I'm able to absorb the blow, and quick enough to grab his foot before he can pull it back. He slips (because he decided to wear dress shoes to a fight) and plops onto his butt.

While scampering to my feet, I try to say, "Nice wing tips—" but another d-bag is swinging at my head, so I shut up and back away just in time. I just whiffed in the same way, so I know his momentum is going to bring him toward me and to my right. I slip to the left and cock back to nail him when he stumbles through. But as my elbow draws back, it slams right into another guy's jaw. *WHAAAMMM!!!*

*Please don't let it be Terry Moss!*

It's the same flop-do from earlier, trying to creep up on me! I'm about to yell something clever about my ninja skills, but my funny bone starts freaking out! Ohhh, that hurts, and I have no idea why. People who say you don't feel pain during a fight are liars . . . or way tougher than I am. A thud in the side of my head sends me down to the ground. I turn and find myself looking at those damn wing tips again. Thankfully, some Top-Siders run up and tackle the guy before he can kick me.

"Thanks, Jeremy!" I say.

"No problem," he replies. "You are really doing great!"

Girls are screaming and glass is shattering as I roll back up to my feet. Terry is beating the crap out of a guy like he's putting on a boxing clinic. The Nortest guys are doing well, but obviously not as well as they thought they would when they stormed into our QuikTrip. A kid has retrieved that 5-iron and he's heading toward Aunt Jenny, before he's descended upon by EJ. I doubt this is the last time Aunt Jenny will come under attack, but she will never have to worry about that particular 5-iron again. EJ breaks the club in two and tosses the pieces into the street.

The last thing I thought I'd be doing tonight is fighting a bunch of dudes *with* Scary Terry, but here I am ramming a guy into the side of a Corsica as he attempts to tackle my nemesis. Terry extends a hand to help me up.

I gasp for air and say, "Thanks, dude. But you should get out of here. You don't want to get in trouble if you're about to ship out."

"I'm in the navy!" Terry replies. "They're disappointed if you *don't* get in trouble when you're on leave."

"Really?!"

He never gets to respond, because my sister yells, "Look out!"

Three guys are marching toward us. Lynn tackles the biggest guy from behind and unleashes a flurry of punches. Terry starts pounding his guy, and I trade punches with mine while Lynn rides her dude around the parking lot, tagging him on one side of the face and then waiting for the other cheek to come around before popping him again. She's played this slapping game with me many times and she's really good at it. The big guy finally stumbles and is just about to fall . . . when Terry swoops in and catches Lynn.

They both tumble to the ground, so he didn't really rescue her from anything, but she looks into his eyes like he just stopped her from falling off a bridge. Their faces are only a few inches apart, and they're both panting.

I run over, yelling, "No . . . No . . . No!!!" but this damn flop-do steps to me again. I'm able to duck his wild punch this time, and I come up with a vicious uppercut that clacks his teeth together and sends his hair straight up. It finally falls back into his eyes when he lands on his butt.

Everyone is fighting like mad, but Scary Terry and my sister are just gazing at each other. I yell, "Quit it!" but a guy tackles me and knees me in the nuts. If I didn't have a terrible romance to stop, and if I hadn't experienced so much testicular trauma over the years, I would just stop and puke for a while. But there's no time to rest. I shove the guy off and yell, "That's dirty, dude!"

I look up just as Terry secures my sister's face with his dirty hands. I yell, "Nooo!!!" But the Nortest guy hits me again and I have to get medieval on his ass for a minute. I'm mad at Terry and disappointed in my sister, and this guy is getting the worst of it.

The guy rolls away and runs from me. In the midst of this crazy rumble, one shot makes me happier than any other. I glance over just as my sister cocks back to her hip and slaps Terry's face . . . *WHAAACCCKKK!!!*

Terry stumbles to his feet and looks down at her in confusion. At that same moment, the guy with the wing tips makes the mistake of his life and punches Terry in the back of his head. Terry slowly turns, and dress shoes start peeling out in reverse. Thankfully, he's knocked out by the first of

Terry's punches, and some Nortest guys come over to drag him away. Terry strides toward his own car. When he fires up the old Cutlass, everyone seems to realize that we can leave this parking lot if we want to. The fight appears to be over. I nod to EJ, and we watch the Nortest guys running back to their cars. No one cheers. Terry's car burns rubber to the left, and the Nortest guys all go to the right.

All of the Merrian guys share my expression: *Did that just happen?*

Two Merrian police cars come flying down Merrian Lane. They pass the Nortest cars and drive right over the broken 5-iron before ripping into the QuikTrip parking lot. You can still feel the energy from the brawl, but the scene doesn't look much different than a typical gas-station get-together. Kids scatter and *most* of us get away. Lynn jumps in with her friends, and I see Abby getting into Jeremy's car before they slip into the Econo Lodge parking lot. But we're still slowly piling into Aunt Jenny when the cruisers box us in.

The two cops who just busted Abby and me climb out. Cop #2 barks, "EJ?!"

EJ and I say, "Yeah?!" at the same time.

Everyone laughs, so I whisper, "Not you."

He replies, "My bad . . . you son of a—"

"Get out of that car!" the other two cops yells. "All of you!"

Eleven of us are sitting on the curb in front of QuikTrip. Old people glare at us as they walk past because the police lights are swirling all around. The clerks keep pointing at me when they're giving their statements. Cop #2 has the zip ties in his hand when all four of them finally walk over to us. It doesn't look good until Cop #1 says, "Hell of a night, EJ. Fires, trespassing, sex, *and* violence."

My boys all rock around trying to look at me, but I don't make eye contact with anyone. I try to say, "It wasn't like that. We weren't really fighting—"

EJ interrupts me. "You've got blood all over your face, dude. Just stick to the truth . . . EJ!"

"What the hell happened?" Cop #1 asks.

I lay it all out . . . without directly incriminating anyone (except the Nortest guys). I tell them about that first football game and the Lou-Owe party, and the Cougar costumes and basketball brawl. They nod as if they were there for all of these events. They know about the graffiti on our school and the snakes that are still cruising around Nortest High. I tell them *we* were not looking for trouble—tonight or any other. "These guys pulled up with golf clubs, man. This is obviously our QuikTrip!"

The cops are thinking about what they want to do, so I keep rambling. I tell them about Amber Lee and Scary Terry and the New York Drama Academy. I start to tell them about the forest fire, but I get kicked from both sides. I'm explaining the plot of *RENT* when Cop #1 raises his hand and tells me to, "Shut up."

He looks at the other officers and says, "Does anyone want to write all of this up?"

The cops glance at each other to see who's going to do it. Cop #1 continues, "The clerks agree that these kids were just defending themselves."

And just like that, we're free to go! And the beat goes on.

We pile back into Aunt Jenny and roll out. I wave to the cops and say to my boys, "You gotta love the Merrian P.D."

Doc asks, "Why do we always run from them? They were pretty cool."

Bag thinks that this rumble will finally stop the beef between Merrian and Nortest, but I think the legend of tonight is just going to feed it. The facts are already being greatly distorted.

# SPRING

# 27. STICK IT TO THE MAN

I'm in the principal's office on Monday. My face is black and blue. It hurts to breathe and I can't make a fist with either hand. I am about to get suspended . . . not for fighting, cheating, stealing, or any of the other crimes I've committed this year. I was fifteen seconds late to American history!

After nineteen Saturday Schools and countless detentions, the attendance office has finally had enough. They're giving me an in-school suspension! I couldn't be more thrilled. Some say karma is a bitch, but I love her. I.S.S. is the greatest study hall ever, and I've got so much to do! Finals are coming up. I also really need to focus on my lines for the play. I'm waiting to be taken down to the dungeons, when I hear people shouting inside Principal Banks's office. I assume it's a kid who's been framed for a crime he didn't commit, but it's a woman's voice . . . a familiar one. Is it my mom? She better not have come up here to defend me! I hop up and carefully walk toward the door to eavesdrop.

The secretary gives me a look like, *Sit your tardy ass down!*

Before I can turn around, the door flies open and Ms. McDougle storms out red-faced. Banks is hot on her heels, saying, "Don't be so dramatic!"

She shows him how likely *that* is by saying, "Oh, screw you, Jim!"

The secretary and I share a look of shock. He doesn't look like a Jim.

The principal continues, "Just change some of the details!"

They're obviously talking about *RENT* because McDougle spins around and shouts, "It doesn't work like that! You don't buy the rights to 'some' of the play! And I wouldn't change one word of that script!"

He replies, "Then you can't do it in this building."

"Fine! You will have my resignation tomorrow."

Tears instantly fill my eyes, and I yell, "WHAT?!"

She looks at me and drops her head before saying, "Oh, Jesus. The New York Drama School is coming to evaluate four prospective students! You are jeopardizing their future!"

Banks says, "No, Ms. McDougle . . . you are, by being inflexible."

I break in. "Nobody cares about that school!"

She asks, "What?"

"You can't quit, McDougle!"

"I can't do it anymore, Carter," she pleads.

"You gotta keep fighting! The drama geeks need you."

She sighs. "I fight for you guys every day, but I'm exhausted."

She has confused me for a drama geek. I confirm her assumption when I say, "You're the only reason I come to this school every day. You're the reason I'm going to be on the honor roll for the first time since fourth grade. You talk to me like an adult!"

She's crying when Mrs. Trimmer enters to take me down to jail. She glares at me like the criminal I am before glancing at Principal Banks. He gives her a nod, and she says, "Get your stuff."

McDougle asks, "What's going on? What happened to your face? Did you get into a fight?"

"Yeah, but that's not why I got suspended. I really need a quiet place to focus today."

She laughs. "You are nuts!"

"I know, but it really helps. Are we really not doing the show?"

She shakes her head and looks back at the principal before she replies, "Oh, we're doing it." She turns to me and says, "Carter, you just try to stay focused in there. Get those lines down. And I'll keep fighting, too. We'll find a way!"

Mrs. Trimmer ushers me into a cinder block cell between the boiler room and the drill team dance studio. I join the murderers, rapists, and other incessantly tardy kids. I nod to J-Low and crack myself up when I remember that he's here all week for watching porn on a library computer. He was so shocked that the video made it through all of the filters that he exclaimed, "NO WAY!" and let it play for about ten seconds too long.

My goal is to write out every line in the show twice. Abby says this will help slow my mind down and force me to focus—and she's right! Before I know it, the final bell rings and I've had a hell of a productive day. J-Low and I are released back into the general population. I'm dying to know what's happened since I went into the hole, so I head straight for the drama department. I hear a saw buzzing from outside the auditorium, and my heart sinks when I open the doors. The cast and crew of *RENT* are cutting down the supports of the loft-apartment set.

I run down the aisle toward the stage and see Abby coming out of the drama classroom with a couple of hammers. She hands me one and explains, "We're doing the show in the parking lot! Banks won't let it happen in the building, but I told McDougle what the police told us on Saturday . . . that the parking lots are owned by the city of Merrian, not the school district. Jeremy's mom is friends with the mayor, so we already have a permit."

"You're so smart!"

She kisses me quick and says, "Couldn't have done that one without you."

The next few days are a flurry of construction chaos. My dad and EJ and a bunch of other people help us rebuild the set. We run cables and transformers and speakers to the corner of the faculty parking lot where the asphalt slopes down to the baseball fields. It's kind of like a huge amphitheater.

Next thing I know I'm wearing makeup and it's opening night. We haven't actually had a full rehearsal of the whole show because there have been so many technical problems. I now understand the importance of a "tech rehearsal" and an actual theater. The atmosphere in the parking lot is insane, though. We've made national news because of the censorship issue and McDougle's awesome reputation. Principal Banks has been doing interviews for days and backpedaling his ass off (that's why we get to use the school's electricity). Almost a thousand people are here to see the show tonight! The

Merrian P.D. had to show up and help direct cars.

We have a big curtain off to the side of the set so the audience can't see us backstage (pooping ourselves), but I'm peeking out to see what's going on. All of my boys are standing together beside the tech booth in the middle of the parking lot. I never expected the audience would stretch that far back, but people are setting up blankets and folding chairs a hundred feet beyond that. My parents and my sister look nervous, but not as freaked as Principal Banks. There's a group of kids that I recognize, but I can't place where I know them from . . . until I see a black eye peeking out from a flop-do. Nortest guys! I can't see their feet so I'm not sure it anyone if anyone is wearing wing tips. I'm a bit worried that they're looking for trouble, until we step out onstage and they join the rest of the crowd in cheering for us. Everyone thinks that we are fighting censorship and "sticking it to the man." But I know we're just obnoxious kids who want to sing and dance in front of other people! The extra drama doesn't hurt, though.

Once the clapping dies down, I take a deep breath and adjust the microphone that's strapped to my head. I wink my swollen right eye at the shocked Nortest guys before I proudly shout the first line: "'We begin on Christmas Eve, with me, MARK!'" And we are off to the races.

I flubbed a couple of lines, some sound cues got screwed up, and we had to move into the spotlights a few times, but it really couldn't have gone better. It felt like old-time Greek theater mixed with a badass rock concert. A bunch of people knew the words to the songs, and they sang along with us.

It was impossible not to be swept up by the energy of that crowd. I felt like I was a part of something real and very special.

When the cast comes out for the curtain call and sings the reprise of "Seasons of Love" all these people are clapping to the beat. I feel like I'm explaining to each and every one of them that a year is just "Five hundred twenty-five thousand six hundred minutes!" and each one is precious and you've got to *fight* to make each minute count. I feel like they hear me.

When the lights fade, it seems like we've changed the world. We get a standing ovation. No one was really sitting on that dirty asphalt, but I think we would've gotten it anyway.

My boys are waiting when I step offstage. There's really no backstage area, so they don't feel the need to wait before they start tackling and punching me with pride. I'm in some pain, but I wouldn't want it any other way. My parents are just shocked again. The Will Carter they know can't remember his own phone number, so the memorization alone is tough to grasp.

I see Abby talking to the New York Drama School recruiters, and I realize that my performance has been "evaluated." I honestly forgot about them during the show, but a wave of stress washes over me now. I really want to go. I want to keep doing this. Not that the rest of my life sucks, but performing is sooo much better than anything else.

After another breath, I break away from my boys and my family, and walk toward them. If I wasn't good enough tonight, I'll never be. About halfway across the parking lot I see the Nortest guys approaching me. I don't think it would look very good for a prospective student to get into a fistfight in front of the recruiters, so I put up my hands like, *I come in peace.* But the flop-do opens his arms wide and throws them around my shoulders. "Excellent work, man!"

"Thanks."

"We tried to do this show last year, but it got shot down," he says.

"Yeah," I say, motioning to a mess of extension cords. "We had a few issues."

Abby motions for me to join her, so I say, "Thanks for coming, guys."

Another kid with a few cuts on his face says, "And sorry for all the trouble last weekend. . . . We got caught up with some stupid—"

"Trust me, I get it."

He nods and we shake hands.

I walk over to Abby and she introduces me to Jeffrey and Diana from the drama school. They're in the middle of a conversation with the other actors, and it sounds like they're making plans for next fall, like they've been accepted to the school. They don't say anything directly to me however. We all talk about the show forever, and we joke about the problems. The recruiters talk about what a "stroke of genius" it was to do it outside, and how "in the spirit of Jonathan Larson" (the dead writer of *RENT*) it was to not sell tickets. They don't say anything positive or negative about my performance. My parents and Abby's come up and say hello, and the small talk persists. Ms. McDougle approaches, and she kisses Diana and Jeffrey on their cheeks like they're old pals. The parking lot is practically empty and I'm getting bored. It almost seems like they're leaving, so I finally ask, "Will you let me know by mail or something? Do you contact my parents privately?"

Jeffrey asks, "About what?"

"About me . . . coming to New York. Do you think I'm worth the academic risk and all that?"

They look at each other with even more confusion. Diana asks, "Is he an academic risk?"

"I don't think so," Jeffrey replies. "You have a C average, right, Carter?"

"Uh, nooo. I've got a B average. I should have all A's by the end of the semester."

"Well, that's fine," she says. "We're more concerned with passion and talent than grades. As long as you aren't flunking out."

I glare at Ms. McDougle and grunt. "I was never flunking out."

"Great," Jeffrey says. "The whole faculty watched those clips of *Down Gets Out* back in the fall, and we're all very excited to work with you."

"You've been excited since the fall?"

My parents and Abby are smiling as suspiciously as McDougle. These bastards set me up! I'm in too much shock to go off on them right now, but ohhhh, I will!

Diana says, "We can't wait to see you guys on our campus in the fall."

"Did you have any other questions?" Jeffrey asks.

I raise my hand and say, "Yeah, I have some concerns."

Everyone looks at me. Diana says, "Sure, it's a huge decision. It's definitely not the easy road."

"Yeah, but that's not what I mean. I don't know if you remember, but Abby came out for a visit in the fall . . . and she's like one of my best friends. And I totally respect her opinion. . . ."

Jeffrey looks at Abby and says, "Of course we remember. She sang a song from *Camelot*, right? And she danced with our advanced class. We were sorry that she couldn't make it last semester, but hopefully she'll join you guys in the fall."

"Did you know that somebody called her fat?" I say. "That's my concern."

They turn red and look at each other. Abby is mortified when she says, "No . . . no they didn't! Well, the movement teacher told me I should lose a few pounds."

"Fifteen," I add.

Jeffrey adjusts his glasses and sighs. "Yes, we heard about that. Ms. Tilly is a brilliant choreographer, but she . . . lacks tact."

"That frankness is not unheard of at a private drama school, however," Diana adds with a slightly bitchy tone that suggests that drama girls will be drama girls, regardless of age or geography. "We don't have time for 'polite.' Recommendations are made and sometimes we're unkind. We may yell at you or put you down. But it's only because we're passionate and we're trying to prep you for a cutthroat industry. You'll need technique and talent, but you'll also need thick skin."

I nod like, *I'm used to that.* But Abby's still scowling, so I continue. "Someone compared her to Adele as well."

Diana glares at Abby like she's been complaining about this for six months and she's sick of it. "I'm sorry you were compared to one of the most beautiful singers of our time. Did anyone else praise you unacceptably?"

I nod at Abby like, *See?*

She doesn't seem interested in the fact that I was right about this; she's more focused on the fact that Diana seems to hate her all the sudden and it seems to be my fault.

Jeffrey says, "We don't need your definitive answers until June."

Diana puts her arm around Ms. McDougle and says, "If you decide to come, you might get to study with our hottest new drama teacher!"

McDougle is smiling like she's been harboring all kinds of secrets. Abby says, "You?!"

McDougle replies, "I'm still thinking about it as well."

"She turned us down flat," Jeffrey adds.

"We have some salary negotiations to work out," McDougle says. "New York is bit more expensive than Merrian. . . . AND if I ever hear anyone call a student 'fat,' it's going to get ugly. But even if I don't go to New York, I'll still be leaving Merrian High. Principal Banks has made it clear that I am not welcome back next year. So it's time to seek new opportunities." She seems to only be looking at me when she says, "I'd never tell you what to do"—even though she's always telling me what to do. "You have an awesome support system here." She motions to my friends, who are running around the dark baseball field. "But I know you can rise to *any* occasion, and I don't think it would be the end of the world for you to get out of your comfort zone."

I look at my parents, and they seem numb yet supportive. So I say, "I'm in."

Abby says, "Really?! Are you sure?"

"No . . . but I'll do it anyway. Why not?"

Abby starts giggling. Which is totally unlike her. Finally she says, "I could handle it too, then. If my favorite teacher and my best friend are there, I think it would be amazing."

I start to do an impression of Abby's mom having a panic attack on the subway, when a strong hand wraps around the back of my neck. I turn to find Cop #2 staring down at me. Everyone freezes. He says, "Hell of a job, EJ. Now I've really got my eye on you!"

I turn back to my parents and teachers and smile as innocently as I can.

# EPILOGUE

My parents were really freaking out about their retarded son leaving home two years ahead of schedule, until they noticed my sister had called the naval warship USS *Hornet* twenty times. It took them longer than an episode of *Law & Order* to put the pieces together because they're so convinced that Lynn is their "smart child." But I've learned that even the wisest girls can be complete dumbasses when it comes to boys (see Amber, Nicky, and Abby).

The nightmare realization that their daughter is engaged in a long-distance relationship with Scary Terry Moss was occurring to my parents about the same time a dream was finally coming true for me. It seems like you can bust your ass for so long that you start to think that busting your ass is the only thing you'll ever do. . . . But all the sudden, something *gives*, and you find yourself moving what you thought was a mountain with very little effort. Of course I'm talking about sex . . . specifically, *me* having it.

Abby pointed out that since we were headed to a performing arts conservatory, we might not ever get to attend a real prom. So my sister gave us her tickets to the dance (because her boyfriend is on a boat just off the coast of Dubai). She paired my black church suit with a fly James Bond bow tie! We went to the mall and picked up a sweet tuxedo shirt and some old-school black-and-white checkerboard Vans. They're way cooler than my dress shoes and much better for dancing.

Abby turned sixteen a few weeks ago, so my cougar picked me up in her parents' minivan. I was staring out the kitchen window like a puppy when she pulled up to the house, so I got to watch as she slid down from the captain's chair. Her skirt rode up a few inches and her high heels made her legs do their thing! She casually pulled the fabric back to its designated length and checked herself in the reflection of the sliding door. She's hot as hell, so no other adjustments needed to be made. Her hair was up and showed off her awesome neck and shoulders. Her dress was simple and black, but tight around the hips and boobs. I wouldn't call it slutty, but I doubt her mom was as stoked as I was about the cleavage.

I walked outside and met her on the sidewalk. My mom went paparazzo on us for twenty minutes, and then we drove downtown to a cool old Italian restaurant. I ordered the seafood tower for us to share because I thought it would be funny, and Nutt is always saying how oysters make girls horny. It was a little bit disgusting to look at, and eat, but all the old people were gawking at us the whole time like, *Who the hell are these pimp-ass kids with the friggin' seafood tower?!*

There's some rule that sophomores are not supposed to be at the senior prom, but we didn't try to hide. We torched that dance (gym) floor! Jeremy and his new (college) boyfriend tried to battle us, but even they couldn't hang. I jumped off the bleachers in the middle of a Flo Rida song and tried to land in the splits. People cheered for my courage, but it didn't go very well and I kind of hurt my leg.

The chaperones were so jealous of our skills that they kicked us out at midnight; either that or there's a rule in our school district that you can't go past twelve a.m.

We grabbed a map to the after-party, but I had no intention of using it . . . even though it sounded really fun. It was at a new indoor water park and it was just Merrian kids, so I could've gone down the slides a million times. Honestly, the only thing that could get between a fake wave pool (that you can actually surf on!) and me was the possibility of actual sex with a real girl.

Things were looking dope as we strolled (limped) across the parking lot . . . but things have looked dope before. The difference on prom night was that I didn't care. I knew that whatever happened next would be great, no matter what. I honestly wouldn't have been heartbroken if we'd high-fived in front of the field house and gone our separate ways. . . . Thank God we didn't!

Abby and I were both dripping with sweat and had been groping each other for hours on the dance floor. The oysters seemed to have worked. It was *on* like *Donkey Kong* and we both knew it. I kind of felt drunk with excitement, but I hadn't had a sip of alcohol. Maybe it was the extra testosterone my body was kicking out, or maybe it was that damn seafood tower, but something was making me giddy and light-headed, and I could tell Abby felt the same way.

We made out for a second before I opened the driver's-side door for her . . . because a gentleman is a gentleman whether he has a driver's license or not! I knew the backseat folded down into a big bed, but I didn't want Abby to lose her virginity in the same place she used to eat Cheerios and poop her pants. I also didn't want to give the Merrian P.D.

another opportunity to interrupt us. So after I helped her into the captain's chair, I looked into her beautiful green eyes and asked, point-blank, "Do you want to get a hotel room with me?"

She didn't shrug. She didn't say "Okay" or "I guess" or "Why not?" She stared right back at me and said, "Yes."

It took everything in my power to not start clapping, but I didn't do it (until I was safely behind the van). On the drive to the Econo Lodge, we stayed pretty quiet until Abby asked, "Should we stop by QuikTrip?"

"You think we'll need Gatorade?"

"No!" She laughed. "I was thinking about . . . protection?"

"Oh, rubbers? Naw, I've got a bunch."

Abby shook her head and said, "You are so cocky! You brought condoms?"

"I bring condoms to biology in case things get out of hand. . . . I don't think prom is that big of a stretch."

She was pulling up to the Econo Lodge when I said, "Okay, our reservation is under the name *Froman*."

"You already have a room reserved?!" she gasped.

"I'm kidding! Is planning one of my strong suits?" I couldn't believe I was able to joke on this momentous occasion.

Abby parked the van while I went in and begged the manager to give me a room. The guy wasn't that old, so he was cool, especially when he saw I had a credit card. Dad told me to use it if I had "an emergency." *If this isn't an emergency, I don't know what is!*

My stomach was churning with nerves, and I was trying to take deep breaths to calm down. I was promising the guy that I wouldn't have a party in the room just as Abby walked through the sliding glass doors. She'd taken her hair down at the dance, so when the breeze kicked it up, her locks looked as if a special effects crew had pointed a wind machine at her. Her boobs were still glistening with a little sweat, and the manager looked at me with so much envy I almost felt bad. He shook his head in disgust, like I hadn't done anything with my life that was worthy of getting to spend the night with a girl that hot. But he had no idea how hard I'd fought to be in that lobby, or how likely it was that I might still screw it up. I didn't feel like getting into it.

He handed me our key card like he was bestowing a lightsaber. He gave us a room on the ground floor, probably because he figured we'd be disturbing anyone underneath us. He was right! We may or may not have broken the bed. All I'm saying is: don't ever attempt a flip between two beds. You think it's going to be awesome, but you could break your neck and die a virgin. I just hope "queen-size bed" doesn't show up on my dad's credit card statement.

Abby and I *might* have made love in Room 134 of the Econo Lodge. . . . We might have done it twice! But I'm not trying to brag about it, and it's nobody's business except Abby's and mine. I don't want to be the guy who does things just to tell other people about it. I'd want the memory of it to be pristine and untarnished by outside influences. I'd want to remember it exactly as it happened. Actually . . . I might want to edit a few things.

I'll say this: *if* it happened, it was more remarkable than I'd ever imagined it would be . . . probably more so the second time than the first. Not to say that the first time wasn't amazing; it just may have been more *to the point*. And this might sound cheesy, but the whole experience was really beautiful and sort of spiritual. Abby and I connected in a way that really surprised me. Like the way EJ and I can talk to each other without opening our mouths. Scratch that. It was nothing like that! But it was awesome. (If it happened!)

I'm so glad that all of my prayers for hooking up with a random slut were never answered, even if when we got to the room, Abby ducked into the little bathroom to "freshen up" and I heard her dress unzip on the other side of the door. . . . I may have pushed my ear against the door to listen to the sweet sound of satin falling to the tile. A brief silence was followed by this gorgeous girl, who I was sooo in love with, moaning seductively, "Ohhh God," before going rogue-diarrhea-ninja in stereo sound: *PLUFFFT, UFF, UFF, PLUFFT, UMP, PEERP!!!*

She was grunting like my grandpa trying to get out of a low chair, but I didn't care . . . until I smelled it. WOW! I only *thought* I was feeling sick until that moment, but I suddenly needed to purge myself of some seafood, and quick! The Econo Lodge doesn't have a crapper in the lobby, so I had to take my business to the parking lot and fertilize their bushes with vomit/chum. The people walking into QuikTrip across the street thought they knew the story. They found it hilarious that a boy in a tux couldn't hold his booze on prom night. They had no idea I was actually dealing with a serious bacterial problem as I knelt on the blacktop heaving my guts up and possibly crapping my pants at the same time! How could they? Would they even believe that a guy who'd waited his whole life for this night would even *consider* eating some weird new cuisine on this important of an evening? I don't think they could.

Once the fireworks were over and I realized I wasn't

going to die, I waddled over to QuikTrip and broke out the credit card again. I wonder if my dad will demand to know why I needed a two-liter of ginger ale, saltine crackers, Pepto-Bismol, two toothbrushes, a tube of Colgate, a pair of NASCAR shorts, and baby wipes at 2:30 in the morning on prom night. I'll have to give my mom some reason that I lost my church pants, but she doesn't even want to know why they're in the QuikTrip Dumpster.

I told the hotel manager there was a funny smell in Room 134, and if it wasn't too much trouble we'd like a different one.

Abby and I may have had a good laugh and a sweet burping contest as we watched two episodes of *Ridiculousness*.

I'm not going to confirm or deny the sex, but I will say that *sleeping* with a girl is way harder than I ever thought it would be. I'm not talking about sex, now . . . I'm talking about *sleep*.

How many hours have I imagined doing the deed, and not one second as to what I would do afterward?! How could cuddling with a hot chick turn into torture? I've seen the action on TV a million times. It seems straightforward: she just puts her head on your shoulder and you talk for a moment. But then that moment drags on and on and she won't get off of your friggin' arm! TV cuddling goes on for a few seconds and then they cut to something else, but I was trapped there for hours. Are you just supposed to drift off with someone's skull pushing into your windpipe? Do you just ignore the hair that's tickling your nose and invading your mouth with chemicals that smell nice but taste like poison?

Sleeping with Abby was kind of like putting a lit Duraflame into my sleeping bag. It made me realize that she's not just hot to look at . . . she's like a hundred and ten degrees, and she twitches like a meth-head in rehab. Also, my collarbone was blocking off part of her nose and making her snore a little bit. That was kind of cute, actually. Hopefully (please, God!), I'll get used to these things.

As light started to creep through the cheap window blinds, Abby stirred slightly, so I was like, "Hey you! Can't sleep? Do you want to walk to iHop? I'm starving."

She didn't really want to get up or brush her teeth, but she really needed to delete some seafood morning breath! She also didn't want to be at a restaurant at 6:15 a.m. in an evening gown, but she's a trouper, and I was so proud to be there with her . . . especially when we walked past the corner booth and discovered EJ, Bag, Nutt, Doc, Levi, J-Low, Hormone, Andre, Timberlake, The Ding-Dong, Coot, Hangin' Chad, and TrimSpa trying to sober up after a long night. I knew Andre would rather have given me a punch in the face than a "S'up?" but he did it anyway. Everyone's got to learn how to lose at some point, and as his friend, I was glad to be of service.

EJ yelled, "I like those Nascar shorts, dude!" Abby and I ignored them and the hash browns that whizzed past our heads. That morning could have been awkward, but it wasn't. As Abby ordered her food, I realized that she is so cool, she can make *any* situation okay, or maybe *I* am cool. I doubt it though. I almost started crying right there in the booth, and I was going to get bacon and eggs even though I love the Funny Face pancake. But I knew my boys would make fun of me for it, and that friggin' seafood tower didn't go very well, and it seemed dumb to order off the kid menu after making love with someone, but at a certain point you've got to make a decision. You've got to figure out who you are and what you want. And if you think that something is going to bring you happiness, you'd be a fool not to be honest with yourself, and I love chocolate chip pancakes. So that's what I got. And I think that makes me pretty cool.

But I'm obviously not an expert.